ANN ROYAL NICHOLAS

More Muffia By Ann Royal Nicholas

This book is a work of fiction. Names, characters, places and events are products of the author's imagination; historical names and information, should either appear, are used fictitiously. Any resemblance to actual persons, living or dead, locations or events is strictly coincidental.

ACKNOWLEDGMENTS

If you're new to *The Muffia* series, then you might not know there's a real group of book-loving, Los Angeles women who call themselves *The Muffia*, which I've been lucky enough to be a member of for thirteen years. These women, whose names have been changed for their own protection, generously share endless amounts of wit, insight, kindness, laughs and food. Most of them can mix a damned fine cocktail, too.

If it were not for the Muffs who are, each of them, overflowing vessels of inspiration to me, this series could not have been written. Many of the incidents in the Muffia books have actually occurred; or they could have happened had events gone slightly differently.

Thanks must, therefore, go first to the ladies of the real-life Muffia: Michelle Joyner, Lisa Mohan, Carolyn Calvert, Sonya Walger, Lysa Hayland Heslov, Denise Gruska, Susan Hoffman Hyman, Betsy Salkind, Clare Foster, Janine Eser and Jann Turner. Without these women, my life would be so much less than it is.

So many others contributed to the book you hold in your hand—either through their inspiration and encouragement, or by virtue of their superior beta reading skills. I'm grateful to Agatha Dominik, Fred Baxter, Arbel Ben Peretz, Cedering Fox, Claire Carmichael, Hannah Dennison and Joyce Mochrie.

Thank you, Liz Trupin-Pulli, agent extraordinaire, for continuing to believe in me and the Muffs. Thanks also to Alex Hyde White, all the people at Punch Audio, and Marc Solomon for their skill and expertise in the recording of *The Muffia* audio book.

Lastly, thank *you*. Your purchase of this book makes a contribution from the real Muffia possible. Ten percent of profits from the sale of this and all *Muffia* books will be donated to charitable organizations benefiting girls and women in the United States. The Muffs will decide, on an annual basis, which organizations will be the recipients of Muffia funds. We are particularly interested in organizations that provide women of all ages with access to education and the means to start their own businesses. Should you have ideas of where we might send our donations, please contact us.

Make suggestions and keep track at www.themuffia.us.

Happy reading,
Ann Royal

More Muffia is dedicated to my son
who's been very patient.

CHAPTER 1

*I*F THERE'S one thing I'm sure of, it's that if *my* dear friend and fellow longstanding member of the Muffia Book Club had called *me* from halfway around the world to tell me that my stupendous Israeli ex-lover—who, by the way, *died* while we were having unbelievable sex—was walking around Narita Airport very much *alive*, I would have jumped on the next plane to Tokyo.

If it had been me who'd been awakened with this news in the middle of the night, I would have been apoplectic and immediately gone online and booked a ticket. How dare Maddie react with her typically unique combination of disbelief and ennui? She should reserve all that composure for her freakin' mediations. What's wrong with people? And on top of that, now I was going to miss my plane! No good deed goes unpunished, right?

"Excuse me, *sumimasen*, pardonez moi…MOVE," I assert with as much conviction as I can muster—though probably coherent only to myself—as I race toward the gate and my plane back to Los Angeles where I live and work and sometimes love. At that moment, though, I don't think it really matters what I say. I just have to say it with enough volume and with the obvious authority I've developed over my career as a talent agent (read: glorified babysitter to celebrities—*not* what I signed up for), so that I can get all these people out of my way.

But they aren't moving. Aggghhhh!

There's a cluster of schoolgirls in front of me—possibly a *Hello Kitty* convention—wearing impossibly hot pink and taking up the entire corridor. I see an opening and lurch toward it, but as I do, "Oh—uh—oh no—!" And down I go: shoes, bag, phone, and the rest of my carry-on belongings scattering hither and yon.

"Shit," I utter with more volume than I intend. *That,* after all, is a word people in every culture understand. I groan in pain, happy I'd given up short skirts, and attempt to pull myself upright, while the *Hello Kitty* contingent stares at my entire *koplotznick* like I'm Lindsay Lohan trying to walk a straight line after failing a Breathalyzer test.

Come to think of it, quite a lot of people, guys anyway— actually it's only been a couple of guys who've hit on me, something that occurs less and less these days—tell me I sort of look like Lindsay Lohan. Only older, taller, heavier, and my hair is auburn and naturally curly, whereas Lindsay's is blonde and straight, last I checked. But yeah, other than all that, I look *exactly* like Lindsay Lohan.

"Here, let me help you," says a bespectacled man with a smattering of freckles spread out over his nose. He has an accent—Australian or possibly South African—I can't tell the difference, and a sorry shortage of hair. He looks familiar in the way guys like Freckles always look familiar. He takes hold of my arm with one hand and helps me to stand and steady myself. In the opposite hand, he's holding one of my shoes, which had flown off when I tripped. He's examining it curiously.

This particular pair of Natacha Marros are not what one would call "traditional" in appearance: Lucite platforms and red metallic detailing over a slipper of gold. People who bother to look down and examine strangers' footwear see them and are instantly put on notice that the wearer is no traditionalist, either. But now, as I follow his gaze, I see the heel of this shoe has completely busted off—something that is *not* supposed to happen with Marros. *Goddammit!* No wonder I'd fallen like a three-legged cow.

Well, one thing's for sure: Yours truly would be making a return trip to the Barney's shoe department in the near future. I had spent far too much of my hard-earned paycheck on these puppies not to make a stink if they refuse to give me a new pair. It hardly seems relevant that I'd been traveling at a speed exceeding the limit recommended for such shoes—some twenty miles per hour, across heavy-duty, multi-colored acrylic carpeting, when I fell. For the price one pays, shoes should withstand a modicum of exertion on the part of the wearer beyond a little pole dancing, the purpose for which they were intended.

I was also going to have a talking-to with that pole-dancing teacher of mine. Great teacher, though she is, it was K-Love who'd convinced me to buy the damned shoes in the first place, saying men preferred Marros above all other brands on the feet of girls twirling on poles. Not that I'd had the opportunity or desire yet to dance for a man, though I was optimistic about one day being ready and able to, once I found the man I wanted to dance for. Success equals opportunity meets preparedness, and I was destined for great things. I just had to keep on believing.

Clearly, K-Love's shoe recommendations were a tad suspect. So, come to think of it, were her promises of increased flexibility and agility—neither of which had been on display in the immediately preceding five minutes. I had fallen on my ass like an uncoordinated giraffe stepping onto dry land after two months at sea. But I was willing to concede that I didn't go to class enough to see any real benefit.

"Thank you," I say to Freckles at last, relieving him of the broken shoe.

"Alright now?"

I nod. He sounds like he's from New Zealand, not that I could tell the difference if he were from Australia.

"Just a minute," he says, whereupon he darts toward a collection of pink *Hello Kitty* lunch boxes, emerging with my errant heel, smiling and shaking his head as he hands it to me. "It's a wonder you can stand in these things. They certainly can't be very good for your feet."

What—he's a podiatrist now? So I twist my ankle in my too-chic-for-shit platforms; that gives him the right to criticize? Granted, maybe I shouldn't have been wearing them for commercial jet travel. But I didn't expect to be *running* for my plane, which was not going to wait just because I went out of my way to call one of my closest friends to tell her some *amazing* news, which she, incredibly, barely reacted to. It's not like I had a choice. And now Freckles is giving me a reprimand? Where does he get off? Literally, where? Come to think of it, I bet I can guess where. He looks like the type of guy who regularly enjoys sexing it up in Bangkok.

I smile at him innocently. "It's not the shoes' fault. They're designed for slightly less rigorous activities—like sex with a pole."

His freckles seem to grow into each other, resulting in his face going entirely red. Must have struck a nerve there. And as I watch him slink away, I'm thinking to myself, *Quinn, you can be such a bitch.* I know I'm supposed to be practicing gratitude.

"Just kidding!" I call after his disappearing form, gesticulating with my broken shoe for effect.

Why do I sabotage the guys who might actually be good for me? This is really the big question I face as I return to L.A. and the prospect, after the Muffs prodding me into it, of signing up on *Match.com* or *E-Harmony*, or any one of an endless number of dating websites in hopes of finding an available—meaning *unmarried*—man, instead of the married one I've been trying to cure myself of. Freckles might even have been a contender in that boy-next-door kind of way, but if I can't be patient with a nice guy like him, what hope is there?

I snarl at a few members of the *Hello Kitty* contingent who stare at me open-mouthed and back away. My right ankle begins to throb, and I'm just hoping that the fall has only caused a minor tweak because I desperately need some exercise to unwind when I get home—a fierce workout on a treadmill or, better yet, a dance class—in different shoes, obviously.

Slinging my over-the-shoulder bag, which had fallen in front of my shoulders, back where it belongs, I grab hold of the handle on my ballistic roll-aboard Tumi case and—*ouch*—start limping, barefoot, in the direction of the gate.

Hobbling as fast as I can, I become aware of a generalized overall body clamminess and that my hair is clinging to my neck under the collar of my white Pink's shirt—so much for that promised crispness. I also realize that I am unable to correct these fashion faux pas without stopping. Not that stopping would really help when a girl is peri-menopausal and under stress— conditions which will likely soon manifest in another vile symptom like hives or swollen ankles. But there's no time to stop. So I forge ahead, my shirt collar pressing against my neck from the shoulder bag as I attempt to move at a limping lope, rolling the case in a reasonably straight line behind me.

It could be that part of my current stress is due to over- reacting to Madelyn's nonplus response to my seeing Udi. But how could she be so blasé, particularly since she claimed that before Udi came along, she hadn't felt a flicker for anyone else in years? How could she let that go so easily? Me—I'd kill to find a guy who sparked my plug the way he had hers.

At my age, fast approaching forty-two years on the planet, I realize how rare those feelings are—more accurately, how rare both those feelings and suitable single guys are. So much so that if I found one who did it for me, I wouldn't be so quick to let him go. Hah! If that wasn't just like a woman carrying on with a married man. Well, at least I can admit the unsustainable nature of my situation enough to say that the whole *meshuggener* mess had led to the decision to attempt online dating as soon as I returned home.

Then again, maybe my romantic notions were getting the better of me, and it was not Udi I saw— only the wishful thinking of the incurable romantic. After all, he was naked the last time I saw him, naked and dead on the day bed in Maddie's house in Agoura Hills. It was more than likely that I hadn't been focusing enough on his face; I do get carried away by their bodies...

"Koon wa ba, Losa Angelisan oni ake tashta. Arigato," a voice was blaring over the loudspeaker.

It sounded like my flight was boarding; I distinctly heard the words *Los* and *Angeles* mixed in with the Japanese. *Oh no.* I can't miss this plane. It's vital that I pick up the pace and I do— but eeow, that ankle hurts—as the voice continues in slaughtered English. "AH-den-shun pweese lady an' gentoomen. Fligh numbah fi-oh-seex to Los Angeles is finohw boading a'gate foteen. Fligh numbah fi-oh-seex… "

Final boarding? What happened to pre-boarding and boarding of people with infants and then all those zones? At this point, the urgency of my situation necessitated actually lifting the rolling bag into my arms—*double eeow*—and turning myself into the biggest, barreling, red-headed broad I could, limping even faster through the terminal and trying to give the impression I had no ability to stop which, in fact, was the truth. People veritably leapt out of the way as I sprinted the final twenty-five yards to the gate.

An efficient Japanese woman of indeterminate age stood in front of the ticket scanner. She had a tidy bun on top of her head, and her hand was outstretched for my boarding pass, a prim look of reprimand on her face. I handed her the boarding pass, heart pounding, ankle throbbing, and bowed my head slightly in the traditional expression of Asian submission. *Hah! If she only knew.*

She says something. It might have been "Welcome to Japan Airlines," or "You look like Amanda Bynes." I don't know which, but I decide it's the former, not only because it makes more sense but because if it were the latter, I'd have to sock her one.

Actually, I'm impressed when people speak more than one language, even if they're usually unintelligible to anyone other than their own culture. It certainly doesn't do much for America's stature in the world when the average American travelling abroad goes around a foreign country uttering the smug, "Why should I speak—*fill in the blank*: French, Russian, Mandarin, whatever—when they—and here they point to the offending native speaker in their native land—speak English?"

Though I can't say I'm fluent in anything other than my native tongue, thanks, in part, to my conservative Fresno upbringing, I'm very proud that I can say, "Hello/please/ thank you/where is the bathroom/ and how much is the wine?" in ten—count 'em, ten!—different languages. I don't know if this is what my parents envisioned for me when, at fourteen, I displayed the educational level of a freshman in college, but like I said, I'm destined for great things.

Now, as I gingerly make my way down the ramp to the waiting plane, I felt like I always do when boarding a jumbo jet, as if I were in a fun house without the fun—no mirrors, no spinning disks or revolving cylinders that give the impression of moving while standing still. No—just a boxy wind tunnel wherein I have to squint and close my mouth lest some FOD fly in, while, dripping with perspiration, I follow the path, like a cow to slaughter, toward the cabin door.

Just before I step onboard, I try to fix my hair before making my grand(ish) entrance. If the seated passengers, including my client, Viggo Mortensen, are going to glare at me for delaying their take off, I might as well look like I'm worth waiting for and prompt them to wonder who the chic woman is who's caused the delay.

Most of the time, I put "the-disaster-known-as" my hair up to keep it from turning into the kind of frizzy, gnarly mess it had now become. But today, I'd been going for sexy—at least that's how I hoped it looked when I'd left the hotel, prior to my physical exertions—because I'd been hoping to get upgraded to business class so I could sit next to Viggo. In that scenario, acted out in front of the hotel's bathroom mirror, I was flinging my must-have locks around and flirting with the charming actor about art and music and living a purposeful life as we winged our way back to la-la land after his stellar performance in a series of Kubota Tractor commercials. Not that flirting on the airplane was going to get me any further than flirting during the shoot had—which was nowhere. But I'd still be angry with myself for not trying, and at last check, he was single; so for me, this would be something new.

I have this love-hate thing with actors: I'm attracted by the larger-than-life, valiant characters they play on screen, but, in reality, so many of them are vain, self-serving, and not even very good in bed unless there's a mirror nearby that allows them to—while gazing at their reflection as they penetrate some arbitrary body—actually make love to themselves.

Clearly, I wasn't going to sit with Viggo, but at least I'd made my flight, which is more than I could say about the time, a couple of years ago, when I spent two weeks in Switzerland for a series of BMW spots with Catherine Zeta-Jones. That time, it had totally been my fault. Nobody had made me have a fling with a remarkably handsome and amusing German microscope company executive who was attending a convention in the same hotel and who, of course, turned out to be married—detecting a pattern yet?—with a penchant for screwing anything over forty degrees that moved. He'd lied so convincingly, I believed him when he told me he was divorced and hadn't been with anyone in a year.

That time, I missed my flight because I felt compelled to do what any self-respecting modern woman would have done under the circumstances: I crashed the Annual Bausch Microscope business breakfast, picked up the lying pig's plate of pickled herring, and broadsided it into his gaping maw. Soon, three other women began hurling water pitchers, coffee cups, and pastries at the louse. It seemed they, too, had succumbed to his charms. They hadn't known about me, and it was abundantly clear they hadn't known about each other. My only regret had been not sticking around to see what happened next.

This singular event may have helped me steer clear of self-destructive relationships with married men while on work-related trips (the only kind I ever go on unless you count infrequent visits to Fresno), but it had yet to cure me of my attraction, unwittingly (and unwillingly, of course), to married men in my own city, like the one I was currently ensnarled with back in L.A.

Now, as I try to move through first class with grace and aplomb, I'm aware of the dirty looks from men in suits and the haughty-looking "women who shop"—the latter probably headed to the U.S. to ransack American stores with their inflated yen, euros, dinars, and pounds—perturbed at having their shopping trip delayed by the likes of me, slowly making my way through *their* cabin to get to the rest of the people of no consequence in coach.

I feel the glare of one of these women judging me and, "Oh my goodness, I'm so sorry!" I say, as I accidentally knock her elbow just enough to ever-so-slightly spill her free Mimosa onto her pale beige haute couture traveling costume with matching designer handbag. *Such a shame…she'll have to go straight to the Balenciaga Boutique in Beverly Hills and buy another.* Well, at least I confirmed her worst suspicions about my character.

Continuing on through business class, I spot Viggo, sunglasses on, head tipped back, enjoying an apparent snooze. Damn, he had looked so fine on that tractor—what an earthmover. But now, he doesn't even know I'm here, the ingrate. I flick my tangled web of hair anyway. *Some*body might be noticing.

And then I enter coach, that engorged mid-section of any commercial jetliner, which veritably swells with people, many of whom have engorged mid-sections themselves. If you squint, blurring your vision, you can sort of imagine an oversized chocolate tin from a big box store—the kind they put out at Christmas—where every compartment is filled with something mysterious you really don't want to take a chance on.

I look up, figuring there will be no place to tuck the Tumi anywhere near my seat, so I'd better start looking. And, of course, it's immediately apparent that all the overhead storage bins are jammed. Kabuki masks, boxes of sake, and duty-free Scotch join the luggage and pieces of clothing, crowding the bins for as far as I can see and pretty much guaranteeing there won't be a spot for my one little carry-on with the perfectly measured three-ounce containers in their quart-sized zip-lock plastic bag. Crap, crap, *crap!*

For all the trouble I went through to call her, Madelyn might have at least *pretended* to believe me. Calling had made me so late, I can't even find a place for my bag. I *hate* that! Why is it everything about air travel is a challenge? The temperature is always either too hot or too cold, and there are always *so many people.* Where are they going, and why are they on *my* plane?

If you're getting the sense that I'm angry, you're right. I'm an angry white woman. Get over it, you say? Granted, things could be a lot harder than they are, and perhaps I shouldn't complain. But things could be a lot easier, too.

Our would-be first female president, Hillary, would agree with me on this. People could be way nicer, smarter, more considerate, and the world would be a better place as a result. But everyone behaves as if they didn't have to share the planet or the not-so-friendly skies with other human beings—not to mention animals, birds, and bugs—including women like me, Nancy Pelosi, and Lady Gaga; not that they fly coach, but you know what I mean—who want all the stuff men have.

I take a deep breath and let it out slowly, imagining I'm back in Los Angeles, clasping a pole in K-Love's intermediate dance class, circling to the sounds of J. Cole's "Power Trip" and loving life. And I remind myself, as I always do in times of stress, I must learn to practice gratitude; I breathe deeply while repeating my mantra in my head: Inhale: *Yes, yes, yes, yes;* exhale: *Thank you, thank you, thank you, thank you.*

I'm moving again, and spot a flight attendant handing out headsets a few rows away on the other side of the plane. So I limp over, smiling cheerily, hoping she can help. Her hair is cut in a bob, and she wears a nametag that says, "Kitty." Seriously, "Hello, I'm Kitty." She can't be serious.

"Hello, Kitty," I say, smiling as genuinely as Reese Witherspoon pulled over for a moving violation. "I wonder if you might help me."

She beams back a not-altogether-genuine smile herself, but of course she's not had the benefit of working with actors as I do, being able to mirror behavior on a daily basis. "Oh-hi-oh, wuh I can do for you?" she asks in heavily accented English.

"Kitty, could I ask you, isn't the rule of the skies that a passenger gets *one* carry-on? Because there are people on this flight who must have more than one. Otherwise, all the overhead bins wouldn't be so full, ya know?" I give her an "aw shucks" kind of shrug, hoping she'll agree and do something about this gross miscarriage of justice.

Kitty's expression doesn't change.

"See, I only have this one carry-on," I continue, speaking a little slower and acting it out with hand gestures in case her English comprehension isn't up to speed.

I realize it irritates non-English speakers when Americans do this, but I really believe it can help them understand better; so I forge ahead.

"And as you can see—" I point to my eyes—"there's no place to put it." I point to the overhead bin and shrug.

"Do you think we could find out who owns all this stuff?" I draw a question mark in the air and indicate all the passengers. "Because I'm pretty sure I few people on this plane have exceeded their baggage limit."

I wag my finger to indicate somebody has been very, very bad. "So if we were to do that, then we could put all their excess stuff under the plane." I end my demonstration with a flourish, swinging a pretend suitcase in one hand, sliding it under the other—simulating the underbelly of the plane—and slamming the non-existent door before finally, brushing my palms together with a smile.

"Sorry," Kitty says, reaching for my Tumi and not the least bit sorry about it. "You late. Take seat and adjust seat belt low cross lap; we taking off soon."

"But—" I protest, holding onto the bag. "I only have one bag!"

She won't let go. "Put under plane."

"No!" I say, realizing I shouldn't be having this fight with Kitty. "I mean—" I try a softer tone. "What are rules if nobody enforces them? Let's get a few people with more than one carry-on to put their unfiltered sake under their seats."

Where was Maddie, the mediating Muff, when I needed her? Oh, right, asleep in L.A., unsympathetic to my plight, unsympathetic to her own plight!

"Sit—down!" Kitty says, trying to take my Tumi. For such a tiny figure, she's surprisingly strong.

"Let me...have my...*ugh*—" I use all my weight to snatch the Tumi from Kitty's clutches. "Bag!" My ankle is really killing me.

We stare at each other for a few seconds, while I'm quite sure she is considering telling somebody in the cockpit there is a terrorist on board.

I compose myself. Inhale: *Yes, yes, yes, yes;* exhale: *thank you, thank you, thank you, thank you.* "I'll just put it under the seat in front of me and have leg cramps and back trouble from your airline's flawed policies and this twenty-hour flight. Thank you for your help."

Once I'm back on the other aisle of the Jumbo Jet, I continue to limp into the bowels of the plane until I finally reach my row—forty-five—and stare at the spot that is my seat. It's a bit of red and purple upholstery, barely visible between a sumo wrestler and a woman in the shape of a tent who met my gaze with an expression that dared me to even try squeezing between them.

Casually, I glance over my shoulder, desperate for another place to put my ass for the duration of the flight, but it's quite clear that every seat is taken. Not only that, it seems like most of the people occupying the seats are huge—even the Japanese passengers.

When did that happen? Japanese people, other than sumo wrestlers, of course, are usually thin. Could childhood obesity be wreaking havoc in Japan, too? With human cargo this size, we might not get off the ground.

Oh, why was there no empty seat next to Viggo? If we're going to crash, it might actually be all right if I could just be near him. If I were to perish in a plane crash, at least I'd be spared further grief from my mother about how I missed out on having kids and how terrible Hollywood is. More importantly, I'd be spared any further thought about how she might be right. *Breathe—I am destined for great things!*

Resigned to the situation, I sigh and fish out my e-reader, on which *The Glass Castle*, the Muffia Book Club's current read, awaited me. There was nowhere to go, and no one was going to help me better my situation. But at least Kitty hadn't gotten me kicked off the plane. *So make the best of it, Quinn. This too will pass.*

I take another deep breath, pick up the Tumi, and squeeze past tent lady into my sliver of a seat, wedging my bag under the seat in front of me. It's going to be a very long flight, but I'm heading home. And though my seatmates' combined mass is four times mine, should either of them attempt to monopolize an armrest, they do so at their own peril. I may have very little control over anything in my life, but my elbows are very sharp.

CHAPTER 2

HAVING SEXUAL intercourse with a very large man has never been something I longed for, though I've often wondered what it might be like; not necessarily a sumo wrestler, but someone of that size and stature who exists on a grand scale and takes up a lot of space—a Pavarotti type of man. My curiosity stems from the concern that even if this large man's penis is perfectly normal in size, as penises go, it's going to look small, buried as it must be—particularly in its non-erect state—in mounds of flesh. It's the visual that I find both amusing and disturbing; amusing, for obvious reasons, and disturbing for less obvious ones having to do with finding the penis—providing, of course, that I was inclined to look.

And how did sex even work with a big man? Did the flesh get in the way? And if the belly protruded substantially beyond the groin, as indeed it usually did with men of generous girth, how was a woman to position herself so as to achieve full penetration without adipose obstruction?

These were the questions that consumed me now, pressed into my seat as I was, essentially trapped by Sumo, a Mount Fuji of a man, and far stronger than I. My first reaction, however, was one of hope—hope that his penis was, in fact, trapped by mounds of flesh, unable to press beyond its rolls; the sumo wrestler's body, in essence, was a buffer against rape.

Where had the tent woman gone? Not that she would have done anything about what was happening in seat 45B. And hadn't I been reading a book? Yes, *The Glass Castle*, on my Kobo e-reader. I needed to find it. Book club was coming up, and this time I was determined to finish the assigned book. This time I would wow the Muffs with my erudite commentary.

I pushed into Sumo's mountainous middle with my fingers. His fleshy folds could certainly house a book, or possibly, such was his vastness, even a toaster oven. It was simply—or perhaps not so simply—a matter of finding which fold he hid things in. Not so simple because it seemed like the inside crease of each fold was some five or six inches closer to the vital organs than the outer rolls. In order to reach that inner lining, I needed to contort my body so as to pry apart the rolls and squiggle my fingers inside. Pressing deeper, I found the crease and kept wiggling my fingers. How *does* one clean in there? The interminable folds were reminiscent of a bulldog's jowls or a sharpei's facial wrinkles, only deeper and wider, like the Shenandoah foothills. I made one last attempt to extend my hand deeper, a little farther and—*kersplatz.*

Jolted awake, I found myself lying on the floor of my apartment. There I was, fully clothed and surrounded by what appeared to be every pillow I owned, which, no doubt, had contributed to the disturbing vision of Jelly Belly copping a feel.

But had it only been a vision? I had the distinct sense that my subconscious was recalling Sumo's porcine presence hovering over me during the flight when I'd nodded off for a few minutes while tent woman was in the rest room. Or had she been there, complicit in his febrile explorations.

With the two warm, fleshy forms rhythmically rising and falling on either side of me, it's no wonder I'd fallen asleep on the plane. Though initially feeling trapped, it turned out that my rowmates' deep, relaxing inhalations and exhalations had lulled me into a state of torpor, during which time Sumo must have pushed himself on me. Now, it was too late to confront him.

Other than the nagging suspicion I'd been violated, however, being able to sleep for a couple of hours during the flight had been bliss, as had the hours I'd spent awake reading *The Glass Castle*. It's rare I finish any book in time for book club, but with Jeannette Walls's memoir—the story of a girl raised by insane people who happened to be her parents—I felt connected to the author in a very real way. We shared a similar past that made reading the book feel like a memory. Not that my father—God rest his bleepin' soul—ever pimped me. No, it was more the tone and the way she reflected back on her childhood with a certain generosity of spirit that made me keep reading until I'd finished.

After learning about all the things poor Jeannette endured on her way to adulthood, I also had a sort of revelation. I say, "sort of," because I've had the thought before, making the word *revelatory* an expression of hyperbole. Still—whatever grounds a person in reality is worth mentioning. What I realized is I felt guilty about all the snarky complaining I'd been doing lately; all that angry white woman stuff.

When I thought about it, I was grateful for so many things. Not the married guy so much, but my friends and even my silly job getting commercials for celebrities. Seriously, I should be ashamed of myself whining about the petty inconveniences of international jet travel—*it was international jet travel!* Some people never get to go anywhere.

Sure, I could be agenting talent on big movies instead of in foreign ads, but at least I still get to hang out with Viggo and Benedict and Brad, occasionally rubbing up against them—even if it's by mistake, and even if they're stinkier and dirtier than you'd ever imagine they'd be. *Uh—there I go again; be grateful,*

Quinn. Yes, yes, yes, yes; thank you, thank you, thank you, thank you! Who cares if they haven't bathed? Some people would kill to get a whiff of Mr. Cumberbatch, no matter what he smelled like. I smiled and closed my eyes. *MMMmmmm....I knew* what he smelled like.

My cellphone was ringing and probably had been ringing for awhile, only I was too sleepy to realize it. Somewhere, lost in all the pillows, was my mobile playing its jazz-era ring tone. *I really needed to change that.* "I Ain't Got Nobody" had turned out to be a self-fulfilling prophecy, but when I chose it, I'd just come off "Girls Just Want to Have Fun," and that hadn't borne any fruit, either. I was trying reverse psychology.

Kicking away a pillow that said "Keep Calm and Wear Spiked Heels," I once again felt the pain in my damaged ankle while my ring tone continued: "...my baby don't care for me."

Spotting the phone, at last I picked it up, fumbling and almost dropping it as I brought it to my ear without checking caller I.D.

"I *knew* it!" said the female voice, further shaking me from my jetlagged state.

"Who is this?" I mumbled, finally getting the damned thing secure.

"What do you mean, who is this? It's Jelicka. Maddie told me you called her from Tokyo, and I just want to be on record as saying, 'I *told* you he wasn't dead.'"

Eeeeerrrrrkkkk—!

Cue SFX of screeching tires. Insert the visual of a car skidding out and coming to rest at the edge of a steep precipice. This is the part of the movie where we might go to a flashback, show the audience how the character ended up in a car skidding to a stop at the edge of a steep precipice; or, maybe we'd start to hear a voice over—perhaps a woman reflecting on the moment everything in her life changed. I don't know about all that; I just want to go back and either refresh your memory, or fill you in on some things before we proceed with the story.

If you're not already onboard with what's happened with The Muffia up to this point, or for some reason, you don't accept my definition of the term, *The Muffia*, let me start by saying there's no hidden meaning. The Muffia is a book club, and that's pretty much it. We are nine women living in the greater Los Angeles area of California, USA, and we've been reading books together for over twelve years. That's it.

We're friends too, of course, some of us enjoying the company of one or more Muffs over and above the others, but that's only to be expected when you put nine women together. We bond, detach, and re-bond all the time. But through all the shifts, what is of greatest importance remains: we all like each other and respect each other's opinions—particularly about books—that is, when we've read them, which we don't always get around to, given the demands of life. This, too, we accept in each other.

We are not, in any way, associated with the group of militant English mothers who call themselves *The Muffia*, whose members criticize bad mothering wherever they see it; nor are we connected to a lesbian porn collective using the name, though we have been known to discuss pornography at great length during book club meetings. In fact, I can recall a particularly heated discussion we had once when we should have been talking about Adrian LeBlanc's *Random Family*. Instead of discussing what might be done regarding the problem of inner city youth and poverty in New York City—hell, *any* major city—we became immersed in a conversation about vajazzling and the pros and cons of vaginal rejuvenation surgery, which after careful review, most Muffs—Jelicka excluded—decided wasn't worth the pain or expense. Deciding on *that* was way easier than figuring out how to eradicate the cycle of poverty.

The Muffia Book Club has been around since 2001 and, as far as we're concerned, even though the other claimants to the name have female power in their mission statements, we feel they've taken their muffs in the wrong direction. And to forestall any additional confusion, let me re-introduce the members of the real and true Muffia Book Club:

You've no doubt deduced, by this point, that my name is *Quinn*, and I've probably told you more than enough about me for now. Maddie, who prefers to be called *Madelyn*, is a divorced mom and mediator who had the wild affair with the guy I saw at the Narita Airport who is supposed to be dead. Maddie wrote about The Muffia in a book called—rather obviously, IMHO—*The Muffia*, which perhaps you've read. Now it's my turn to write about us, and I'm calling my story *More Muff*, which granted isn't all that original either, but my excuse is I *represent* talent—I don't have any of my own. Despite my parents' contention that I was destined for great things, their sanity was later questioned when I was the only child of five who didn't have an arrest record by age eighteen. "Great," after all, is relative. But I thank them anyway because even though I turned out far more ordinary than they'd have you believe, their conviction gave me the confidence to succeed, and it did, after all, get me out of Fresno. Not that there's anything wrong with Fresno. It's close to Yosemite. The truth is, I probably would have wanted to get out of wherever I grew up. Even though I have no plans to return, Fresno now seems like a refuge from all the insanity in Los Angeles. *Oops—didn't mean to start talking about me again.*

Lauren is the member of The Muffia whom some of us secretly refer to as "Rich Muff." She married an heir to the Anheuser-Busch dynasty—before they sold it to Germany. She doesn't act like a rich girl, though, not that I have any deep knowledge about how girls as rich as Lauren act. She's down to earth, has a couple of kids, and is starting a non-profit aimed at curing Alzheimer's that has a too-long name. If it were a movie, it would bomb for sure, but just because you name your organization the *Alzheimer's Search for the Cure at the Sweet-Busch Center for Neurological Research* doesn't mean it's going to fail. I was simply concerned people would hear Sweet and Busch together, and not even read the mission statement.

Sarah worked her way up to mid-management at Williams-Sonoma and regularly hooked us up with expensive Balsamic Vinegars and biscuit mixes, but gave it up to raise her son, Nate Jr., which was unfortunate for us, though clearly better for Natey. We're all a little concerned about her too-modern open marriage to Nate Sr., which the rest of us think involves swinging and seems to be collapsing under the strain. *Rachel*, the youngest Muff at thirty-two, is a painter. She's very talented but super-opinionated—especially about books, which can get sort of tedious. She's a blonde bombshell who's dabbled in the same sex arena, but lately always seems to have a new guy in her life. Next up is *Kiki*, who is married to Saul with a son named Troy who is, or was, a vegan. She used to be an actress—a pretty good one, too— but now she's training to be a nurse practitioner, which all of us are happy about since we don't know what kind of health care we're going to be able to afford in our old age, with or without Obamacare.

Then there is *Paige*, who is the unofficial Muff boss. She teaches tennis and is in a highly dysfunctional relationship—or so the rest of us think— with a guy named Richard, but we all give her props for trying to make it work. She has a couple of kids under ten from a previous relationship and is a total hands-on mom with the school—volunteering and carpool and school trips to every museum in California. She's a great girl and a fantastic cook and has been known to throw her weight around on book choices. The Muffia's most inspirational member is, without question, *Vicki.* She's divorced with a grown son (she married young), and she's also a cancer survivor. It's not her style to whine or complain, and she is filled with that sense of gratitude I'm still working on. *Yes, yes; thank you, thank you.* Maybe it helps to feel like you've been given another shot at life. Vicki has always worked, and now she's decided to go back to film-making and, for some reason, has been shooting our book club gatherings. All of us are hoping she never does anything with the footage because it would be devastatingly embarrassing, if for no other reason than it would be too boring to watch; how embarrassing is that?! But it was Vicki who said she'd try online dating with me. We figured we could help each other, away from the scrutiny of some of the other more aggressive, serial dating Muffs who might think they knew best and tell us what to do.

And finally there's *Jelicka,* the Muff who just woke me up. Jel is a character out of *Desperate Housewives.* Recently divorced, she tends to overdo it on the Botox and lip injections—at least as long as her spousal support holds out—and who knows what other kinds of procedures, such as the aforementioned vaginal rejuvenation. Wacky as she can be, her intentions are honorable and her heart is pure. She's also The Muffia's very own resident conspiracy theorist—a label that has only increased in aptness since her husband left her for an *older* woman. According to her, this was *not* supposed to happen! Though encouraging to older women everywhere it has, in no small way, tweaked Jelicka's entire worldview. She has seen multiple UFOs, is convinced the government staged the moon landing in the New Mexico desert— not to mention masterminding 9-1-1—and swears there's a consortium of international scientists who have developed a cure for cancer, but Big Pharma won't release it because cancer care is a gazillion-dollar business, the loss of which might destroy our tiny hold on positive economic growth.

She could be right about some or even most of these things. But while I appreciate that she has us thinking about topics we might otherwise not pay any attention to, life's too short to be that paranoid.

"Quinn, are you listening? Oh, *Qui-inn!*" Jelicka was practically chanting my name on the phone.

"Huh? I'm here," I said, still trying to figure out how I ended up lying on my living room floor.

"I want to be on record as saying, 'I *told* you so.' "

"*Mmm*, you told us so. On record; duly noted."

"Now you're patronizing me."

"I'm not." I yawned. "I just need coffee."

As you might expect, Jelicka's assuming that Udi was still alive meant about as much as saying the Big One's coming which, by the way, she tells us at every book club gathering, along with warning us to replenish our earthquake kits. But neither Udi nor earthquakes can we do anything about, save for, in the case of earthquakes, trying to make ourselves feel better by stocking up on water and canned goods. From the moment Jelicka heard about Udi having a heart attack and dying while he and Madelyn were having sex, followed soon after by his getting carted off by his so-called friends, Jel was already on record saying he wasn't dead.

"You guys just thought I was being my typical, overly-vigilant self," she was saying now. "But voila—turns out he's alive the whole time, just like I said."

I yawned loudly for effect.

"What's the matter?"

"I'm exhausted. I just flew twenty hours next to a sumo

wrestler and woke up thinking we had sex."

There was a beat. "Seriously?"

"Seriously the flight, or seriously I had sex with the sumo?"

"The sex, silly."

"I don't know…it's possible."

She paused again. "I don't know what to say…good for you?"

"How did you hear I saw Udi?" I decided that no good could come from continued thoughts of sex with the sumo.

"Maddie has a date with a new guy, so I asked if he was as hot as her sexy, dead-slash-not-dead Mossad agent boyfriend—you know, a logical question I thought—and she told me you called her. I got the distinct impression he wasn't."

In my current mental state, she was talking too fast for me to keep up. "Wasn't what?"

"As *hot*, of course. Anyway, I was very impressed you recognized him, particularly considering he was playing dead when you met. I'm hoping now that he's back and alive. I'll get a chance to see that bad boy for myself."

"I don't know how. The guy I saw, if it *was* him, could be in Kazakhstan or any number of other places by now."

"The way you and Maddie carried on about his body—it was like he was Michelangelo's David, you know? Like some awesome marble statue." She paused. "What does that even mean? Women say that kind of thing all the time. So-and-so's boyfriend is like a Greek statue. Most of those Greek statues are missing limbs, so I don't exactly see it as a compliment."

"He was kind of like a statue…I guess; except he had all his limbs, of course. His abs were amazing, and his ass was Zeus-like."

I really needed coffee. My head was now throbbing to the same beat as my ankle. "What time is it?" I pulled the phone from my ear to glance at the screen. *Shit—it was noon!* Talent Partners had little sympathy for any employee's problems, not even those with injuries and accustomed to different time zones. I had permission to come in late, but I was pushing it. "I need to get going."

"Now that he's risen—" Jelicka went on obliviously. "Wait, if he's Israeli, that means rising again would be a religious impossibility, wouldn't it? Only Jesus did that, I mean if you believe in Jesus. Don't tell my Rabbi. I can't remember anything I'm supposed to from my Bat Mitzvah. Which reminds me, do you want to sign up for *Lumosity*? They say it keeps your brain exercised; it's sort of like Pilates for your pre-frontal cortex. They're doing a two-for this week."

"I can't even make it to the gym and pole dancing on a semi-regular basis, let alone a Pilates for the brain class."

"You can do the exercises from your phone! Anyway, it's something to consider, especially now that Alzheimer's has struck the Muffia family."

"My grandmother had Alzheimer's, Jel, and Sarah's grandfather and who knows who else's aunts and uncles. It's not just Lauren's mom."

"That makes this next thing I'm going to say even more vital to understand!" *Oh, no, she was impassioned.* "Lauren is doing all this work—putting together the non-profit and the benefit—to try to halt her mother's disease before it's too late, right? And yes, I admire her for it. But what people don't understand is that Alzheimer's is another disease created by the government to get rid of old people. They want to stick 'em in a facility and get the taxpayers to pay for their meds until they eventually fade away."

See what I mean about Jelicka and her conspiracy theories?

"Isn't there a genetic component to Alzheimer's disease?" I sort of recalled reading this somewhere, but fittingly, not remembering where. "I'm pretty sure there is."

"Minor," Jelicka quipped. "If you only look at the genetics, we all have it a little. But they're doing something to make it turn into full-blown Alzheimer's."

This can't be true, but just because Jelicka's paranoid, doesn't mean I don't agree with her some of the time. I'm terrified of getting the diagnosis. Lauren's mom isn't even "old." Seventy is the new fifty, or whatever. Exercising my brain suddenly seemed extremely important. "Send me the info," I said. "I'll check it out."

"The good news is that by starting her organization, Lauren will have a chance to redeem herself and her family after turning on her country when she and George became little Mr.-and-Mrs.-watch-us-sell-the-great-American-beer-company-to-the-highest-bidder."

"George's *father* sold the company, Jel. And what does it matter now in our globalized world? The French buy Japanese companies, the Germans buy American, the Chinese buy…"

"The Chinese buy *everything!* They just bought the Pulaski Skyway, for God's sake. That's like buying New Jersey. What's next—the Grand Canyon?"

"I'd like them to buy my car." That stopped the rant, if only briefly.

"And what are *we* buying?" *She was on a roll now.* "Cheap clothes made by under-aged, under-paid workers in Bangladesh just before their factory caves in killing them all. Do we really need more crappy clothes? We don't *make* anything anymore."

"We make great cupcakes."

"Ha, ha." She was not amused.

"Jelicka, it's too early for this. My brain can't handle it. Besides, don't we make Botox? I'm pretty sure we do. There's a growth field if there ever was one. Think about all the Chinese we can sell it to."

"The Chinese don't get wrinkles. They won't buy our Botox."

I gave up. "Listen, I really have to get to work."

"George is a wimp," she said, ignoring me. "Sorry, Lauren, but your husband is a wimp. He should have stood up to his father. It's anti-American what they did. He should have stood up to the old man and said, 'No. No, no, no, no, NO!' Every country needs a national beer, and ours was Budweiser."

"So now it'll be a different brand. Things change; we have to adapt. I personally couldn't care less about beer."

"What's going to happen to the Clydesdales?"

"The what?"

"The horses."

"Oh, they'll be okay. Someone will want them."

"It's a shame… just a shame. Somebody will probably *eat* them!"

She was taking this way too personally. "You could start one of those online petitions people are doing now: 'Bring back our beer' or 'Save the Clydesdales.' "

She snorted. "Not a bad idea. I've actually been thinking about running for office—on this and a whole range of issues; I'd do a better job than a lot of these people getting elected and not doing anything. At least I have no desire to Tweet my naked body all over the planet, as if that helps get a bill passed."

Pulling the phone from my ear, I checked the time again, then put the phone on speaker so I could get going while she continued ripping holes in a growing list of individuals and institutions. I stretched my body to its full length, and a searing pain bolted through my ankle. "*Yeaowrwh!*"

"What's the matter?"

"Rolled my ankle running for the plane."

"Ouch."

Sitting up, I saw that my ankle had swelled to the size of

an eggplant. "No heels for me today," I sighed. "Hey, you're a shoe aficionado—can I wear Crocs to work?"

No answer. I rolled to pick up the phone and glanced at the screen, where it appeared the connection was still good. "Jel?"

"How is it possible you even own a pair of Crocs?" she hissed.

"I'm too tired to deny it."

"How about some cute gem-encrusted flip-flops? Wear those if you've waxed your legs recently."

"My legs are clean, but my toes are swollen together and shooting out at odd angles. Not quite as bad as Julianne Moore's did at Cannes, but still really unattractive."

"You're right; people will remember that and have a negative association. I recommend staying home."

"Not possible."

"How 'bout this: wear one good shoe and put the Croc on the other foot and maybe glue Swarovski crystals on it so it looks cute."

Swarovski crystals? Where did she think I was going to get Swarovski crystals to glue on my Crocs? "Can we talk later? I gotta go."

"Wait, *Quinn*! One more thing—what makes you sure it was him? I mean, can we *prove* it was him? What was it about the guy that told you he was the same guy who died, or supposedly died, at Maddie's and who we are referring to as Udi?"

She was not helping me start my first day back at work with grace and aplomb.

"I'm hanging up now." I needed to go into the agency appearing rested and polished with my best, only functional foot forward.

"Please?"

Clearly, this woman needed something more to do with her life. A Muff intervention might be called for.

I sighed. "Because I dressed him. I got a good look, and there were certain aspects I noticed beyond the abs and ass. Like he was kind of hairy, and he had this sort of thick stubble on the back of his neck covering a mole. The guy at Narita Airport had the same thing."

"Whoa."

"Okay, bye! See you at Rachel's for Book Club."

"Did he see you?"

"Jel!" Like a terrier, she was.

"I thought he looked my way, but I don't know if he looked *at* me. And if he did, I don't know how he would know me because obviously when I got to Maddie's, he couldn't open his eyes…I don't think."

"Oh, there are lots of ways around that. Tiny cameras get put in the craziest places now. He could have one in an eyebrow—possibly even surgically installed in his retina."

"Okay, enough." I had to stop her. I'm pretty sure that was only in movies. After all, I'm in the business.

"He had the chip in him, right?" she said.

"That never got verified."

"Don't forget the Israelis are very advanced. OMG, this is huge! Do you realize just how huge this is?"

It was like she'd received confirmation that the CIA had been holding Elvis in a controlled area.

"The thing is—then I really do have to get off the phone," I said, trying to be diplomatic. "The thing is, we need to let it go."

"How can we let it go?"

"It's none of our business is how. Even if you and I believe Udi is still walking around out there, in order for Maddie to keep moving forward, she needs to believe he's dead. Because if he's dead, he can't call her; but if he's alive and not calling her, it means he's not that into her, you know? Like that book—*He's Just Not That Into You.*"

"I couldn't get into it," she said without a trace of irony.

"But you know what it's about—when you're really crazy about somebody and he's not calling or treating you the way you want him to, it means he's just not that into you and you have to accept it and move on. Because if he *were* into you, he'd not only call, he'd tell you how nice you smell, remember your birthday, bring you flowers… "

"I wouldn't know. I guess no one's ever been that into me."

"That's not true; Roscoe was into you, and Sam-what's-his-name; Lots of guys have been into you… "

"Maybe."

"Anyway, it was obvious to me she didn't want to hear that Udi might be alive, so we need to carry on like I didn't see him. Otherwise, it's just going to be upsetting to her."

There was a beat, which I knew better than to infer that she agreed with me. Her tactic was to change the subject. "You still seeing Steve?"

I guess the topic of "guys who are just not that into us" put her in mind of my married lover. I'd told all the Muffs a couple of weeks ago that I'd broken it off with him, which was true, for the most part. But being as I'm weak, the situation remained "fluid." Funny thing—Steve seemed pretty into me, considering he was completely unavailable.

"Not really," I said.

"How do you *not really* see someone?"

"I'm still working on it."

"Who would think that women as cool as we are would have difficulty finding worthy men?" said Jelicka.

"Maybe we're not as cool as we think we are."

"No, we are."

I reached down and gingerly palpated my ankle, feeling another pain shoot up my leg. "My ankle is a mess."

"Want the name of a good ortho guy?" She might be a know-it-all, but she was always ready with a doctor recommendation.

"Maybe I should just go see Kiki."

"She's training to be a Nurse Practitioner, Quinn, not a foot and ankle specialist."

"How hard can it be to tell if it's broken?"

"It's probably just sprained. Wrap it up, take some Advil, and stay off it."

"Fine." I slowly pressed myself up to standing, putting as little weight onto my injured limb as possible. This would be brutal, but somehow I had to make an appearance at the office or Jamie Harris, my boss and one of the partners at Talent Partners, might be that much closer to replacing me with her ambitious assistant, with whom at least a few of us at work are sure she was having sex with.

"You know…" Jelicka started back up, "we wouldn't have to tell her we're investigating on our own."

"Jelicka, I gotta go. The Velocoraptriss said I could come in late, but at this point, I'm beyond pushing it." I hopped on one foot toward the bathroom. "And it doesn't matter to her if I can walk or not."

So we're just going to drop the whole thing? What if there's something going on that's a threat to national security?"

"If it makes you feel better, call the NSA or Homeland Security or whoever."

"Useless," she snorted. "They didn't do anything when the FBI agents told them there were terrorists in the U.S. learning how to fly jumbo jets."

"So maybe now they've learned their lesson. What else can

you do? Infiltrate the Mossad?" I immediately realized my mistake. "I take that back. Jelicka? Don't. Hear me? Don't."

She grunted what I hoped was her assent.

Splashing water on my face, I toweled off and studied myself in the mirror. Tired and drawn, my skin looked splotchy, reminiscent of scorched earth. The weather in Japan had been gray and gloomy, and now I saw both in my eyes, not that I should necessarily be blaming the weather.

Ugh—what day was it? I always lose track when I cross the International Dateline. Let's see...if I left Tokyo on Wednesday and they're sixteen hours ahead...the flight lasted twenty hours so that would mean it was still Wednesday. No. It was Thursday. *Oh, shit.* Thursday was usually the day I saw married guy. Not today, though. This Thursday I am going to be strong!

I stare at the hollows under my eyes—forty-two going on sixty, and what did I have to show for it? Even Jeannette Walls, who started with nothing but burn scars, has surpassed me. So what if her mom is a dumpster diver. My own mother has glaucoma and macular degeneration and just moved to a retirement facility outside Fresno. Jeannette has a great writing career and a husband who loves her. Me? I ain't got nobody save somebody else's man for an hour a week.

It's true I have great friends and a good career that I enjoy—a career a lot of people would be desperate to have. After eighteen years booking "C" and "D" list actors on commercials for everything from douche to donuts, I'm now booking the "A"-listers. I work at a prestigious talent agency with top talent, and I'm considered skilled at what I do. You'd be surprised just how many movie stars are willing to sell out to big corporations so long as the deal states the commercials will only air in foreign markets.

But now, with the proliferation of online video, ensuring *that* is well nigh impossible. The idea that any commercial will remain unseen by a star's core audience is ludicrous these days.

But I digress. At this point in my life, I'm able to afford the lifestyle Hollywood and non-Hollywood types alike dream of, and I know I shouldn't complain. The thing is, other than the Muffs and pole dancing, I don't have much else. No husband, no kids; my dad died, my mom might as well be dead, and my brothers are either in jail or in religious cults. So what do I do? Apparently, I thought it was a good idea to have an affair with a married man whom I meet up with on Thursday evenings for fast and furious sex, hoping one day he'll leave his wife. The whole thing is beneath me, beneath any woman of my stature. How does a smart, successful woman like me get herself into such a situation?

Well, in my case, married guy is smart, sexy, and he owns a cutting-edge architecture firm with offices in L.A. and Milan and a factory in Malaysia where his company makes prefab houses with built-in solar panels. He's so far ahead of the curve that he's doubled back on himself before the other guys have started. And he doesn't just run the place; he *owns* it. In the industry, people call him Mr. Greenhouse. He understands higher math and physics, which is just too sexy. But, like a lot of geeks, he can be a social nitwit. I must have a soft spot for nerds since I lost my virginity to the biggest math geek at Fresno High who wowed me with Pythagoras, Pi, and polynomials. He even showed me the mathematical significance of the name Quinn, which, suffice it to say, made me cream before I even knew there was a word for what was happening between my legs. And ever since, math makes me horny.

For the past two years, the object of my misplaced affection is one Steven Zucker—not any of THE Steven Zuckers—the producers and bankers and other rich and famous Steven

Zuckers. No, this is Steven I. Zucker. And the "I" does not stand for Ives or Irwin or anything like that. In married Steven's case, the "I" stands for Ignatius. *Who does that to a kid?* And I didn't find out from him, trust me. One Thursday, when I realized, for the 100th time, that our affair wasn't going anywhere, I went through his wallet while he was showering—just to see how much I could torture myself. There were the pictures of his family and, of course, they were all lovely. The woman was gorgeous—perfect hair, perfect smile, perfect body—as were the two beaming kids, which only made me feel more insecure and horrible, no matter how many times he tells me his wife is frigid and won't have sex with him and that he wants to run away with me.

The bottom line, and what's been hardest to admit to myself and anyone else I talk to about it, is that he *doesn't* run away with me, nor does he talk about how we'll do it if he were to actually follow through. The pain of that admission is the fuel that stokes my denial. If I stop denying, I have to change, and change is hard.

What's most ironic of all is that if one day he ever did follow through and announce that he'd worked it all out—our life together lay ahead of us, stretched out like a beach towel—I don't think I'd be able to follow through myself. I'd feel guilty. I know it's messed up, but it may be the drama and unfulfilled, unfulfillable illusions about each other that have kept us together.

This is my fault more than his, and I know I have to break it off once and for all, which is why I started telling the Muffs I stopped seeing him when I technically haven't. It's also why I agreed to try online dating with Vicki, even though success will elude me unless I get a total attitude reboot to simply get over feeling that there's no one else out there for me.

I unplug my phone from its charger and stick it in my purse.

This whole thing with Steven is so boringly predictable, that's what's so irritating. I should know better. In fact, I *do* know better; I'm just not doing it. *Yes, yes, yes, yes; thank you, thank you, thank you, thank you. I am destined for great things.*

Well, at this point, I've pretty much given up on great things, but I *am* going to become a better person.

CHAPTER 3

WITH MY damaged foot in a purple croc, I limped off the elevator and onto the fifth floor offices of Talent Partners, Inc. as gracefully as I could. Everyone, save for the receptionist, a recent college graduate named Daniel, seemed to be at lunch, which was just as well since when Jamie returned, I'd be at my desk, looking industrious, possibly negating the reality of how late I was.

Making my way across the mostly-open floor plan, over the tasteful wall-to-wall wool carpeting in muted shades of gray and grayer, I reach my office—an enlarged cubicle, really, which we who have one call a 'cubiffice'—and sit down. If half of life is just showing up, I'd made it. I'd shown up and my ankle didn't even feel too bad, the double dose of NSAIDs having done wonders and delivering on their advertised promises. Too bad all the anti-wrinkle creams I'd purchased over the years had not.

My mobile vibrated, and I looked down to see Steven's name on caller I.D. I considered picking up but let it go to voice mail. That was one place I would *not* be showing up today.

Other than making an appearance at Talent Partners, the only task I had to complete that particular afternoon was the paperwork for the Kubota shoot so that everyone involved on our end could get paid. You'd think that in the latter half of the first quarter of the 21st century I could have finished up the job from home with my ankle up on ice, but even with all the technological advancements and our faith in online transactions, believe it or not, some of what business required was still done on real paper and required real signatures.

As people slowly returned from their lunches, I chatted with colleagues who were curious about my shoe selection, Japan, and how Viggo looked on a tractor.

Sameer Kumar works opposite me in a cubiffice the size of mine. He's a soft-spoken, dark-skinned guy of about thirty-five originally from Sri Lanka—a former cricket player turned agent who basically does the same thing I do at T.P. except instead of dealing with A-list actors, he books athletes—Tiger Woods for Nike, for example. He handled that quintuple-timing, under-par husband throughout his multiple sextscapades.

Carolyn Marcus, with a slightly smaller cubiffice, is the go-to person for PSAs—also known as public service announcements. When various charities or causes need a mouthpiece—wanting one of our clients to speak out against smoking, or to be the new face of "Got Milk" or whatever—Carolyn is the one to field that call. She's whip smart and might one day call the shots at T.P. unless somebody hires her away to another agency first, which is probably what will happen since hiring from within seems to be threatening to those passed over.

The three of us—Sameer, Carolyn, and me— are assisted by a recent mailroom graduate named Rafe who puts out calls and basically takes care of our every non-sexual need, including indulging our caffeine addiction by driving to Peet's Coffee several miles away, even though there were three Starbucks installations within walking distance.

After an exchange at the water cooler, I hobbled to my desk, realizing the only person in our immediate area who had not returned from lunch was the newest member of our immediate team—Titania Cibulkova, a Moldovan immigrant by way of the

Ivy league, who had become Jamie's exclusive executive assistant—the very same assistant some of us suspected of having sex with our boss. And, as it happened, in a twist that I would soon come to find out was related, Jamie also had not returned from lunch.

Carolyn must have spotted my quizzical expression as I glanced from Titania's desk to Jamie's office—no cubiffice for Jamie— because she suddenly said quietly, "Things really heated up while you were gone."

I felt my eyebrows rise. *Very interesting...* "Do tell."

Carolyn took a sip of her Kombucha, got up, and strolled over.

Titania had arrived at Talent Partners four months earlier and worked a few different desks in the theatrical and literary divisions of the agency before landing with Jamie Harris. Titania was pretty and smart, and she dressed like a high-class secretary, but she did not strike me as gay. Not that I'd ever been particularly skilled at pegging a woman as lesbian unless her wardrobe was that of a bull dyke.

Both Carolyn and I noticed the furtive glances exchanged between Titania and Jamie prior to my leaving for Japan and surmised the two were beginning an office romance. Now, clearly, there had been developments.

Carolyn stood poised within whispering distance with her open bottle of Kombucha. "You like that stuff?" It smelled awful.

"It's so good for you," she said. "All the probiotics."

"MMMmm." I'd heard the latest spiel about how we need to put more bacteria into our guts because our food is, in fact, too clean. We must eat dirt is what they were saying. Dirt tasted better to me than Kombucha.

"Anyway," she said sotto voce, her eyes on the entrance. "This is the third day this week the two of them have taken an extended lunch."

"Are you sure they're together?" It seemed like the logical question.

"I haven't followed them, but watch what happens—Jamie will come back and half an hour later, Titania will show up." Carolyn glanced up toward the entrance and immediately pivoted back to her desk. "Here we go."

At that moment, Jamie strode across the floor, her burgundy leather Longchamp shoulder bag swinging alongside her. Peering beyond Jamie, I did not see the lovely Titania. I looked over at Carolyn who shrugged and mouthed the word "watch" before turning back to her computer screen.

Jamie Harris, if not the beauty so many of the agency's clients were, knew how to maximize what she had. Average in every way, she was always well-coiffed and impeccably dressed—usually in expensive earth-tone suits by Jil Sander or Armani—always carrying a bag that enhanced what she was wearing. The Longchamp was my favorite.

She stopped at my desk. "Good trip?"

"Great trip," I said, keeping it short. Jamie was not someone who enjoyed hearing an elaborate breakdown of events.

"What's with the purple Croc?" she asked, clearly perplexed, having grown accustomed to seeing me in heels.

"Rolled my ankle running for the plane."

She grunted unsympathetically. "Sorry to hear that. All the documents ready?"

"End of the day," I said.

She looked like she might protest— that this was far too long—but she just smiled. "Good. When they're ready, just give everything to Titania." And with that, she turned toward her office door.

"Where *is* Titania?" I called after her.

"She'll be here," said Jamie over her shoulder.

A couple of hours later, my work still unfinished, Titania had not only returned, she was now inside Jamie's office with the door closed. Thinking about what might be going on in there, I felt distracted and picked up my mobile without checking caller I.D.

"Hey babe, am I seeing you this evening?"

Steven. If truth be told, picking up had less to do with not checking caller I.D. than sensing who it might be and picking up anyway—in other words, I picked up at one of those moments of weakness I'd been suffering.

"I've been thinking about our favorite piece of furniture," he teased, his voice seductive.

Furniture was the furthest thing from my mind at that moment but, just to explain: I have this solid old dresser/sideboard thing that sits just off my kitchen and once belonged to my grandparents. Supposedly, it had been the focal point of the dining room in their Fresno farmhouse where buffet items were put out for big family dinners. Steven, however, liked it for sexual reasons because when I sat on top, naked and spread-eagled facing him (okay, it's a little premeditated), my poontang was at the perfect height for his cock.

"Steven, please—we're not seeing each other *any* more, remember? Besides, something's come up."

"You make me come up, I'll give you that. Just thinking about putting your ass up on that dresser has me really needing to see you."

"Then don't think about it. I'm at work, and I have a lot to catch up on."

"Why didn't you tell me?"

Realistically, I didn't have to tell him anything; I knew that rationally. But I heard his voice, and all the good stuff flooded my brain, none of the bad. This is why *I must never pick up when he calls!*

"I would have thought it might be sort of obvious," I said, "with the trip and everything. We had an extra day in Tokyo and with the time difference… Plus, I rolled my ankle running through the airport."

"Oh, Babe, you all right?"

"It's a little swollen, but I'll be fine." *Good, Quinn. Not a trace of encouragement.*

"Do you want me to come over later and take care of you? I miss you, Babe, and I can think of a few activities that don't require an ankle."

"Sounds nice but…" It did sound nice—the perfect antidote for all that was irksome, including the budding office love affair happening in front of my face at work. Irksome because when love was new, it was known to be infectious, and proximity to Steven would be very dangerous to my recovery. "I don't think that's a good idea."

I imagined him sitting at his glass desk in the corner office of his glass castle—hey, *The Glass Castle*—his dark, close-cropped curls with the start of gray catching the setting sun. A handsome, successful, married man in the prime of life, and I liked him—very much. In truth, I loved him. But he wasn't mine; he had a family, and continuing on would just pile on bad karma. And since coming to the conclusion he would never leave his wife, despite all his protestations to the contrary, I'd decided that anything that might happen between us in the future would have to be on my schedule. *Ugh, what am I thinking?* Thinking something *might* still happen between us in the future was disturbing and self-destructive.

"I can't," I said again, my Better Me winning this round. "There's an international corporate issue that's come up, and

I have to do due diligence." This was not altogether untrue.

He gave it a couple more tries, but my resolve held.

So far, so good; I'd put him off. But I knew if I didn't take further action, I might still cave to his will and my own longing. So I hung up and immediately decided to call a Muff for moral support. Which one, though? Well, including me, there are nine of us Muffs. Six have kids, three are divorced, two never married, a couple haven't worked in years; one's a vegan, one used to be into women, two still sneak cigarettes, one's Buddhist, one's Catholic, one's Protestant, two are Jewish, two are Atheists, and all of us enjoy a good cocktail. We Muffs consider ourselves women of today who are smart and/or talented and/or attractive and/or lucky and/or of some means, even if those means are meager. But which member of Muffia should I call to help me deal with my weakening flesh in the face of adversity?

"*Match.com, Nowlove* or *PlentyofFish*? Which one should we sign up for?" I asked Vicki, the Muff I'd chosen for the online dating adventure.

A motor whirred into use in the kitchen on the other end of the line, the creation of a fresh anti-oxidant juice in progress. "Vicki?"

"Hold on, I'm checking the blogosphere."

"What are you putting in that juice?" I hoped to be heard over the din. "Sounds like tree trunks."

"Carrots, kale with some probiotic and wheatgrass thrown in. But I'm reading the opinion blogs while I'm doing it." *Another probiotic freak.*

Vicki was the best Muff to share the slings and arrows of

online dating with because: (A) She had experienced adversity and would be able to withstand the probable vicissitudes of searching for love on the Internet; (B) Of the single Muffs with whom I might share this experience, her marriage had been over long enough to give her a healthy perspective; and (C) She was game.

None of the other Muffs was the right choice for one reason or another. Madelyn didn't want to, Rachel was off men, and Jelicka was still wounded after her recent divorce—no matter what she said. Plus, she was pushing *Cougarlife.com* like she owned it. While I may be the right age for cougar status, I'm totally the wrong temperament. And I would never give money to a company that ran a jingle with the lyric, "Cougar life dot com, so many women to try." So many women to *try*? What were we—a pu-pu platter? Clearly it was a site set up for cubs, not cougars.

The motor continued. If Vicki was talking, I couldn't hear her.

"Should I call back?" I yelled.

The juicemaster went off.

"According to this blogger," she said, "I think we're good to go with any of those three. I know women who've met nice guys on each of 'em, which proves… " I heard her slurp her juice concoction. "*Mmm,* tastey. Sorry. I guess, you know, theoretically, there are good men to be found anywhere."

Theoretically was a little speculative, but I was determined to remain upbeat about the prospects. "So you're saying, 'just pick.' "

"*Whoa…* " Vicki was obviously reading something on her screen but offering nothing more.

"Bad review?"

She took another slurp. "The little bot fishes, or whatever they're called, know I'm looking at dating sites, and suddenly

I'm getting pop-up ads for other sites. I just got one asking me to try *Dateafarmer.com*."

"If the idea of dating a farmer wasn't just plain odd, that would be really creepy."

"Don't worry. When we hang up, I'll search for gluten-free restaurants, missile launch systems and adult diapers. That will keep the data miners busy wondering about my ulterior motive."

"You sound like Jelicka," I said, slightly concerned. "You know, dating shouldn't be this hard. I hope we don't turn into a bunch of whiny, crotchety old women who start every sentence with, 'Back in the good ol' days… ' "

"Here's one," Vicki plowed on. "*Singlechristianteapartiers.com*. I'll take *Dateafarmer* over *Singlechristianteapartiers*, I'll tell you that much. What do you think about farmers?"

"Farmers are great and totally necessary, but to *date*?" I just didn't see it.

"Aren't they the new venture capitalists?"

"I don't think so, Vick. In L.A., the definition of a farmer is a guy growing hemp on reclaimed land in Compton."

Sameer appeared at the edge of my cubiffice, looking slightly put out. "My parents are farmers in Tamil Nadu, and my grandparents before them. Farming is a noble profession where I am from."

"It's noble everywhere." I covered the phone. "When we were in Japan and I saw Viggo on that tractor, I thought, *where would we be without farmers?*"

Sameer waggled his head, turned and walked away. I watched him, wondering how much he'd heard.

"What if you could meet an organic egg producer?" Vicki was saying. "Or somebody growing sustainable aquaculture? That would be sort of cool."

"If I had to choose, I'd take the entrepreneur cultivating

superior quality weed in Mendocino. Weed might just save America. That's not my line, by the way. I read it on *The Daily Beast.*"

"The product is appealing, but Mendocino is geographically undesirable," replied Vicki.

"Let me look." I typed *Dateafarmer* into the search bar. I still couldn't envision myself with a farmer, but maybe if I saw some pictures.

"See the hottie in the overalls with no shirt? He raises organic chickens."

Mmmmm, I sure did see him—Calvin—handsome, ruddy face, windswept sun-bleached hair, adorable crow's feet at the corners of his blue eyes. "Good looking," I agreed. "But why do I suddenly feel like a character in *The Grapes of Wrath*?"

"One wouldn't think you'd be such a snob, growing up in Fresno."

"Guess you *can* take the farm out of the girl, huh? Besides, my dad was an accountant."

"I could see myself with a salt-o'-the-earth type like Calvin," she said. "A strong man with big hands able to help us survive the coming apocalypse."

"If there's an apocalypse, no one is going to survive," I pointed out, "big hands or not—that's why it's called an apocalypse."

"Don't tell Kiki. She's working on the Brownie points so as to be saved."

I continued clicking around *Dateafarmer*, and the presentation was pretty slick—the definition of "farmer," rather generous— kind of like calling Kim Kardashian an "artist."

"I think they're using the word *farmer* as a metaphor of some kind," I suggested. "Beaver mining, for example. Or digging for orgasms."

"Such a skeptic." Vicki laughed, not taking the bait as Jelicka would have, which is another reason I'd chosen her to talk this through with in the first place. She was a far more serious sort—not one to encourage my cynicism, which only seems to be getting worse despite my commitment to becoming a better person.

Sure, my ankle hurt, and I was suffering from jet lag, but why was it so hard to be less cynical? The brief reprieve I experienced after reading *The Glass Castle* was now *Gone Girl*—which happened to be another Muff read, only slightly less enjoyable.

Clearly, working on eliminating my snarky attitude was getting the same amount of focused energy I would be devoting to those *Lumosity* exercises Jel told me about—which is to say, *none*. I was quickly transitioning to being a snark with no memory. Then I realized that maybe my memory was the *cause* of my snarkiness. If I had no memory, there'd be nothing to snark about! Suddenly, not having a memory seemed very appealing.

"We need to just choose a site and commit," said Vicki. "Every person I know who's dated online says that commitment is the most important part; which site you choose is beside the point. You have to get in there, read the profiles, have the conversations, go on the bad dates and kiss the frogs. But if you stick with it, you'll ultimately be rewarded."

"How long 'til *ultimately*?—I mean, best case—if you could hazard a guess."

"*Quinn*." She didn't need to say another thing. The reprimand was built in.

"All right," I acquiesced.

"This is going to be fun."

Fun? Unlikely. The whole enterprise sounded like work. Being lazy and back in bed with my married boyfriend seemed like the much easier—albeit worse—choice.

"I better go," I said abruptly, looking at the clock. "She-who-shall-not-be-questioned could walk out of her office with her new girlfriend at any second, and it's almost time for me to call Moscow. Get this—they want Joseph Gordon Levitt to do a commercial for Kentucky Fried Chicken."

"Will he do it?"

"No way. My job is to get them to consider other Joseph Gordon Levitts who sorta look like him."

"Sounds like fraud."

"You have no idea. It's wrong on so many levels, but I don't think the average Moscovite would know the difference. They still think of him as the little kid from 'Third Rock from the Sun.' "

Before we hung up, we agreed to choose our site, sign up for a webinar about online dating, write our profiles, and talk again in a couple of days, once the profiles of our dream dates started pouring in. Though significant energy would likely be expended before I met someone I liked, I needed to distract myself with at least the idea of another man if I was going to resist Steven. And having Vicki doing it with me ensured I'd follow through. This time, I vowed to myself, just like the woman who goes on and off her diet, I would turn my life around.

CHAPTER 4

FOOD AND alcoholic beverages are a vital part of any gathering of The Muffia Book Club. Talking about what book we were supposed to have read is just value added. The real reason we created the book club is to give ourselves a pretext for seeing each other and doing the aforementioned eating and drinking.

I needed to see my Muffs. It had been six weeks since the last book club gathering, and a few of the women I hadn't talked to since. That's far too long, especially when I need them for moral support so as not to fall off the Steven abstinence wagon, as I was in danger of doing. In my mind, our next book club meeting couldn't get here soon enough.

Pre-book club meal planning is the job—but mostly joy—of the hostess who selects the book to be discussed at the next meeting. With book club coming up in a few days at Rachel's, there were bound to be a flurry of emails going back and forth to get the details straight about who was bringing what. Sometimes it could take half an hour or more to figure out what was happening, what with all the double-entendres and tangents the Muffs went off on in their emails. It was easy to miss some piece of critical information, or worse, assume one had an understanding of what was happening, only to have everything change a few emails later. So that evening after work, I sat down with a glass of Sauvignon Blanc to find out what was what.

> From: rachelbakerart@mac.com
> To: The Muffs
> Re: Next Meeting
> Just a reminder ladies—Next Muff meet is Tuesday, 7:30,
> chez moi. Hike to the Hollywood sign beforehand if anyone's
> interested? LMK We'll have a white trash meal in honor of
> Jeannette and will make poulet frite (bear with me, I'm learning
> French). We need drink, bread, hors d'oeuvres, salad, and a
> veggie dish, so let me know, s'il vous plait. Quinn, are you back?
> BTW, every painting from "Nude Men without Faces" sold in
> under two hours. Isn't that outrageous?! The next series could
> either be "More Nude Men Without Faces" or "Nude Men Miss-
> ing...?" What do you think? Looking forward to seeing everyone,
> with faces on.

Rachel went through guys faster than seemed healthy, but is this the reason she reduced them to mere bodies—now possibly without body parts? Why did she take their faces away? This latest series of paintings had a few Muffs concerned.

> From: kookykiki@hotmail.com
> To: The Muffs
> Re: Next Meeting
> Will bring vegetarian dish, as I am still "no meat" in solidarity
> with Troy. Can't wait to talk about Jeannette, who spent so
> many years going to bed after eating only weeds! ~ K.
> PS—Happy to report Saul and I are working it out, yay! And
> you cannot believe what's going on next door to me. Will tell all
> at roundy-round.

Troy is Kiki and Saul's son who just turned fourteen and is

a serious animal lover— to the point he almost got killed getting out of the car in freeway traffic last year to save a dog. I was happy to learn her marriage was on the mend, but more explanation was needed on that as well as what was happening with her neighbors.

> From:Sapizz11@connect.net
>
> To: The Muffs
>
> Re: Next Meeting
>
> I'll bring a pie! Kiki, great news about you and Saul! I think I can be there for the hike, but I'm probably not going to finish the book (what a surprise!) even though it's really good. The author makes my house problems seem ridiculous.

Sarah rarely finishes any book we read, but she can always be counted on to bring a delicious dessert, despite her crisis-to-crisis lifestyle. Her biggest problem, in my opinion, is that wandering husband of hers. What irony—considering I'm an adulterer myself. Anyway, lately Sarah and Nate Sr. have been having money problems, which seem to have morphed into house problems. I hoped this didn't mean they were getting foreclosed upon. What was tragic about the situation was that if Sarah hadn't quit her high-paying job with Williams-Sonoma, money wouldn't be an issue.

> From: MissjelickaG@aol.com
>
> To: The Muffs
>
> Re: Next Meeting
>
> I want one of your faceless men, Rachel, so yes, paint more, but don't take off anything else. BTW—hunky costume guy is finished. Am now officially single again and back on Cougarlife. com. Bringing white trash pigs in blankets (poubelle blanc porcine?) along with a few empty blankets for Kiki, 'k? xJ

From: victoriamendoza@mac.com

To: The Muffs

Re: Next Meeting

Loved the book. El cerdito en una manta in Espanol. Will bring
camera to capture more of the Muffs in action.

This capturing of our book club meetings—for what,
posterity?—was a relatively new thing. Vicki started shooting
our gatherings, capturing the dramatic and the truly dull—
mundane jabber about skin conditions, kid and husband problems,
and gripes about reduced volume for the same price at grocery
stores—when she was still recovering from breast cancer. Without question, the Muffs agreed to let her shoot us because she'd
been feeling low, and we thought it would help her heal. But now
that the last few tests had come back clean, a few of us felt we
needed to get her another film gig—developing a script or shooting something that had nothing to do with us. For everyone's
sake. It was getting uncomfortable. I was even hoping the online
dating might draw her away.

From: LBSweet@aol.com

To: The Muffs

Re: Next Meeting

I'll be there, speaking English, and will bring whatever's needed.
How 'bout chili fries in honor of white trash? Would love to hike,
but I have a meeting for the non-profit so might need to buy,
rather than make. Have exciting news to share re: the location
for our gigantic fundraiser next month! ~L

Lauren is from the Midwest, and the kind of meal Rachel
was envisioning was just her kind of feast. She didn't work and
would be hard pressed to take on a *real* job even if she needed

to, which she most definitely did not after the big brewery sale. She has two young kids and is dedicated to being a hands-on mom. So what does a rich, philanthropically-minded woman do? Like I said, she forms a 501 C 3.

From: MSC@MSCMediate.com

To: The Muffs

Re: Next Meeting

I'll bring some delicious Grenache I just discovered. Quinn, what was that phone call from Japan about? For those of you who don't know, Q called me from Tokyo to tell me Udi was at the airport. Do I need to remind everyone about the state he was in when he was removed from my house? What were you on?

xo Madelyn

Maddie always brings wine to book club, never a prepared food item unless she's bought it. I'm not one of those who gets irritated by this because the wine she brings is always delicious, and when we go to her house, she never asks us to bring a thing; it's a feast. Of course, she lives in freakin' Agoura, miles and miles from anybody else, so she feels like she has to bribe us. As for the phone call and Udi, well, 'nough said.

Paige had yet to weigh in on the upcoming meeting, which was odd because she was sort of the Muffia's mother hen—the one who kept the rest of us on track with dates, rules, who the next hostess was, and remembering what books we read, which would become more and more relevant as time went on. Not even brain Pilates could help me remember all the books we've read. I figured she would get to it soon enough and decided it was my turn to "Reply all ":

From: cunningquinn@Talentpool.com

To: The Muffs

Re: Next Meeting

Hello, ladies. I've returned from the land of Toto. You can't believe the shrines they build to toilets over there; they have a potty museum. Viggo M. tractor shoot went well, but the vigorous Viggo himself alas remains only a fantasy. Glad to be home, despite twisting my ankle (better now), lack of sleep, and other peri-menopausal symptoms. And guess what? I finished the book!!! Loved it. Helps to be trapped on a plane. Sorry for the call, M. I'll bring a bottle of Bourbon, and we can pretend it's moonshine.

After perusing several more emails—deals from Amazon Local, a group conducting dating webinars, signature requests from watchdog groups, solicitations from what seemed like every site I'd ever been on, no matter how many times I've unsubscribed, and requests to wire funds to save the royal family of Burkina Faso—my eyes were glazing over. It was all I could do to retrieve my Kobo reader from the Tumi bag and put it next to the front door so I'd remember to bring it to book club.

Exhaustion finally caught up with me and, after attempting to read through The Dating Company's ten tips for successful online dating, all further thought was banished as the laptop slipped from my lap.

What I didn't yet know, as I crashed into the first deep slumber since my return from Japan, is that unseen by me when I'd pulled out the Kobo, burning a hole in the Tumi roller, was something that could change the course of the Muffia.

CHAPTER 5

*T*HE FOLLOWING morning, Jamie Harris strode through the mostly open floor plan of Talent Partners, Inc., per usual. Her hair appeared newly highlighted, and she was wearing a slimming navy suit that hung like nobody's business, with a perfectly accessorized black Lauren bag swinging by her side. She gave me a nod in acknowledgement and made a beeline for the door of her corner office where, once inside, she deposited the bag on her desk and pivoted to return to the open door.

All of us who work on the fifth floor within shouting distance of Jamie's office know to look down at such a moment, hoping not to be called upon, prone as she was to addressing us like schoolchildren. This time, though, I felt the full heat of her withering glare.

"Well, Quinn, were you going to tell me about this?"

My head snapped up to face the threat, for in her tone there was an audible note of impending danger. But what was she talking about? What was "this"?

I glanced over my shoulder to the few members of the Talent Partners team—my mostly self-serving colleagues—who were at their desks, heads bowed: Sameer, Carolyn, and Titania included.

"They can't help you," Jamie said, and started backing into her office. "Would you come in here, please?"

I rose slowly, putting the computer on sleep mode, and looked over to Sameer who gave me his signature head waggle, which simultaneously said, "Uh-oh," and "Don't worry."

Once inside Jamie's office, I closed the door.

"Ankle better?" she asked, getting the niceties out of the way.

"Yes, thanks. Much." I'd graduated to my lowest heels.

"What exactly happened in Tokyo?" She sounded almost accusatory as she walked around to the far side of her desk and assumed an attack stance.

"Nothing. I mean beyond the shoot, which went really well, as I told you. Kitomo Matsuhashi was very happy with Viggo's work on Kubota, and they might want him back for their new bulldozer campaign."

"Never mind that," she snapped. "We heard that one of our agents in Tokyo was misbehaving last week."

"Really? Who?" Best to play dumb while I tried to figure out how she could possibly mean me, which it was clear she did.

"*Who?* Are you serious? *You* are who."

I hadn't misbehaved; *I don't think*. As quickly as I could, on only one latte, I reviewed the four-day trip. Had I eaten too many *daifuku*? If I had, so what? Did I splurge on the expense account? Not at all. It's possible that I went by Viggo's hotel room a few too many times, hoping to catch his door open, and he thought I was stalking him. Even this didn't really rise to the level of punishable offense.

"Who told you I was misbehaving?" I asked. That's the way to do it; cast blame on the messenger.

"Doesn't matter who told me." She pulled out her chair and gestured to the one I found myself already gripping the arm of. "Sit."

I slumped into the seat.

She smoothed her hair and took a breath. "You were our only agent *in* Tokyo last week."

"Whatever it is, it's not true!" Somebody was feeding Jamie lies; but why? And why was Jamie believing this person?

"Talent Partners' code of conduct demands that every member of our team, from the partners to the lowliest mail room Harvard grad, maintains a spotless reputation and does nothing to throw any unwanted attention on the agency. You *know* that."

As she was saying this, she picked up her iPhone, her fingers flitting over the touch screen. "You came to TP as a high-grossing booker with Commercials Plus, but maybe this was too big a move for you, our clients too rich and famous, and you haven't been able to keep things in proper perspective."

Jamie had always been a snob.

"How do you know another agent wasn't in Tokyo? Talent Partners is a pretty big agency," I pointed out.

Jamie gave me a withering glare.

Had I forgotten some altercation I was involved in? I couldn't think of a single event. Maybe this was the kind of thing *Lumosity* was supposed to help with. I flashed on how snarky I'd been with that flight attendant about peoples' excess baggage. Perhaps Japan Airlines was considering a commercial campaign with one of Talent Partners' clients and they'd captured the whole thing on CCTV. *Oh, shit!*

A sinking feeling came over me, and I felt sure I was about to be "let go"—that annoying euphemism for getting fired.

Keep your mouth shut, Quinn. When in doubt, don't crucify yourself.

"These pictures arrived in my email inbox today." Jamie turned the phone around so I could see.

It was me, all right—a disheveled mess with the broken Lucite shoe in my hand. *It was coming back to me.* These shots must have been taken at the airport in Tokyo, and from the angle they were shot, it appeared as though I was holding the distressed Natasha Marro at a threatening angle while four or five *Hello Kitty* girls cowered beneath me. I felt my eyes bug. *Who could have sent these? And even more curiously—who took them?*

"Where did they come from?" I tried to visualize the airport scene a few days earlier. I couldn't remember anybody with a camera per se, but everyone had a smart phone, so realistically, everyone had a camera.

"Doesn't matter. You read the caption?"

Peering at the screen, I read:

Talent Partners' agent, Quinn Cunningham, terrorizes Hello Kitty convention in Japan.

I stared at the photos and the absurd logline, incredulous. Maybe with a little advance warning and a second cup of coffee I could have thought of a way out of my current predicament, but I was without words to defend myself. The evidence was damning, and there was absolutely no getting around the fact that the woman in the pictures was me.

The only thing I had in my favor was a previously unsullied reputation and demonstrated ability to make millions of dollars for Talent Partners and its clients. Unfortunately, neither of these things made me irreplaceable. In Hollywood, *everyone* is replaceable, and though this fact interferes with many an industry insider's hubristic belief of his own value, it's wise not to forget it. The script gets rewritten, new actors hired; the show really does go on.

"So," said Jamie, "we have a problem. Dakota Johnson will *not* be booked for *Hello Kitty* if this gets out."

I wanted to say that once Dakota Johnson stripped down in *Fifty Shades of Gray*, *Kitty* would be saying "Goodbye." But my mouth remained closed.

She pulled the phone back and put it down on the desk. "You agree it's you?"

"It's me but... "

"The person who sent them wants you let go from the company."

Sometimes I really hate it when I'm right.

"Did Viggo say something about me? I thought we got along well. You know, we had a good working relationship. All I did was make sure he showed up on time, which meant waking him up before he wanted... "

"It's not Viggo. He likes you."

He likes me? That was nice to learn, especially since he'd been sort of cold toward me most of the trip. But if it wasn't Viggo, who took the pictures and somehow dashed to the plane ahead of me; who would want me gone?

"I guess I just don't understand," I protested. "I mean, I'm a *nobody*. I book actors who shoot television commercials in foreign countries. Am I a threat to the balance of trade?"

"It is a bit of a mystery," she agreed, admiring her manicure job.

"If you don't tell me who sent them, I *really* can't explain it."

"I don't actually know who sent them...yet. The Internet people are working on it. But the fact remains," she glanced at her computer screen, "it IS you in the pictures and if this were to get out, it could damage us—the department—if not the entire agency."

"I don't really see how," I said, and immediately wished I hadn't.

"Quinn, we are a talent agency, and you must remember that as a talent agency, we exist to help create entertainment for the masses—entertainment which is a vehicle for corporations to market their products. It is a corporate *commercial* enterprise. Corporations don't want anything out there in the media that will damage their brands. Your yelling at people in Japan damages our relationship with every corporation that is Japanese and every corporate entity that does business with the Japanese, not to mention any other corporation that's offended by your behavior. If this gets out, they will use other agencies' talent. Do you understand?"

"Even if they really, really want one of our clients?" I asked hopefully.

"They'll go somewhere else," she repeated. "So I need you to clean it up."

I nodded my head. I *did* understand.

A thought hit me. I opened my mouth and just as quickly closed it again. If I'd learned anything about human relationships—which wasn't much if it had taken me this long to break up with Steven— it was that you should never bad-mouth your friend's or boss's sex partners.

In this case, the only person I could think of who'd want me gone was Jamie's pretty little handpicked dog's body and Moldovan Molotov cocktail, Titania. Their affair was not a secret; everyone already knew Jamie was gay, so no biggie there, either. But when Titania had arrived in the TP offices four months earlier, most of us had taken an immediate dislike to her. Her scantily dressed body—and even more scantily cloaked ambition—made Eve Harrington look like Melanie in *Gone With the Wind*.

"Doesn't matter where they came from or who sent them, just clean it up," Jamie said, interrupting my thoughts. "Get some help. Get Reputationdefense.com, or whatever it's called. If these pictures hit the Internet, I'm telling you right now, I can't save you."

"I'll handle it, don't worry. Absolutely." I stood, none too sure about how I was going to do it nor if I'd be able to halt the implosion of my career.

"One more thing—"

I sat back down as she scrolled beneath the pictures and once more presented the phone:

**You must terminate Quinn Cunningham's contract,
or this goes live in three weeks.**

My chest constricted; my throat tightened. *Where were my aphorisms now? Yes, yes, thank you, thank you?* They'd abandoned me.

"Three weeks," she said, just in case I'd suddenly forgotten how to read. "That's how long you have, or I'm afraid we really will have to *let you go.*"

I realize euphemisms are supposed to grease the wheels of social discourse, but *let you go* in this context is flat-out insulting. At least she hadn't *let me go* immediately. I had time to get proof before exposing Titania as the culprit.

"Thanks for giving me a time to fix things." I stood once more and headed for the door.

"Don't thank *me.* Thank your persecutor for giving you some time."

Of course—why hadn't I thought about thanking the person responsible for making my life more complicated?

"Right." I didn't know how Titania, or whoever it was, had gotten my pictures, but I *for sure* was going to find out. But why the delay? That was a mystery, too. *Find the culprit; find the reason.*

As I left Jamie's office, closing the door behind me, Sameer suddenly appeared. "I won't ask you what happened in there," he said to my relief. "I just want to know, did you decide to date a farmer?"

I stared at him. He had obviously heard far too much of my conversation with Vicki and had been preoccupied by its content.

That made me feel uncomfortable, but I was still glad for the distraction.

"Thinkin' about it," I said, feeling my phone vibrate in my jacket pocket.

He beamed. "Excellent choice. Sometimes I wish I was still a farmer. At the end of the day, you make something that people need."

He had a way of putting things in perspective.

CHAPTER 6

IS HANDS clasped either side of my low-rise thong printed with multi-colored peace signs, and he pulled it down, over my thighs, past my knees, and off, lingering for a few moments at my damaged ankle, caressing and kissing the pain away. He glanced up, his eyes meeting mine, whereupon he came high onto his knees before me as his lips took hold of my pussy, his tongue making the plunge.

Yes, I'm weak. But OMG, it feels good.

I sat perched on Gran's sideboard/dresser thing—naked, spread-eagled, my skirt hiked up around my hips. Only instead of his cock availing itself of my throbbing pussy, he was demonstrating his oral skills. And he was so good at it—all the sucking, kissing, and licking that goes into orally getting a girl off.

"I missed you so much," he said, pulling back, his entire face shiny and wet with me.

I didn't say anything; I was trying desperately not to think about how weak I am, but instead to simply find a few minutes of escape.

Steven kissed the soft insides of my thighs—both sides, of course; equal time. He kissed my ankles, giving greater care to the swollen one. "Poor baby," he said, before moving toward my clit again.

I groaned. This was no post-flight dream. This was happening, and it felt great.

"You taste so—fucking" — he sucked on my clit—"good."

"I'm...so glad you...like," I said haltingly.

"Oh, yes," he said between licks. "Very...much."

"Kiss me." I pulled him to his feet.

And we kissed. The taste of our flavors mingling got me almost as riled as his engorged penis impatiently throbbing against my thigh. He took my earlobe between his teeth.

"I want you inside me," I said, and his body responded, his cock moving toward my wet, warm center of its own volition. No five-finger assist from either of us. Like I said, I was at the perfect height on this thing, and his penis was as hard and directional as a rudder on an America's Cup catamaran steering for home.

He thrusted.

"*Agghhhh*," he growled.

"*Oooohhhhh*," I responded.

His cock found its mark, high and deep inside me. It felt like it was pressing on my lungs, forcing me to take a sharp inhale.

Thrust.

Again I felt penetrated fully. How could I be expected to give this up when there was no one else? And I'd had such a bad day! He must care because it wasn't even Thursday.

I know, I know; he's married. But please don't judge me too harshly. I'm working on it. I have some of my profile written. And anyway, it's my karma that will be affected, not yours. If he wanted me this bad, I must be doing something good. He said his wife doesn't like sex, so perhaps I'm actually being charitable.

"Oh, my God, that's good," he said. I don't question his God.

I told myself this wouldn't happen, and I do feel weak, but

I needed some loving after being confronted with those pictures and the possibility of losing my livelihood. Any normal person would need a tension release. And, due to my ankle, neither dance class nor the treadmill was an option. Perhaps those of you who are single, with stressful careers like mine, with a shortage of romance, might relate. Or maybe you'd just say I'm rationalizing my bad behavior.

Thrust and *hold.*

"Oooooh."

"Ahhhh." Yes, this could get me there.

Thrust.

Madelyn told me, after Steven and I broke up the first time, that I should just use a vibrator to release tension. We even had a date to go vibrator shopping, but I blew her off to go on another bad date with an actor; how tacky of me.

Thrust.

I did finally buy a vibrator but...

"Oh, yeah!"

"Oh, *God*—I just can't get the hang of the thing. And it's called *The Rabbit*, which—""Oh, Quinn, you're so wet!"

—"I'm sorry, even with the clitoral—stimu—it's not a... "

"Fuck—"

"I look at the thing, and it's like having sex with the Easter Bunny, all pink and—"

Thrust

—"which, in turn makes me think of a lot of little kids in pinafores watching and pointing, counting their jelly beans."

Thrust

Suffice it to say, I remain weak where Steven's concerned. I want my very own man, but my options for this kind of release are—

"Oh!"

—limited. None of the Muffs knew I'd taken back up

with him; I was too embarrassed to—

Thrust.

Ahh—tell them.

"*Oooooohhhhh*," he moaned; *thrust.*

Yup—you got it; *weak again.*

"Aaahhhhhh." So good.

Thrust—thrust—thrust—

He started moving in that way that told me he was about to come—*it's not that hard to tell.* And lately—well, probably since we made love for the fourth time, actually, he comes pretty quickly, and often—like today—leaves me in the dust. Then he says, "I love you," in a perfunctory manner and gets dressed, while I pick my clothes off the floor.

Oh, but the feeling! Thrust . . . thrust . . . shudder . . . drive. In and out, make me feel alive!

I didn't want to stop him. I didn't want to stop myself. Truth be told, I've never been one for three-hour sex. I have too many things to do. I think ten minutes is just about perfect.

"You feel outrageous," he said, moaning.

But one minute?

"You're so hard," I moaned back. "So...*hard.*"

"Oh, my God. I'm gonna—"

"No, don't—"

"I'm going to—"

"Not yet—"

"Going to—"

"—No, don't—"

"I'm going to—Oh!"

"—come yet, please—"

"Here I—"

"No—"

"—come!! I—"

"Please, not—"

"Yes!"

"Not, oh—"

"I'm cooommmming."

"Ohhh, God, you—"

"I'm coooomming."

"—kill me—"

"I'm *coming.*"

"Wait!"

"Here I come—"

"Please... "

Thrust. "Aghhhhhh!"

"Oh!"

"Rrruhh—" Thrust.

"Not yeeehh… "

Thrust. "Fuhbla…ahhh… eyaiischloooeee—"

"Arghhhh!"

Deeper, longer thrust . . . shudderrrrr.

I hadn't come.

"Sorry. I couldn't stop myself. But that was amazing," he said, amazingly. "You had me so riled up, and I love this piece of furniture."

After another minute, he swept the hair from my face, leaned down, and caressed my lips with his own. "I love you, you know."

"*MMMmmm,*" I *mmmmmmd,* noncommittally.

He really was a sweet man, even if he lied like a corporate titan. *Stupid Quinn, he is a corporate titan.* To his credit, though, he genuinely seemed to care that I thought well of him, which, in truth, no longer mattered. I'd made up my mind finally that what he did—or more accurately, did not do—trumped what he said he would do. Obviously, I had found it difficult to pull myself away because he was the only man I knew of who made me feel this good—even without an orgasm. There were other men out there, my rational pre-frontal cortex told me—hence the nascent attempts to find one—but my amygdala was telling me something different. And right now, with "Picturegate" hanging over my head, perhaps I should forgive myself this one-time backslide. Good as Steven was, this really had to stop.

He glanced toward the kitchen, where the bag of goodies he'd brought sat on top of the counter. "Hungry?"

I was starving, but not for anything that food or sex was ever going to satisfy.

CHAPTER 7

*T*HE SUN was setting on what had been an abnormally warm April evening as Kiki and I waited for the Muffs to return from their pre-book club hike to the Hollywood sign—a site which even the most put-upon Bangladeshy garment worker knows is situated in the hills above the original tinsel town.

We were sitting on the front stoop of Rachel's rented house on a windy street off Beachwood Canyon, and I'd already started in on the bottle of bourbon I brought, telling Kiki I was just getting into the theme of the night—*white trash*. The real reason, of course, was my life—Picturegate—with me playing the part of a crazed shoe wielder, which put my job on the line, and my relapse into Steven a few hours ago. Thus far, I had yet to tell any of the Muffs about either development, but my plan was to definitely avoid the topic of Steven. Too embarrassing.

I held up my metal, reusable coffee mug in which three fingers of bourbon awaited my consumption. "Cheers."

"Cheers." Kiki clinked her vegetarian, gluten-free pasta casserole against my mug. *Sweet woman; didn't want to make me feel I was drinking alone.*

"To white trash." I sipped the deliciously-strong, peaty liquid and swallowed. *Ahhhh…that's better. Yes, yes, yes and thank you, Maker's Mark.*

"Do you think the term 'white trash' is racist?" she asked,

disturbing my little respite.

"To who…w*hom*?" I sputtered.

"I mean in a sort of reverse racist kind of way."

Lowering the mug from my lips, I assessed her expression. *Was she serious?* "Only a beautiful, wealthy, twenty-first-century Black woman could ask that question."

Kiki was well educated and always dressed like three million bucks. Tonight she had on a pair of her typically expensive-looking, covet-worthy boots, a gorgeous tan leather jacket, and diamonds glittered from her ears and fingers. Correction: *four million bucks.*

She met my gaze. "You're right; trashiness crosses all racial dividing lines. It's more a way of life."

"You have no idea." I reflected on my own definitively white trash upbringing just down the block from the greater Fresno trailer park. "It's a little like being born into a religious sect."

"Well, I have a story that gets into a specific kind of human trashiness, which I eluded to in my email, but I'm going to save it for the roundy."

"Can you give me a hint?"

"Let's just say it's juicy."

"Well, you've certainly piqued my curiosity." I took another sip of bourbon. But I guess I have to wait.

The roundy-round was that portion of every book club gathering dedicated to updating each other about everything going on in our lives. It was a way to reconnect and see if we could help each other. And it's what the Muffs who never read the books show up for—both to hear and be heard.

"And you wait," I said. "I have a hell of a story for you, too." *The roundy-round was going to kick ass tonight!*

From our vantage point, the fading light glinted like a ray gun off the letters of the Hollywood sign rising above us. It was always shocking to see how large those letters were when you got close. Each could provide enough shade for a hundred coyotes, three of which had just strolled by, nonchalant and bold as could be. And they clearly weren't starving, subsisting as they did on the small pets of neighboring hillside dwellers. I knew people whose dogs had disappeared through supposedly protected outdoor enclosures. Seeing a pack of them gave me the creeps.

Soon the coyotes had tucked out of sight, and it was a pack of Muffs strolling toward us—Rachel, Sarah, Jelicka, Madelyn, and Lauren—all slightly damp from their exertions but not the least bit creepy. Rachel's blonde curls were pulled back into a ponytail, and all the women were dressed in at least one piece from Lululemon. We greeted each other with our usual joy and warm feelings.

"I hope you saved us some." Rachel eyed the open bottle of bourbon. "I was lookin' forward to a Whiskey Sour."

Holding up the bottle, it was clear we had more than enough bourbon left to put us all under the table, if that's what we wanted.

"Where's Paige?" Madelyn said.

"Should she be here by now?" asked Kiki.

I pulled out my phone to check to see if Paige sent an email, but there was no Internet connection. It was almost shocking these days to find pockets in this high-tech town where one still couldn't get online. How quickly we forget that not very long ago, few people had mobile phones—let alone handheld computers on which one can also carry on a conversation on the other side of the world. The bourbon was having its desired effect, however, and neither this, nor much else, seemed to matter.

"We'll check when we get inside," said Rachel opening the door. "And Vicki's coming but said she'd be a little late."

Before long, we were seated around Rachel's Indonesian table with a veritable white trash feast in front of us—fried chicken, saucy peanut coleslaw, marshmallow potatoes, and biscuits. Kiki's casserole was the only offering that could be referred to as part of a healthy lifestyle. The sun had gasped its last, and the lights in the houses perched on the canyon hillsides below us were beginning to twinkle. We were happily chowing down, and most of us were in our cups, thanks to the Whiskey Sours whipped up by yours truly, a pitcher of which sat on the table before us.

Vicki finally showed—with her video equipment, of course—dressed in black with her hair spiked up, looking a little too 1980s for comfort. In that get-up, I thought *Dateafarmer* seemed like the last website she should choose to find a mate. Before we'd sat down, she took me aside while setting up a couple of lights and whispered her approval of the rough draft of my online profile, which I had emailed first thing in the morning, before Jamie ruined the day with those pictures.

"Did you pick a site to put it on?"

"*NowLove*. I'm hoping that having the image of an arrow getting shot from a bow will encourage me to just pick somebody."

"Or shoot somebody," said Rachel, passing by with an empty bowl for the chicken bones. "I don't know why it's a secret, but I won't tell."

Vicki looked at me. "I didn't say anything. Swear."

"It doesn't really matter." And it didn't; I just didn't want eight opinions about what site I should go on. "How 'bout you?" I asked. Where's *your* profile?"

She looked like she was going to say something but was interrupted by Maddie.

"Rachel, it's Paige; she sent an email."

Rachel went over to the computer and read aloud.

From: vonhooter@gmail.com
To: rachelbakerart@mac.com

Subject: Tonight

Dearest Muffs, I'm not going to make it. One of my students treed a forehand, and the tennis ball slammed into my eye. I'll be fine but will just have a massive shiner. On top of that, the creep who hangs out at the club has turned into a full-fledged stalker and when he followed me to my car with ice bags, I got so freaked out, I almost had an accident on the way to the doctor. I know neither of these things is an allowable excuse, but trust me—you don't want me there. Loved the book, though, even if she made it up.

Love, Paige, your repentant book club Nazi

"Well," said Rachel. "I guess we don't have to wait."

"That had to have hurt," said Kiki. "Poor Paige."

"Yeah, poor Paige," agreed Lauren.

"What is she talking about?" I said. "Jeannette did *not* make it up. She's not James Frey saying she went to prison when she didn't. She really *lived* all that insanity."

"Supposedly," said Rachel. "But memoir is not *necessarily* truth. It's truth through the lens of memory."

"Which means it's definitely *not* true," Kiki said. "Memory is faulty."

Vicki's camera was pointed at us, moving nimbly from woman to woman as the conversation flowed.

Lauren held up a piece of chicken. "So true—dang this is tasty." She took a bite. "Why do you think I started a non-profit for Alzheimer's?"

"At best, memoir is revisionist history at the micro level," said Rachel. "But it's the genre of our time. Each memoir is its author's truth, so you just have to read it as a story."

"Nice...revisionist history at the micro level. Don't we sound smart," said Jelicka.

Sometimes Rachel, the English major, literary aficionado

of the group, gave us the impression she merely tolerated the rest of us. What she didn't appreciate sometimes was that there were far more readers like us in the world who just want a good story well told; and far fewer snob critics who praise drivel as "must read," when it's a load of crap. I couldn't think of a particular title just then, but we'd read a few.

"Jeannette's is one of many truths." Typical Madelyn—always playing the mediator whenever conflict arises. "But it's no truer than anyone else's. Chances are each member of the Walls family remembers events slightly differently. "If there were a conflict—in the Walls family or any other—I'd have to listen to each person and try to piece together the real truth of the conflict. But even if I did that, whatever I came up with would only be my truth about their truths, you know?"

Gotta love her.

"Jeannette never ate this well, I'll tell ya that much," said Lauren, helping herself to another piece of chicken. "Tomorrow it's back on the diet—four weeks until the Benefit."

Some of us mumbled a few words about how, yes, we should be concerned about what and how much we were eating and drinking but agreed that tomorrow seemed soon enough to do something about it. Now that my ankle was better, I'd be back working the pole in a day or two.

"I was going to make hot dogs, in honor of Jeannette's sacrifice," Rachel said, "but I didn't think anyone would eat them."

"That's right!" Sarah exclaimed. "She caught fire making hot dogs. Wasn't she only four years old when that happened? How crazy is that?"

"Totally irresponsible parenting," agreed Madelyn. "Not to mention, the dad had the kids robbing banks, and he practically pimped Jeannette."

"I don't know how you mediate that, Maddie," Jelicka said.

Vicki swung her camera lens from Sarah to Maddie. "Could

you guys have that exchange again?"

Maddie and Jelicka repeated their lines, and Maddie threw me a glance that said: *What is she going to do with all this footage?*

I shrugged.

"My dad always used to say, 'crazy parents make sane kids,' " Rachel said. "Which must explain why I'm a little nuts—they were only half crazy."

"I don't think it works like that, Rachel," I said.

"I liked how her dad taught her to shoot," said Jelicka, who herself made regular trips to a shooting range for target practice. "In fact, we should encourage Paige to come out to the range if she has a stalker."

"Okay, well…Paige is a grown-up, but Jeannette was five years old when her father stuck a gun in her hand!" Madelyn was incredulous.

"And it was probably still scalded from the hot dog incident," Sarah adds, equally put out. "You don't let a five-year-old cook!"

Exercising great restraint, I helped myself to more of Lauren's coleslaw, rather than another chicken thigh, telling myself the dressing wasn't fattening.

"At least she wasn't afraid of guns, which can be just as dangerous," said Vicki, who'd grown up in New England and was, incongruously with her overall vibe, into skeet shooting.

"All I know is, if I ever saw my mother dumpster diving," Kiki interjected, "especially in my own neighborhood, I don't think I would have handled it as well as Jeannette."

"Ah, but maybe her mother didn't actually dumpster dive," said Lauren. "I mean if she made some of it up."

"Did you see her mother?" Kiki asked. "I Googled her, and I'm pretty sure she did."

"What I loved most about Jeannette's mom was, even though

they were poor," Sarah said, "she always managed to save a little money for those special things that made life more bearable, you know? Like a tasseled silk throw or a cut crystal vase."

"Yeah," said Jelicka, sardonically. "Much smarter than buying food for her starving family."

"My white trash mom had the same motto," I said. " 'The surest way to feel rich is to invest in 'quality nonessentials'—even though, in my mom's case, it meant new plastic to go on the couch."

I was about to reach for the last drumstick, when Vicki snagged it from the platter.

"Jeannette Walls is a testament to the human spirit," said Maddie. "Maybe you wouldn't want her upbringing, but she proves that the human will to survive is so strong, we can get through almost anything." This was a sentiment we could all agree on.

When Sarah's peach cobbler was served, we started in on the roundy-round. Sarah herself was in couples' therapy, trying to repair her marriage with Nate Sr., while their house problems, which she'd intimated in her email, turned out to be enormous. Upside down in their mortgage, they thought it might be better to abandon the whole thing and risk foreclosure. Consequently, she might have to go back to work, which a few of us were in favor of, even if it required the working out of childcare details. Rachel was indeed painting a new series of nude men—body parts intact—and "all was grand," even though she'd broken up with the newest boyfriend—a swarthy Greek—and claimed she was now taking a break from the boys. Then she read us a fairy tale she'd come across, saying it was her new motto:

"Once upon a time, a guy asked a girl 'Will you marry me?' The girl said: 'NO!' And she lived happily ever-after and went shopping, dancing, to the theatre, drank martinis, had high self-esteem, always had a clean house, never had to cook, did whatever she wanted, didn't get fat, had lots of lovers, and all the hot water to herself. She never watched sports unless she wanted to, never wore friggin' lacy lingerie that went up her ass, never yelled, looked fabulous in sweat pants, and was pleasant all the time. The End."

When she finished, the rest of us sat silently for a few seconds. Wow. Was she serious? Should we be concerned? Or was everyone thinking—as I was—how good that sounded, wondering why any woman would live her life any other way. Perhaps I needed to rethink my rationale for online dating.

"I like it," said Vicki, smiling. "Can you email that to me, Rachel?"

Kiki cleared her throat. "Okay, ready? The house next door to me is a porn set," she announced.

Apparently, she began noticing some strange goings on a couple of months before and suspected, at the very least, that the neighbors were operating a business out of the house. There were deliveries of office furniture, sightings of the giant industrial truck the cable company only sends out when installing major bandwidth; things like that. She told Saul who, agreeing with her, called the city to come out and enforce the law. But when the inspectors came out, they claimed there was a "lack of viable evidence"—that the occupants of the house, in fact, invited them in and introduced them to their "friends." Kiki was livid. All the cars lined up every day, owned by the "friends" (read: employees), was "evidence of nothing," said the inspectors. The ongoing frustration, and the guttural paroxysms of the "actors" as they performed their erotic scenes, had brought Kiki and Saul closer together. She was happy to report the sideline benefit of the activity next door had contributed to some exciting fireworks going off upstairs in the master bedroom of their own house.

"The Muff posse will come over and shut 'em down." Jelicka volunteered all of us to assist in busting the naughty neighbors. It seemed like Kiki had already consulted Maddie, who said she was looking into the legalities and warned us to wait before doing "anything too crazy," which included Rachel's wanting to dress up like a porn star in hopes of entrapping somebody. Kiki seemed calmer when she was finished, happy to feel like she wasn't alone—which she wasn't.

Maddie told us about the guy she met from Scotland who, she insisted, while glancing at Jelicka, was "too new to even discuss, so I don't know why certain people feel compelled to talk about him." She claimed to have no personal knowledge about what a Scotsman wears or does not wear under his kilt—much to Sarah's disappointment and mine— but if Diana Gabaldon's *Outlander* books were to be believed, it was nothing.

Vicki, who was no stranger to foreign guys, having been married to a Spaniard, wished Maddie luck with the Scot before segueing into her various film projects, including the Muffia project, and telling us about becoming a mentor for a teenage girl named Solange, who was getting out of foster care. We all thought she was incredibly generous and noble but worried it might be too much, as Vicki was still supposed to be avoiding stressful situations. Jelicka began her turn in the roundy-round talking about what kinds of jobs she might get now that her divorce was final and she had to go back to work. She gave us a full report on *Cougarlife.com*—the cubs were cute, but the cougar was getting bored—and she thought she might be getting stalked just like Paige. Unlike Paige, however, if Jelicka was being stalked, God help the stalker.

"Does anyone else think Paige might not be here for a different reason than the one she gave us?" Jelicka asked. Talk of stalking and Paige must have triggered that question.

We stopped, glancing around at each other for understanding.

"Like what?" asked Sarah.

"Like, do you think she might have, oh say, had her eyes done?"

Maddie frowned. "Where do you come up with this stuff?"

"I think it happened," Lauren said. "At least the part about the stalker—Paige's stalker. I don't know about yours, Jel. But I've seen Paige's a few times when I dropped Gavin off for his tennis lesson."

"You're starting 'em young," said Kiki.

"You did too, Kiki," said Lauren, probably referring to Troy's sax playing. "These days, if you don't have your kids doing something extra-curricular really well by the time they're fourteen, you can forget about getting them into a decent college."

"Agreed, but why would Paige lie about the reason she wasn't coming?" said Maddie. "Especially considering she's never missed a Muff meeting."

"Right. She would have told us," said Vicki.

"She's actually kind of an oversharer, which makes it all the more odd," I said. "Remember when she told us about peeing on her friend's horse?"

Sarah's jaw dropped. "Really? I must have missed that. What did the horse do?"

"She was riding this horse," I said, "and suddenly she looks down and the saddle is completely wet. She looks around, can't figure it out, and suddenly she realizes it's her. And she's not just leaking—the floodgates have opened, and she didn't even feel it happening."

"It's a common problem after childbirth," Lauren said. "She just needs a bladder sling."

"A bladder *what?*" Jelicka raised her brows, though due to Botox, they did not raise very far.

"Bladder sling," said Maddie. "It rhymes with bling, Jelicka."

Vicki pointed the camera at Jelicka, who said, directly to the lens, "Who knew?"

"They go in and sort of lift up your bladder into a, well, into a sort of sling thing," Lauren explained. "I'm going to need one, too, so we were discussing doctors. The good news is, once you get one, you stop peeing at inopportune times, like whenever you laugh, cough, or take too big a breath."

Jelicka didn't seem to follow. Plastic surgery, she understood. Any kind of surgery where you couldn't see a visible improvement to your looks—that was a waste of time and money.

"I told you when I had my eyes done," said Vicki. "But for me, it was a medical necessity—because of my Nordic folds, which are hereditary and can eventually interfere with vision."

It's always struck me as funny how some people who undergo cosmetic eye surgery claim it's a *medical* necessity, blaming something called Nordic folds—extra large folds of eyelid skin— for their future failing vision, even when they have absolutely no Scandinavian blood.

"I tell you all about my Botox injections," said Jelicka. "Is that oversharing? I'd just call it sharing."

"I wanted to talk to you about that," said Sarah. "The Botox. Do you like it? Not that I can afford it."

"It's so cheap now," said Jelicka. "These days you can get it done at a foot spa."

Madelyn leaned toward Sarah. "You don't need it—especially not from the Vietnamese lady who does your pedicure—nothing against the Vietnamese."

"Some dentists are offering it, too," Jelicka said.

"Foot spa—dentist—you can probably get the guy behind the meat counter at Ralphs to work on your face," said Maddie.

"Not that it's a good idea." Jelicka delivered this line to Maddie, with whom she was clearly having some sort of tiff. The rest of us carried on, pretending they weren't. "You just have to go to an artistic type person who knows where to stick the needle."

"I plan on telling you all when I get a facelift," Lauren said. "But if it looks horrible, you must, must promise to be totally honest with me. I don't want to turn into one of those women who keep on having procedures and have no idea how other people see them."

"For the record," said Rachel, "I'm never having plastic surgery."

A few of the older Muffs groaned at this proclamation. At almost thirty-three, Rachel was the youngest and, as such, the least in need of any facial "maintenance." Most of us thought she'd change her mind in another ten years.

"Your statement has been duly recorded," Vicki said. "And when you have something done, we promise we won't say 'told you so.'"

"Speak for yourself," said Jelicka, giving Rachel a gentle push. "Kidding. I have no horse in this race either way. It's not like I own stock in Allergan."

She knew too much about this stuff.

With that digression over, it was my turn and, as wowed as everyone had been about Kiki's porn-making, next-door neighbors, when I told everyone about Picturegate, they were astounded. Nobody they knew so intimately had ever been…well, in essence, blackmailed. Hearing that I had three weeks to fix it or get canned, made everyone furious and adamant that I must fight the injustice done me with everything I had, and they vowed to assist in any way they could.

By this point in the evening, however, we all needed to get going, so a Muff sub-committee agreed to meet me the following night to help hammer out a game plan.

"Who's next?" Lauren asked, as we began packing up to go. "I feel a little lost without Paige here to guide us. I'll go see her this week and see how she is."

"Hold on." Rachel reached for her laptop. "I think I have her list."

"It's gotta be my turn," said Vicki.

"I haven't hosted in *years*," Jelicka chimed in.

"Me neither," Lauren said. "I haven't hosted since *Max Tivoli*."

"Well, you're all wrong." Rachel slapped the laptop closed. "It's Quinn. Any ideas for a book?"

At that moment, I didn't have a clue what to choose. Of all the Muffs, I think I stress out the most about choosing what we read because I'm the most fearful of picking something people won't like. There's just not enough time in a life to spend it reading bad books—which, in the Muffs' case hardly matters since, even with great books, they rarely read them.

"Is it too much for you right now?" Sarah said, sensitive to my situation. "Somebody else could go, and we can come back to you."

I looked at their expectant faces. With everything I had going on, it was understandable they'd be concerned there might be one too many things on my plate. But I felt happy to have positive distractions. "I'm good. Just give me a couple days."

CHAPTER 8

ARLY THE next evening, Madelyn, Jelicka, and Lauren met me for an emergency strategy session at Firefly, the popular Studio City bar/restaurant with the close-cropped-vine-covered exterior, which gives the place the appearance of a giant chia pet.

The three of them sat opposite me, each holding one of Chef Jason Travi's themed cocktails, speechless after listening to my woeful tale, which I'd fleshed out from the "highlight reel" version of the night before.

"I've been thinking about changing careers anyway," I said, hoping to wipe the shock off their faces. Leaning back in the plush, velvet-upholstered banquette, I picked up my drink. "This just forces my hand."

The alcohol soothed away the stress as it went down—granted, not the healthiest way to unwind, but it's all I had at that moment since swearing off sex with married Steven. It was true—I had been thinking about changing jobs; for years, if I was honest with myself. But until I said it out loud, my idle musings hadn't gained any traction. Now that my departure from Talent Partners might be imminent, I needed feedback about what I could do to fight the threat, but also to prepare for what might happen if I lost the battle.

"What would you do?" Jelicka said, aghast. "It's not as if

jobs like yours are easy to come by. Then again, *I've* been out of the labor force so long, I'm not qualified to do anything." She took a long pull from her bourbon-infused Orange Bomb with egg white foam while gazing longingly at the attractive twenty-something bartender. "Except Cougardom."

Lauren's gaze drifted over to the bartender. "Oh, *my*, he is hot!"

"Being a cougar doesn't pay," said Maddie, who was behaving like she had additional information. "I know because I mediated a case, that's all. Disappointed cats all 'round."

"But sometimes those little cubs are *sooooo* much fun." Jelicka smiled wickedly.

"So you told us," Maddie said. "In great detail. You also said you were tired of it."

"Just a little." Jelicka smiled.

Lauren gestured to the cute bartender. "Did you...?"

"Not that cub there, no; but I have indeed," said Jelicka. "And they're well worth the price of dinner."

Clearly, being a cougar was not a sustainable pastime, but Jelicka's previous career as a sometime screenwriter had arguably never been a *real* job, either. Selling scripts in Hollywood— no matter how good they are—has always been a crapshoot and has, for the most part, pretty much been a career relegated to young, aggressive males with a penchant for action and violence. This is not to say that women *can't* succeed, only that the business is run by, and primarily caters to, men and boys. Now that Jelicka, a *female*, was going through a divorce and was past the age the entertainment industry considers viable to begin with, none of the Muffs liked her chances of going back to screenwriting. Even at the peak of her success, she never made more than enough to get by. And now her love for the finer things in life—leaving aside her addiction to Botox, Restylene, and her Audi A8—ensured she'd have trouble going back to her struggling "poor-me" writer lifestyle.

This point would have been driven home when Lena Dunham walked in, entourage in tow, but fortunately, I was the only one of our little group to see her. Dunham, known for creating the HBO series "Girls," is one of those writers, arguably not even particularly talented nor doing anything to advance the stature of women, whose early efforts met with instant—and to me inexplicable—commercial success. This always irritates people who've been slaving away for years, not that that was Jelicka.

"Cougardom is also dangerous," said Maddie. "But let's get to *your* job prospects next, Jel. Right now, let's focus on saving Quinn's career."

"No need," said Jelicka. "I've decided to get my real estate license."

"That's a great idea," said Lauren, generally a *glass-half-full* sort of person, but now she just appeared relieved to be off the subject of boy toys.

"I don't know if getting a real estate license is 'great,' but what the hell, right? People need houses." Jelicka once again lifted her cocktail. "L'chaim."

She and Lauren clinked glasses while I repeated, "L'chaim," after which I took a large gulp of my pomegranate margarita. *Mmm, l'chaim indeed!*

"L'chaim, already. Now let's get back to actually *living* that life we're drinking to—" Madelyn turned back to me. "Do you have a plan?"

I put my drink down. "Sort of. If Jamie fires me, I was thinking I might become a personal manager for a couple of my clients."

"Which reminds me," blurted Lauren. "I need to talk to you about Viggo Mortensen."

"*Hello...?!*" reprimanded Madelyn. "Can we stay on topic?"

"Hold on, Maddie, just one more thing," Lauren said. "I have this other idea, about a way to find out who sent the pictures, but I have to run it by George. That's it; that's all I wanted to say." She picked up her drink and sat back.

Maddie glanced around the table. "Anyone else want to say something; comment on a hottie at the bar or the new line of Spanx?"

We sipped our drinks, not wanting to rile her further.

"Sorry," she said. "But can we try to focus on Quinn first and her own ideas about what she might do if they fire her? You can ask questions, but just hold your suggestions until after. Everyone will get a chance to talk."

Gotta love Maddie. She's tough when she's on a mission, and right now the mission was me. She rarely had an evening off from the duties of raising her budding fourteen-year-old daughter, Lila, and I was grateful she'd made the effort to join us. This evening, Lila was under the care of her dad—Maddie's ex, Brian—which could be the reason for Maddie's shorter-than-usual fuse.

"Okay, so say you become a manager; what happens if your clients stop working? Then what?" Jelicka asked.

"Then I gotta get a *new* new job."

Lauren hrumphed. She never *needed* to work, so she was not the most reliable opinionator on the subject of gainful employment. As far as most of us could tell, she'd married her prep-school sweetheart—who just happened to be heir to America's foremost beer dynasty.

"Any other ideas?" asked Maddie, taking notes.

"I could start a sort of speechy-lecturey sort of booking agency."

Maddie wrote that down.

"Sounds vaguey," said Jelicka giddily, clearly getting tipsy. "Sorry."

Madelyn threw her a look. "All options open. We're brainstorming."

"It would be the kind of thing where I'd arrange for people—you know, actors, athletes, ex-presidents—to appear at events. I'd book them to talk at annual meetings on the lecture circuit—that kind of thing. Think TED, but smaller, and no YouTube," I clarified.

"Wouldn't there be a lot of competition?" Lauren asked. "I just know that from researching for the Alzheimer's benefit."

"I am SO looking forward to the benefit," Jelicka said. "Will there be some eligible bachelors—?" She caught herself. "Er, excuse me—my mistake. We'll table that for now."

Maddie rolled her eyes indulgently and turned back to me.

"Yes," I said, apropos the glutted field of booking speakers. "There will be competition. But think about how many speeches are given every day at corporate retreats, meetings, society luncheons, schools, old folks homes. I think there's room for a new specialized agency."

"I like the idea," said Jelicka. "These days, people can't seem to get enough speeches. No matter what they're about—saving the world, bug anatomy—doesn't matter. I watched a TED Talk about procrastination. *Boom,* a million views! What do they call it? Oh yeah, *viral.* And guess what? There's no cure." Jelicka laughed, slapping the table. "Cheers!" Then she picked up her Orange Bomb and knocked it back.

I glanced at Maddie, concerned if this was Jelicka's first or second drink. She instantly got what I was thinking and leaned toward me. "I'm driving."

"Why *are* speeches so popular all of a sudden?" Lauren asked. "Every single day, somebody sends me a link to somebody yammering on about something. Do you think it's because when other people are speaking, we don't have to?"

"That would never work for the Muffs," Jelicka said. "We all want to talk—well, Sarah not so much." Her words were beginning to sound garbled.

"All right, we agree speeches are currency." Maddie turned back to me. "But let's get back to the task at hand. Any other ideas?"

"I have a little money saved, so I thought maybe I'd do something totally different. Go back to school; study landscape architecture maybe, or cooking. Also, sort of related to all this—I signed up on *NowLove.com*. Maybe all my problems will be solved by meeting a rich guy."

"That doesn't sound like you," Maddie said, only half-joking. "You'd really take the coward's way out? Where's the challenge in that?"

"The feminists would not be pleased," echoed Jelicka.

"I'm not a coward; I'm forty-two," I said. "And I'm still a feminist. But I'm tired and no longer want or need the challenge. I'd like for things to be a little easier, and if I met a nice guy with money, it wouldn't necessarily be bad, would it? I'm barely able to save any money, and if I lose my job, then what? Unemployment? I mean, I'm about ten paychecks away from becoming a bag lady like Jeannette Walls's mother."

"That's not going to happen," Maddie said.

"On NPR today," I said, "they reported this study on Women, Money, and Power, and they said that half of American women over forty fear becoming bag ladies. *Bag ladies*—that's the term they used. At least I'm not alone."

There was collective agreement amongst the three of us singletons and a look of—what was it, guilt?—on Lauren's face.

Despite wanting to make it on our own, have successful careers, build that nest egg, and be totally self-sufficient while at the same time finding worthy mates—at our age, the reality of just how hard that was to achieve had struck us all.

At that moment, a strapping young actor type got a little

too close to the table, bumping it and causing it to shake. "Sorry," he said, turning up the wattage on his smile. "Ladies… " He nodded, made a slight bow, and departed—all of us gazing longingly after him.

"On the other hand," I said, feeling wistful. "I wouldn't mind dying next to that."

"Don't misunderstand; it can work—that older rich guy thing," Maddie said. "I mean, it doesn't really seem like you, but it worked for Jelicka; for awhile."

"Until I was undone by a conniving, husband-stealing secretary nine years older than me!" Jelicka snapped.

"I didn't set out to marry a rich guy," Lauren said with no prompting. "I just got lucky. And I really *love* George, you know? He's just…big and loveable and—I feel so blessed." She shook her head and started to tear up. She suddenly stood—the expression on her face suggesting she'd forgotten something. "I'm sorry, but I'm gonna have to get going."

Jelicka winked at Maddie and me. "Any idea what's on her mind?"

"Oh, it's not like that," she said, her face visibly flushed despite the low light. "I just remembered that Lourdes—she's the kids' nanny—she asked for the night off and, well, I should have been there already."

Lauren had what appeared to be a charmed life. She loved her family and was a happy, vital woman. And, now that she'd started her foundation aimed at curing one of society's biggest medical problems, she'd become one of those people—like Vicki mentoring a foster kid—who was doing something that mattered. She was completely filled with love and purpose. I could hate her if I didn't love her so much.

I stood up and gave her a hug. "I'm sorry Paige couldn't join us."

"She's still swollen and doesn't want to be seen in public." She turned to Jelicka. "She did *not* have her eyes done, Jel. I'm going over to see her tomorrow."

Jelicka put her hands up, palms facing out. "It was only speculation."

"Thanks for coming and hearing my saga," I said, and we all asked Lauren to give Paige our love.

"Of course," she said. "I hope I said something useful."

Just having her there helped, and everything she, Maddie, and Jelicka said would get worked over in my brain until I came up with a plan.

"Go home to your adorable husband and children," I said. "Thanks for coming."

"It's going to work out. You're going to figure out who's trying to screw you, and one day you'll find somebody to love. *Believe* it. I'm just so glad you broke it off with that married guy, once and for all, and that you're moving on."

My focus drifted away, mostly out of fear of being exposed as a liar, and I caught a glimpse of a man in a trendy fedora on the other side of the bar. He seemed to be in his thirties or forties; it was hard to tell. But he looked familiar—like I'd seen him somewhere recently— but maybe he was just a guy in a hat.

Lauren brought me back. "And when you *do* start dating, make sure that every time you go out with somebody, you tell one of us where you're going to be!"

"Right," Jelicka said. "In case you go missing."

"That's thinking positively," said Maddie.

Jelicka sat back in the banquette, considering. "She could have a chip put in. You know, like Udi. Then we'd be able to track her."

Maddie took a long, deep breath. It seemed to me that ever since she had let Jelicka persuade her to break into Udi's friend's house in pursuit of information about her missing lover, there had been a noticeable chilling in their friendship. The Muffs didn't really "fight," but from time to time we switched confidantes—like me talking to Vicki about dating. But we always found our way back to the group, eventually.

"I'll tell someone," I said. "Promise."

"Okay." Lauren pulled out her wallet, depositing too much money on the table, per usual. "I'll be checking that you do. Hope all this helped, Quinny. By the way, what's the book we're supposed to be reading?"

"I'm still deciding." Truthfully, I hadn't started.

"Thank God. I'm so worried about getting Alzheimer's myself, I thought you might have told us last night and I forgot. The disease is hereditary, you know, and with my mom and everything, you can imagine I'm on constant guard."

"*Nnn…* " Jelicka shook her head. "They don't know. They also think it could be something in the water, or maybe fluoride in the toothpaste." Leave it to Jelicka to know the conspiracy theories on the causes of Alzheimer's disease.

"Really?" said Lauren.

"No, they don't," Maddie said firmly, effectively shutting down the topic.

"I'm telling you, they don't really know."

"Anyway," Lauren continued, "you know how long it takes me to read. I need maximum time, especially now with the benefit coming up. "

"We all need maximum time," Jelicka said, as both she and Maddie rose to say their goodbyes. "You know how we get distracted."

Did I ever. "Next week, latest," I promised.

"I'll call you," said Lauren, backing away. "About Viggo and my idea for catching the person who sent the pictures. I just have to run it by George."

After she'd gone, we sat down and Jelicka clunked down her drink. "I know we're supposed to be focusing on Quinn's job prospects, but can we, just for a second, talk about *why* she might be fired? I mean, I know most of the Muffs think I'm always looking for hidden meanings and motives, but the thing is, they're usually there. And don't you think it's odd that somebody would send an email to Quinn's boss with pictures that made her look like a crazed psychopathic shoe-wielder? Think about it. Something's not right about that."

"I have to agree with you there," said Maddie. "And by the way, Jel, apropos another of your many conspiracy theories—namely Udi not being dead. Agreeing with you in *no* way suggests I agree with any of your *other* conspiracy theories, or that I will act upon anything you might say. Do you understand?"

Maddie seemed worked up, all of a sudden, like she'd rehearsed this in her head. I gave Jelicka a nudge under the table in an attempt to keep her from talking.

"I liked Udi a lot," Maddie said. "If I were a teenager, I'd probably even say I loved him, but he *died*, you guys. I felt him die on top of me. He's gone."

I put my hand on her arm. "I'm sorry, Maddie. I didn't mean to dredge the whole thing up again when I called you from Tokyo."

"I know." She smiled. "I know you didn't."

"All right, let's move on," said Jelicka, starting to appear more sober. "Udi is in a better place now. And you have your new Scottish guy, the hurler." She threw me a look that told me none of this was close to being over.

Maddie took a sip of her drink. "Now, getting back to the pictures—any ideas about who could have sent them?"

"Jamie's new assistant is the prime suspect," I said. "I can't think who else has a motive."

"Why do you think it's the assistant?" asked Maddie.

"Because she and Jamie are sleeping together."

"Ahhh…" Madelyn nodded knowingly. "So she's possibly trying to capitalize on her relationship with the boss and get a bump up at work?"

"Exactly."

Jelicka looked confused. "Your boss is gay? I didn't know that."

I shrugged. "It's not a secret. And it's not exactly shocking these days anyway. I mean look at Rachel."

"Rachel's not gay; she's just pissed at men so she experiments."

Even as Maddie said it, I got the idea that Titania might also be an "experimenter."

"Okay, so it sounds like the assistant is angling for your job," said Madelyn.

"Poison could work," Jelicka said, appearing all too serious. "I'm *kidding*."

"What's sort of weird," I said, "is sure, the assistant is a suck-up, and she totally rubs most of us on the floor the wrong way. But even if she's the one who's trying to make me look bad, she's not going to get my job if I'm fired; she doesn't have the experience."

Maddie and Jelicka were either deep in thought, or I'd lost them completely. But I pressed on. "The thing is, the agency is downsizing, and it *could* be that having a reason to fire me—even if it's a sort of trumped up reason—helps Jamie's bottom line. So, in a way, it still gets the girl *points*, even if she doesn't get my job."

"Don't you make the agency a lot of money in commissions?"

"That's another thing; I *do*. Though they'd probably say that all I'm doing is booking *their* talent and that a trained monkey could do it. Not true, by the way. And the last thing is, if Titania *was* the one who sent the photos, and doing that leads to my ouster, she would get credit for my demise. Even if she didn't get my job, she'd move up the ladder faster. They'd just spread pieces of my job to the remaining agents."

Another pause with the two of them staring at me blankly. "Makes a sort of sense," Madelyn said. "Do you think it could be one of the other agents who's competitive with you?"

"Possibly," I said. "But I doubt it. Titania is still the most likely perpetrator."

Jelicka smirked. "*Titania?* Really—that's her name?" She sat up a bit taller, assuming the countenance of her version of an enraged monarch. " *'What, jealous Oberon! Fairy, skip hence. I have forsworn his bed and company.'* " Jelicka was transformed into another Titania—this one the Faerie Queen from *A Midsummer Night's Dream.* She reminded me of Jennifer Lopez.

"If I were you, Jel, I wouldn't make fun of unusual names," Madelyn said gently.

Jelicka considered this. "Actually, it's precisely *because* I have an unusual name that I am uniquely qualified to—" She pushed her drink away. "Even I recognize how stupid that sounded."

"What I haven't been able to figure out," I said, "is who *took* the pictures? Even if it was Titania who sent them, who did she get them from?"

"That is freaky," said Jelicka. "Do you remember seeing anyone at the airport who looked out of place? I mean, other than Udi? God damn it. Sorry, Maddie."

No one came to mind. I shook my head.

"Maybe if you snoop around her desk, you'd find something to get her back with," Jelicka suggested.

I considered this. "I like that. I just can't get caught in the act."

"Obviously," she said.

"Legally, I'm not sure what you can do," said Maddie. "Corporate sabotage was never my field of expertise. You need to get proof that there was some sort of malicious intent, I think. However, the fact remains, there are photographs out there showing you in an unflattering light, and they're real. On the other hand, what you have going for you is you are not a public figure and so even though you handle public figures, you are not one yourself and shouldn't be put in that category. I don't think Talent Partners can legitimately claim your behavior has damaged them."

"Could your boss have arranged for the photos to be sent?" Jelicka asked. "For one of the reasons you mentioned?"

"Jamie?" I hadn't thought about that. "I guess it's possible." But I didn't really think so. And there was something about the way Titania had been acting today at work. Usually she was both aloof and smug, but today she was being way too nice to me. Something was up.

"Well," said Jelicka. "I have to say, you're right not to let her know you suspect anything until you get proof. But what I really think—between what happened with Udi, threats from the deranged office staff, and the minefield of Internet dating—is that we've reached that time again."

"What time is that?" Maddie asked with trepidation.

"Any guesses?" Jelicka tried once more to raise her eyebrows.

"Koreatown massages?" I actually knew full well what Jelicka was about to say.

"I shudder to think" Maddie winced.

"It's time the Muffs paid another visit to Shooters Paradise," Jelicka beamed. In her element, she now appeared to be completely sober.

"Of course it is," said Maddie. "Silly me not to get it."

Though hardly a zealous advocate for the NRA, Jelicka was still The Muffia's link to gun culture. Don't get me wrong, she believed in making it tougher to buy a gun; but she already had hers. In any event, she was always on the lookout for the opportunity to share her gun and her knowledge with us. She thought she was simply being realistic.

After six weeks spent in Israel in her late teens, Jelicka had come to the conclusion that everyone should know how to shoot so as to protect oneself against threats both known and unknown. She would launch into her gun spiel upon hearing any word that might possibly be interpreted as militaristic. Words like *rifle* (as in search), *shoot* (a film or syringe), *kill* (as in perform brilliantly) and *aim* (have a goal) were the *trigger* to get her *fired* up. Most of the Muffs were amused and left it at that. But both Maddie and I had taken her up on previous offers to teach us how to hold and shoot a gun. And now we both felt reasonably equipped to handle one.

"I'm in," I said. With this latest threat to my livelihood, I don't fear for my life—I just wanted to get through the next couple of weeks. Almost any distraction was welcome, which is why I doubled down on acquiring them.

CHAPTER 9

*T*HE NEXT morning, I slipped into the office an hour earlier than usual, planning to go through Titania's desk in search of anything that would prove she was complicit in the attempts to take me down.

To my knowledge, Talent Partners had not yet put cameras on every floor, but only at the elevators to track comings and goings of angry producers, divorcing actors, and any errant agents, messengers, and delivery people—just in case one of them went "off" one day. So I felt reasonably certain that the minutia of what I planned on doing would go unrecorded. There's just not a lot of suspicious activity that occurs on the floor of a talent agency.

As I stepped off the elevator, averting my eyes from the lens of the camera, my cellphone rang, giving me the perfect opportunity to appear nonchalant and otherwise engaged. Pulling out the phone, I saw Steven's name. Since our last rendezvous, we'd had two very short conversations, the second of which occurred last night while I was driving home from Firefly, during which I informed him, in no uncertain terms, that *this* time I was serious—I was breaking it off. But here it was, early the next day, and he just had to make sure.

It was my fault. We'd been here before, and I'd always been too weak to hold my ground for long. But this time, I thought

I'd made it clear that I was turning over a new leaf, wiping the slate, cleaning my clock, frying a different fish—however you wanted to say it. I was determined this time not to let myself be drawn in. I hit "ignore," imagine someone like Chief Justice Sotomayor patting me on the back, deposit the phone into my bag, and keep walking.

Using my passkey, I opened the back outer door to the office floor and strode through the carpeted corridor off the break room—which all the agents, subagents, and assistants share—and from there, moved into the main workspace. Most days, when everyone was busy, we were so close we could overhear parts of each other's conversations, which was what usually discouraged gossip. This was probably why management only put those who'd been with the company a long time—the people who are, in essence, partners—into private offices with a door to close; like Jamie.

Titania's desk was the closest to Jamie's office, whereas mine, inside my cubiffice, was against an interior opposite wall, positioned nearest Sameer. I figured if someone came onto the floor and saw me near Titania's desk, it wouldn't look completely wrong for me to be there. After all, Titania is Jamie's assistant, and Jamie is my boss. So it was within the realm of possibility for Titania to have something on her desk relating to *my* work—even if I were the one to put it there. Anyway, that's the story I had ready if someone *did* come in.

The assistants at Talent Partners all have the same type of desk—the partners insisting on uniformity. They're birch with tasteful chrome details and, on the non-working side of the desk, each is finished with a clean shelf about eighteen inches higher than the desk surface, which means you would only know if someone were working at one if you got close enough.

On the working side of the desk, there are numerous slats, slots, and compartments under the shelf, and all those compartments are filled with things the partners don't want to see when they walk through the floor—papers, pen holders, tchotchkes—hence the design.

Titania's desk was no different, though her stuff was arranged more neatly than some of the other assistants'. Amongst all that "stuff," I was hoping to find a clue to her guilt.

Scanning the vast floor one last time for movement, I walked a little closer. I wasn't sure what I was really looking for. Maybe a receipt that said, "One compromising photo of Quinn Cunningham, $500?" No. But Lauren's semi-offer of help, provided George agreed, might not pan out, and the girls had convinced me that doing something was better than waiting around. Even though I'd made up my mind that I was both ready to accept the situation and adapt to whatever change was coming, I wasn't about to let that fair-haired Moldovan transplant get away with her plan without a fight.

There didn't seem to be anything obviously amiss on her desk; certainly no receipt. I pulled on a drawer—locked. Then another—also locked. I pulled the chair out and suddenly heard a door close somewhere on the floor. *Damn it!*

I scooted back to my desk just as Sameer turned the corner. "Do you have to call a faraway place as well?" he asked. For a split second, I thought he might find it odd I was there so early... might even suspect something.

Recovering quickly, I said, "Preparing to, yes." I really hated to lie, but I figured it was best not to tell the truth, for Sameer's own protection. "Singapore."

He wagged his head. "Tiger is going to be a spokesperson for Scottish whisky, but there is a bidding war transpiring. Orkney wants him for Bruichladdich and Islay for Bunnahabhain."

"Better you than me. He should get both just because his agent can pronounce them. All I've got is Sarah Michelle Gellar for a new vacuum cleaner."

"Good luck." He glanced at his watch. "We will see who gets the Tiger."

He skittered away and with him, so went the day's attempt to probe Titania's desk. Obviously, I'd have to try again.

The rest of the workday passed uneventfully. Titania was back to her aloof self, and Jamie once again brought me into her office to ask if I'd made any progress, to which, of course, I replied, "No." Lauren hadn't called, so whatever she had in mind to get me out of my predicament remained a mystery. Vicki and I connected about online dating—I'd posted my profile, she'd done nothing— and finally, it was evening, and I headed for dance class for the first time since my return from Japan and injuring my ankle. It was still a little sore, but within fifteen minutes, K-Love had me searching for, finding, and releasing my inner goddess. The lights in Studio A were turned down low, and up went the rhythmic sounds of Paloma Faith, Four Tet, and Rage Against the Machine. It was perfect; I needed to rage.

K-Love is a thirtyish multi-hyphenate with a million followers on Instagram, and she gets an instant 200 likes for any pic she posts with a pole dancer in it. She's a beautiful soul and talent, and like so many in L.A., hasn't gotten her due. The warmup she leads us through might seem to the uninitiated to be a glorified masturbation session, and maybe it is a little. She tells us to run our hands over our spandex-clad bodies, allowing our fingers to really feel what they touch and encourage our bodies to respond—*ha! Like I need any help.* My take is, when you have no one lovin' on you, lovin' yourself becomes even more critical, but any actual masturbation, removal of spandex, would need to wait until we got to our respective homes. Tonight, however, sex was the last thing on my mind. In fact, freeing my mind of anything except freeing my mind was the only thing on my mind. When I walked into S-Factor so twisted and tense, K-Love had come over to the mat to unwind me. It didn't take too long, though, before I was back into it—the music, the candles, the deep breathing of all of us together in the room, the inner release. Soon I was just being and moving and expressing myself for nobody but me. Like a lot of people, I just needed a little encouragement—more so now that I've entered my second half. Gone are the days—I hoped not forever—when cutting free seemed easy.

As I held onto the pole, I allowed my body to slowly unshackle itself from all the constraints life had put on it, most of which were self-imposed and which I considered—in large part, wrongly—to be necessary to succeed in the world. I tried to push away the thoughts of why doing so had become so much harder. Why, since I hit 40, did it seem like I have more and more excuses to close myself off? I didn't want to be thinking about this now. Doing so was incongruous with the lithe bodies moving around me and the driving, pounding music.

They say we have to release or we'll explode. So there I was, leg around the pole, head stretched back, hair flowing, wondering if my lifestyle was causing me harm, and OMG I started to cry. Everything I was going through hit me at the same time—Picturegate, Steven, Titania, online dating profiles, the no-go with Viggo—I hadn't even picked a book. All of it broadsided me like I'd been hit with a—well, like I'd been hit with a pole. I clung to it and sobbed.

Whatever comes up in class for any of us is fine with K-Love. No one judges. We're there to release ourselves through the dance; that's her mantra. Granted, it doesn't usually mean somebody is clinging to a pole and crying, but she's okay with that when it happens, too. The mere act of release did the trick. The dam broke and I flowed free.

Pretty soon I became aware of a familiar, sensual, teasing guitar lick coming through the speakers, and I felt like a ton of crap had been lifted off me. "Baby, take off your dress—yes,

yes..." It was Joe Cocker, of course; *You Can Leave Your Hat On,* one of my all-time favorites. *Yes, indeed.* You find your joy where you can.

CHAPTER 10

SOMETIMES, THOUGH, you have to make your own joy. Re-energized after pole dancing, I dodged another call from Steven, and when I got home, I was ready to take the next step toward online dating success. This meant sitting down with a glass of Sauvignon Blanc and logging onto *NowLove* to see if anyone appealing had responded to my profile. I'd posted it at lunchtime, after a bit of suggested tweaking from Vicki, changing the "About Me" portion to read: "I can cook a couple of dishes really well," instead of what I had—the truer, but more off-putting: "I hate to cook." She claimed there was plenty of time to tell a guy I didn't like to cook *after* he'd fallen in love with me.

Typing in my password, I reminded myself it didn't need to be love at first page view, but if I was patient, gave the process time, and resolved to be a *little* less picky, I'd find the right man.

Deep breath, hit return and… Wow, was I shocked to see 100 "matches" in my inbox, along with men "winking", sending me "flowers," or otherwise selecting me as their "favorite." Plus 30 messages! *Sheesh*, this was going to take awhile. I sipped my wine and told myself to stay positive. After all, I had a choice in this game—far better than a lot of women on the planet.

Scanning the long list of men who were lonely or horny or, most likely, both, I waited for a name to jump out at me.

I envisioned my perfect man in a house or office somewhere, scanning down the long list of women—lonely, horny, most likely both—hoping for a name to jump out at *him*. I opened the first message and knew right away I needed some sort of screening mechanism.

"What's with their handles?" I asked Vicki ten minutes later. "Do they really think *Beachbum2453* is going to nail more babes than *Beachbum2452*?"

She snorted. "Why would a guy think a woman's going to be attracted to somebody called Beach Bum in the first place?" There was the sound of ice clinking in a glass.

"Seems like a minor groundswell; there are at least 2,453 of them. That's a lot of Twitter followers anyway."

"They should be so lucky. Hit *delete*," she said.

I tapped the delete key. Bye-bye Beach Bum. That was one way to cull the herd.

The ice clinked again, followed by the sound of a glass touching down on a table. Was Vicki drinking alone? Not that her doing so should shock me; *I* was drinking alone.

"What are you drinking over there?" I asked as my computer generated an unfamiliar *ding* sound.

"Just water. The doctors still advise not to drink anything stronger than ginger ale, which makes it tough for someone who pre-cancer only drank coffee and alcohol. I try to pretend it's a vodka martini with a twist."

"The power of positive thinking writ large."

"I like *your* handle," she said. " 'Miss-underscore-Quinn.' It says exactly who you are and the underscore, you know, *underscores* and gives it some personality."

"What did you choose for yours?"

"I haven't decided yet."

"Come on, we're supposed to be doing this together." I sensed hesitation but hoped I was wrong. "How's your profile coming?"

"I'm getting there. So do you see anyone interesting among the available offerings?" She was definitely stalling.

"Interesting is a good word; anything more than interesting...I don't know. And as far as who's available, it's kind of hard to tell." I was well aware that some of these guys were not, in fact, available. Negotiating which ones were was part of the minefield a woman had to contend with on her way to capture the flag. Some men were married, "in a relationship," or otherwise *una*vailable. It was safe to say that what every guy streaming by on my computer screen was doing was exploring other options. Any woman proceeding did so at her peril.

I paused the stream. "Here's a guy who calls himself *Letstalkaboatsex*. Get that? Instead of 'about' it says 'a boat.' Do you think he has trouble spelling or just wants someone to go sailing with?"

Vicki snorted again. "Or have boat sex?"

"I'd get sea sick."

"Either way, give that guy a wide berth."

"Ha. I don't know anything about boats. Fresno's land locked." I hit *delete* again. How easy it was to dismiss people when they're not right in front of you.

"Did you know Paige met Richard online," said Vicki.

I did *not* know that. "I thought they were set up."

"It was a setup, all right, provided by *Plenty of Fish*. They met online, and *they* set up the first date."

Not that Paige and Richard's relationship was any sort of testament to the success of online dating, in my opinion. "What's happening with them now? I can't keep track."

"She's too embarrassed to talk about it, but I think this month they're engaged." Paige and Richard's engagement had been on again-off again for three years, and during that period, their status had vacillated several times between the two states, with the only variant being whether they were living in the same house.

"Have you talked to her? She's been uncharacteristically quiet, don't you think?"

"I haven't," said Vicki.

"I'll call her tomorrow. I should have called already, but with everything going on… I'm beginning to think Jelicka might be right about her having plastic surgery."

"So, any other possibilities?" Vicki asked, getting back to the manhunt.

I sighed. "I made the mistake of responding to a guy who had a bunch of visible tattoos—and I'm sure there were plenty of others you couldn't see—who wrote saying he wanted to, 'Put me on the back of his Harley and ride me—double entendre probably not intended—around this wacky world as the wind played in my hair'—something like that. I felt like I had to respond because there's no way he read my profile. It clearly says, 'If your means of transportation is a motorcycle, or your free time is spent on your bike, please *do not* contact me!' "

"They don't *read*, Quinn," she said. I heard the ice clink again and the glass hit the table. "Ugh, I really need something stronger than water."

"If this is upsetting, I don't have to trouble you with it. It is kind of depressing that these guys can't even read a woman's profile."

"Maybe they don't read because what we have to say is irrelevant in their all-important quest of getting into our panties."

"That sounds like male-bashing, Vick. Are you male-bashing?"

"I love men; I'm just not sure I like them all the time, you know?"

"I absolutely do." Exactly.

"Hey, speaking of reading, have you picked a book yet?"

It kept slipping my mind for obvious reasons. "I'm narrowing it down." This was mostly true. I'd eliminated any book over 350 pages from consideration, which only left about seven hundred million choices.

"I need a good book to get lost in."

"After we hang up," I promised. "Top of my list."

"We need a rule that the new hostess has to pick a book within two days of the last meeting."

"Okay, I'll pick a book. Now help me with these guys."

As I watched the name of a new suitor hit my inbox, I realized the now-familiar ding was *NowLove* sending me another candidate's wink, flower, or message.

"Anyway," I said, "I felt compelled to tell tattoo guy—*Highwaytolove* he calls himself—that he couldn't possibly have read my profile or he would have known, you know? But he ignores that, too, and writes back asking me what I'm afraid of. What I'm afraid of?"

"Couldn't admit he didn't read," said Vicki. "If he hadn't written to you, I'd wonder if he even knew how."

"So I make something up about an ex dying in a motorcycle wreck and how I couldn't handle it happening again."

"And, of course, that was a challenge he just *had* to respond to."

"*Mmm-hmm*—to tell me the best way to handle my heartache was to get back on the bike. He wanted to 'free me from my sorrow.' "

"How kind."

"Sitting on a motorcycle behind someone I barely know, trusting that person to guide a six-hundred-pound piece of metal through other pieces of metal weighing anywhere from two thousand to twenty thousand pounds? Not my idea of a good time."

"Not to mention, in L.A. it's suicide," said Vicki. "Is that it?

There's gotta be somebody interesting."

"Lots of trawlers—guys like *SideshowBob* who go for the low-hanging fruit—too lazy to read a profile or write a personal message, they click, 'Wink' or, 'Tell *GoodtimeSally* you want to meet her.' So *GoodtimeSally* gets a wink—whatever the hell that is. But in reality, *SideshowBob* is winking at every woman on the freakin' website. He's just lazy and doesn't want to expend any emotional or intellectual energy. And if he can't even do that, what hope is there he's going to do his own laundry?"

"Out with the winkers." Vicki sighed. "Why are we doing this again?"

I knew my reasons, some of which were crap, but I said, "Because we want to prove Rachel's wrong about her fairy tale?"

"Oooh...that's going to be hard. I liked that fairy tale and I read on *HuffPo* that 'Single is the new Black.' Supposedly, single people like us are going to define the mainstream trends of tomorrow."

"Vicki, we're doing this together! You promised."

"I'm sorry, Quinny. I know the goods are out there, but the goods are odd, and finding someone who isn't requires that level of commitment we were talking about before. I realize I don't have it."

"Oh, come on. If I can squeeze it in while trying to clear my name and keep my job, you can, too."

"And you know," she said in a quieter voice, "it's only been four years since Ricky and I split."

Here we go... Vicki and Ricky had been married for close to twenty years before getting divorced. Apropos Rachel's fairy tale, maybe after such a long time, Vicki was enjoying her freedom and didn't want to give it up—whereas a woman like me who'd never been married felt like she was missing something. Whatever the reason, it still sounded like an excuse.

"I'm just into a lot of stuff right now," she continued. "I want to do my art for and make movies. And don't forget, I'm mentoring Solange, so I don't really have the time."

"All right." I certainly wasn't going to argue about it.

"I'll still be your sounding board. Any time. How's this? You can be my inspiration. If you find true love, I'll try it."

"I wish you'd reconsider," I said. "Life is so short. You know that better than most of us."

I decided not to mention that one of the main reasons we were doing this together was so we could vet guys for each other—something we could only do if she was on the same site with me.

"I'll think about it, I promise." She paused. Something else seemed to be on her mind and I waited her out. "The other thing is, I *do* really want to do something with all the footage I've been getting. It could be my last chance." *Ah, now I got it. Stupid I hadn't figured it out.*

"It is not your last chance; stop it. Your cancer's gone; that's what you told us. These last few follow-up appointments—there's nothing there, right?"

"Right," she said in a very small voice.

"Look, I know you're worried, and I'm sure that's completely normal, but gosh, Vicki, statistically you've already beaten the odds. Yes, it could come back, but there's also a very good chance it won't. You'll have lots of chances to make movies—though, I have to say, you could probably find more interesting subject matter—not that the Muffs aren't endlessly fascinating *to us.*"

"You're sweet, Quinny, but I guess the overall point is, right now a guy would just get in my way."

There had to be more to this, but I didn't want to push it. Of course she was trying to protect herself—and some mythical man she might fall for—from heartbreak in the event her cancer did come back. But that might never happen. *I* could get cancer;

it runs in my family for Godssake. And either of us could be in a car accident. The reality is, any of us, at any point, could be caught in a situation where we're injured or killed, irrevocably destroying or simply changing our lives. At least for myself, I'd figured out that this plain fact, made more and more real with each passing day, was no longer a reason to postpone the rest of my life, even if it was difficult, and even if it hurt.

"You'll know when it's the right time," I said. "And hopefully by then, I'll be able to help *you*."

She let out a long breath. "Okay, let's review... Narrow down the candidates by deleting the winkers, anyone who's a beach bum, anyone who rides a motorcycle or has too many tattoos, and anyone who obviously hasn't read your profile. And just delete any email from a guy who doesn't post his picture because he's probably married, and you've already done that." *Nice of her to remind me.* And with that we hung up.

The process of finding love indeed seemed overwhelming, but I was determined to remain, at least in the short term, un-daunted by the challenges. And it was amazing what shopping for a guy was doing for my self-esteem. There were hundreds of men in my inbox every day to choose from. Even if 80% of the guys who had written to me weren't worth the bother, the mere fact they'd contacted me felt good.

I slathered an age-defying, detoxifying mask on my freshly-scrubbed face, poured another small glass of wine, and sat back down in front of the computer to assess my choices—determined to find at least one man, out of the thousands out there in cyberspace, looking for love, with whom I might go on a date. I only needed one. And I had to believe he was out there.

CHAPTER 11

ESPITE PICTUREGATE hanging over me, the days seemed to whip by, and today was no exception. I still hadn't been able to scope out Titania's desk thoroughly, but I'd decided if I couldn't do it soon, I would have to confront her, one way or another. This decision coincided with Lauren finally leaving a voice mail saying she'd call me at lunch. Apparently she had good news about the matter she'd brought up at Firefly—something she said might help me get to the bottom of who was trying to sabotage me.

Until she called, I busied myself with two conference calls and finalized terms of a contract between P. Diddy and *Toys R Us* for the new P. Diddy Doll. Fortunately for all parties concerned, I was not in charge of marketing the new toy because the only tag line I could think of was, "You'll have hours of fun diddling your Diddy." Though this was infinitely better than diddling your "Daddy," it wasn't likely to fly with the advertisers. The marketplace, however, would probably love it, just as they had the stuffed, trash-talking Honey Badger.

And speaking of diddling, if our online repartee was any indication, let's just say I was looking forward to meeting someone I'd "met" online: *JohnV202*. If his picture was any indication—*did I dare hope?*—he had masses of dark hair and a style that might belong to a doctor or the owner of a small artisanal Bourbon distillery. According to his profile, he was in information technology— I.T.—but beyond that, the subject remained vague as I.T. always does. I hadn't pressed him, figuring it was tacky to be overly concerned with what people *do*, rather than who they are.

From his first direct message, he demonstrated that he was smart, witty, *and* that he had read my profile. What an enticing combo after the earlier lazy creeps. John and I took up an easy correspondence over the following few days, with the time between missives shrinking and the content of those missives getting more and more revelatory.

And with no additional threats from Jamie for the time being, I eagerly accepted his invitation to dinner. And so, per Muff edict, it was time to tell the girls about my upcoming date.

From:cunningquinn@Talentpartners.com

To: Muffgroup

Subject: Date night

Dear Muffs, I have been warned by a couple of our esteemed body that I am to inform you when I am going on an Internet date or risk flogging. So you are hereby notified of my impending date Saturday night at Boa. No need to watch from the bar. Just send out the search party if I don't answer the phone Sunday morning. xo Q

PS—No new news on Picturegate.

That should cover it.

From: vonhooter@gmail.com:

To: Muffgroup

Subject: Date night

Great on the dating but bummer on the employee sabotage. Lauren filled me in. Sorry to miss you all last week. My face still looks like I got run over. You'd think I got smacked down with a frying pan rather than one fuzzy yellow ball, but doc says it's because of where the little beasty hit me. Something about my occipital sensory apparatus going into overdrive. Pick a book, Quinn!!!

Oh, right. The book.

From: cunningquinn@Talentpartners.com
To: Muffgroup
Subject: The book
Will pick book by the weekend, or you can shoot me.

Jelicka wasn't done with date night.

From: MissJelickaG@aol.com:
To: cunningquinn@Talentpartners.com
Subject: Date night
Saturday night? Sorry to crash idea of steak dinner at upscale, trendy, expensive restaurant, but shouldn't you start with coffee on a weekday afternoon? He's probably going to expect a quid pro quo. And what's going on with Titanic Titania's desk? I stand ready to help sink that ship when called upon. BTW— Speaking of shooting—next week at the range. Who's in?

So far, no emails from Muffs declaring their irrepressible desire to shoot guns, but everyone did have something to say by way of support for my upcoming date—the Muffs are my girls, after all. Jelicka wasn't the only one to warn me about the dangers of scheduling a first date on a Saturday night. Obviously, I just didn't realize how sacrosanct that particular night of the week was for some people.

Madelyn, who'd done a bit of Internet dating herself, said

she knew of three studies that determined there was far more pressure for a date to succeed on Saturday than any other night, and one of those studies even suggested there was increased incidence of suicide if a date didn't work out. For my part, it had been years since I'd gone out, alone with a man, on a Saturday night, and I was just being practical. It was the only night of the entire week that I didn't have to either recover from the workweek or prepare for the one ahead. It was the only day I could wake up late and go to bed late and have enough time to take a pole dancing class and get a manicure—all without rushing like the fiend I am the rest of the time.

So despite all the prognostications and potential dire consequences, both known and unknown, I was going ahead with my plan. Most of the time, I create so many reasons why *not* to do something, maybe going out on a Saturday night would make me try harder.

Jamie and Titania left early for lunch, acting as normal as any other gay female couple in Hollywood—which is to say, rather unusual—but there were still too many people on the floor to make it possible for me to conduct another search of Titania's desk.

I made a few calls—one to Kiki to find out what was happening at the house next door and to ask when the Muffs might come over to help catch the neighbors in the midst of a porn shoot. I also called to check in on Vicki and, though she was happy I'd found somebody to go out with, she was still reluctant to join me online. The girl she was mentoring was turning out to be more than she'd bargained for.

"Solange's foster father is a pig so she did a little time, but she's a really sweet kid."

"Hold on. She's an ex-con?"

"Not really. Her foster father was a scumbag."

"Was?"

"He's alive but see, he tried to rape her, so she defended herself—hit him with a football helmet and he lost an eye."

"Yeow."

"She should have gotten off completely, though. I bet Maddie could have gotten her off. The Public Defender was terrible. Anyway, I volunteered to help her, you know, to get on a better track."

"That's so generous, Vicki. I really applaud you. Be careful, though—what if One-Eye finds out where she is and comes after her, and *you*?"

"Restraining order—I'll be fine."

Despite being concerned for her, what I mostly felt was envious. Because in addition to trying to become a better person—*I'm destined for great things*—one of my other un-acted upon resolutions was to get involved in a cause, or some worthy charitable group. My excuses for not having done so thus far were lame and included the idea that there were so many worthy causes that I couldn't choose; either that or I'd talked myself out of each of them. I'd considered working to preserve land for animals and birds, but if the human population kept growing, all that protected land would eventually get taken over by people anyway, with the excuse that people are more important than animals, even though people got us into the whole mess in the first place.

I could work to stop global warming, and even though I was willing to drive an electric car—that is, if I could afford one— the planet was still doomed because of all the rich people who run the world and won't turn the lights and air conditioning off in their high-rise office towers and refuse to give up their private jets. The rich have a far greater carbon footprint than some poor illegal immigrant who drives an inefficient truck. How could I make them stop?

The American Cancer Society or some other organization aimed at curing a dreadful disease was a possibility—like Lauren and her Alzheimer's foundation. After all, curing disease is a noble goal, but do we really need *more* people living beyond the age of 95? Just think of all the carbon-exuding activities needed to keep blind, brain-addled, methane- spewing, bedridden people breathing through tubes until they finally, one day, drift off to the next world costing their families and society hundreds of thousands of dollars. No, that didn't seem sensible.

This kind of reasoning got me thinking about stopping unwanted pregnancies, which was not exactly politically correct and, therefore, verboten for any employee at Talent Partners to get involved in. Maybe I could work to preserve historical build-ings…that probably wouldn't offend anyone.

Meanwhile, my friends were out making a difference in the world. I felt like a slacker. "You're out saving souls, if not lives, and *I'm* worried about Internet dating!"

"You can date *and* save the world," Vicki suggested.

"You just got through telling me you can't date and save one girl. How am I supposed to date and save the world? I can't even save my job. I don't even know how to date anymore."

"You're right," she said. "Just do what you can."

After we hung up, I realized Lauren still hadn't called, and I was beginning to think she'd forgotten about me. I had prob-ably invested too much hope in thinking she could fix my problems at work, but that was only because I was short on ideas about how to fix them myself. It looks like I'm going to have to spend some money to dig into the matter—money I'd probably have to borrow. Big inhale: yes, yes, yes, yes; and exhale: thank you, thank you, thank you, thank you. *Just do what you can.*

Opening my eyes, I glanced around and lo and behold, it

looked like Daniel was the only other person still on the floor. And he was clear across at reception busy with his takeout salad. *Hmmm…* Did I dare? With the droning purr of the HVAC creating white noise all around me, I stood up and walked to the break room. Again, surprisingly empty. I strolled back toward my cubiffice, encountering no one, and made a beeline for Titania's desk. With luck, she'd left some drawers open.

Yes! First try—center drawer, unlocked. Slowly, I eased it open, but there was nothing in there other than pens and blank Post-it notes—useful, I suspected, for jotting down all those chores Jamie wanted her to take care of. I pushed it shut, listened, scanned the floor again, then ducked down behind the desk where I'd only be spotted if someone came out of Jamie's office, which I was sure wouldn't happen with the lovebirds out at lunch.

I rifled through a bunch of papers lined up in one of the compartments—nothing but gym and yoga schedules, menus from different restaurants, and brochures from waxing salons and lash extension offers—*better to bat her baby blues at Jamie with.*

I put that stack back and moved on to another cubby. More mish-mash, but not the mish-mash I sought. *If only people kept incriminating photos around.* But these days, people keep their pictures on their phones. I briefly allowed myself the thought that if the planet suddenly stopped, and all Internet server farms ceased to function, any future civilization would assume we all died off in the 1990s, or else they'd wonder why we suddenly stopped taking pictures of each other.

I was about to give up when I noticed a small vase with a couple of artificial peonies sticking out. As I picked it up, I heard something rattle at the bottom and shook it. There was something in the vase other than the plasticene peonies. Tipping the vase, out poured the fake flowers and one of those wearable buttons you can get at a portable photo booth: Two people kissing—really kissing—and one of them was clearly Titania. The other was a *guy*—Titania was kissing a *guy!*

Wait, Titania was *gay.* Or was she bisexual, only pretending to be gay so she could manipulate Jamie? Did Jamie know her girlfriend had a boyfriend?

Maybe Jamie considered herself incredibly hip and evolved for dating a bisexual. *No,* that was unlikely. Based on what I'd witnessed of Jamie's past romantic liaisons, she needed to *own* her lovers—including Titania—and she didn't strike me as the type who would share, especially if her lover's lover was a guy.

Hmm...I just might have found something useful. If its authenticity was to be believed, this photo badge might just undermine the relationship and possibly cast suspicion on Titania's motives. But I needed to consider just how to use it. In any event, I felt better knowing I had something on her, as I gave up on Lauren's call and went to grab some lunch.

CHAPTER 12

STEPPING OUT of the elevator, as I considered how best to use my new find, I felt my mobile vibrate, and Lauren's name finally popped up on caller I.D.

As much as I couldn't wait to hear her idea about uncovering who sent the incriminating photos, I felt like I needed to wait for her to offer.

"Hi, how goes the party planning?" I asked.

"Today we booked the band, secured the flowers and a couple more huge auction items. Get this—a week in a villa on one of Richard Branson's private islands."

"Wow!"

"I know, and we have various people on the board drumming up money and guests for the primo tables. But I wanted to talk to you about Viggo Mortensen. You have a minute?"

Patience… "Sure." I crossed the lobby, dodging three lawyer types walking abreast, oblivious to the possibility that they might be blocking traffic.

"Have any idea how he feels about Alzheimer's disease?" she asked.

I pushed through the revolving door and onto the street, heading for Chipotle and a steak bowl, a few blocks away. "I'll betcha he doesn't like it."

"Funny. But seriously, how do you think he'd feel about being auctioned off for the cause?"

"Bid on Viggo and he'll paint your kitchen?"

"This would be more like: 'Bid on Viggo and go on a date.' He wouldn't have to spend more than an hour with the highest bidder, promise," Lauren went on, clearly trying to minimize his commitment.

"Knowing Viggo, I think he'd rather paint a kitchen. He *is* an artist, you know. I'm sure he'd do an awesome job."

"Will you ask him? Or is it awkward? I know people must bug you all the time about your famous clients."

She was right; people did bug me all the time. But in this case, maybe getting Viggo on board could be my contribution to the greater good—or at least *a* contribution. OK, it wasn't like going all-in and relocating to Africa to bring healthy drinking water to the indigenous populations, but if my connections and contacts might bring in dollars for a cure to Alzheimer's, this would be a good thing.

"I'll ask. Want anyone else? Matthew McConaughey? Johnny Depp?"

Suddenly, there seemed to be forty Chinese tourists on the sidewalk in front of me. They were exiting the Nike store, laden with shopping bags and bound for their limousines, impeding my progress toward Chipotle. *Talk about conspicuous consumption.*

"Are you kidding—could you? They'd both be great," Lauren was saying.

A large panel truck rattled by, obscuring all other sounds. "What was that?"

"I said, 'Fantastic!' We'd probably have to ask Johnny to leave his dead crow at home though, don't you think? We wouldn't get much for him with that on his head. No Captain Jack Sparrow routine, either. Oh—and he can't bring his dogs." Lauren bit her lip and looked at me apologetically. "Come to think of it, maybe not Johnny Depp."

"You'd be surprised how much you could get for Jack Sparrow, but as he's a protected character subject to licensing fees, so leaving him at home won't be an issue. I'm happy to ask around, though, and give you some more names. I'm sure we can get an appealing group of guys to auction off."

"That would be amazing, and I really appreciate it. Having those handsome Hollywood hunks could bring in a lot more money."

"No doubt." For a change, I wasn't getting asked for tickets to premieres or award ceremonies—events that, granted, helped the economy but did very little for the greater good. Getting some of my celebrity clients on board for the benefit made me feel good, would surely make the guys donating themselves feel good, and would also raise cash for Lauren's foundation—a triple "win."

"Would you like to come?" she asked.

Of course I did, but she'd made it clear none of the Muffs could go for free, and the ticket price was pretty steep.

"I *want* to come, sure, but... "

"I'm happy to comp you."

"Really?"

"Only seems right, don't you think? You're doing all this work for us."

"I'd do it anyway, Lauren."

"I know but...just let me comp you. But please, don't say anything to the other Muffs."

"Promise. Hey, if my date doesn't work out on Saturday night, maybe at the benefit you can point out all the rich single men with Alzheimer's to me."

"Are you serious? *With* Alzheimer's?"

"Kind of? No. I'm not. Anyway, I'd love to come and thank you. Besides, you'll probably need me as celebrity wrangler if the guys say 'yes'."

"Good point. Okay, new subject. Remember how I said I was going to work on that *idea* I had? I mean, about your situation at work?"

"Yeah...I remember." Ever since Jelicka had the idea to make The Muffia an ersatz amateur crime-solving entity, I've been wary of any Muff *ideas*—including my own.

"Well, I finally pinned him down," said Lauren.

I came to a stop again—this time outside Barney's—only a few doors west of Talent Partners. "Who?"

"George's dad, of course. George was fine with it. But Pop was out of the country, so I had to wait until he got back."

Rather than straining to hear over the traffic noise, I pushed through the glass door into the Barney's make-up department—a mere thirty feet from Shoes, where I still needed to go to deal with my broken shoe.

"Dare I ask what this idea is?" I sprayed some of the new Marc Jacobs cologne on my wrist and sniffed. Wow, that's...*floral.* Hoping the sales people would ignore me, I began to stroll.

"Okay, here we go. Even though George's family sold the parent corporation, they're still involved with day-to-day beer-making activities, and they keep a kind-of private investigation company on retainer for corporate espionage—to avoid the theft of beer recipes, I guess, things like that. So my thought was, maybe you could sort of *borrow* one of the investigators, you know? Maybe the family hasn't met their minimum billable hours this quarter, and we could get somebody to scope out Picturegate."

"Do you think they'd allow that?" The idea sounded great.

"It's done. That's why it took so long, but George's dad likes you, and George loves that you're helping with the foundation and the benefit and everything, so they want to help any way they can."

I hadn't actually said I'd help until ten minutes ago, but I guess that was a minor detail. "Oh, Lauren, this is great. Really? When can he or she start?"

"Right away. And I'm pretty sure it's a he. All I have to do is tell them you're game, and they assign the person officially. Whoever it is will contact you directly."

"Do you know what this person's name is?"

"No, and I won't know. It's all very spy novel, espionage-y, you know…on a need-to-know-basis type of thing. But he'll be in touch, and I think you'll know the guy when you see him."

I wasn't sure what that meant, but a visual of Bradley Cooper in "American Sniper" popped into my head. *If only.* We ended the call, and I looked up to find a severe, overly made-up young woman with short dark hair staring at me over the Clarins counter.

"Can I help you?"

Though I didn't think I'd been standing there talking on the phone for very long, apparently she thought I owed her a purchase. I like Clarins, but it's a little pricey for my budget.

"Not today, thanks." I turned on my heel and walked out the way I came in, quickly covering the remaining two blocks to Chipotle where I stood in line outside the crowded restaurant. Though I wished there was no line, because I would now be late getting back to work, I was very glad I'd bought twenty shares of stock in the company.

Scanning the street, I wondered how long it would take for the investigator to make himself known, and if—dare I hope—he might indeed be a handsome former Navy Seal or Special Ops hunk. I scrutinized the men in line with that picture in my head, but no one fit the bill. And since this was the only type of guy I was looking for, I failed to notice someone else watching me.

CHAPTER 13

"ANY WAY I can convince you not to go?"

Jelicka was on speaker as I zipped up my black pencil skirt and finished getting ready for my date with *JohnV20*. We had yet to meet in person—yet to even talk on the phone because he thought it was more romantic. But our email and direct message exchanges had led me to believe he might be right, and I couldn't wait to meet him.

"No way. I'm going, and if he turns out to be a fraud, I'll still get a steak dinner for my efforts. *He* asked me, *he* suggested the place, and I'm not going to feel guilty if I don't want to put out afterward."

She let out an audible sigh. "That's good to hear anyway. What does he do again?"

"He's in I.T. I don't know exactly what."

"I.T.," she repeated. "Like the rest of us *aren't* into 'it.' What's with the *JohnV20*? Is the "v" for versus or is he on the twentieth version of his operating system?"

"Who knows?" I said, sucking in my belly." I've stopped trying to figure out their handles."

"What does he look like?" She was persistent.

"Not that it's important, but he's good looking—dark hair and eyes, probably fifty-five—though I'm assuming he's lying about his age, which he put at fifty. Probably also lies about his height, which he says is five-eleven."

"They all lie—not just about their age and height, either. Beware of all pictures on the Internet."

As an agent, I was all too familiar with photographs that don't accurately represent their subjects, but right now Jelicka was just being a doomsayer. "Do you have any words of encouragement?"

"Sorry, I'm being a witch, aren't I?"

"A little witchy, yes. But you sincerely care, so I can't get too mad at you."

Though I was projecting, I knew Jelicka was still smarting over her divorce from Roscoe. That was why she played the part of the cougar so vociferously, hanging out with hunky young cubs and drinking a little too much. Neither the cougar nor any of her cubs took such dalliances seriously, but it also seemed a little self-destructive.

"Sorry, Quinn. I really hope it goes well. That said, I'm organizing a search party if I don't hear from you by midnight."

She made me laugh. "I'll be fine. My plan is to park a few blocks away and take a cab to and from the restaurant—just in case he tries to follow me. I learned this technique from my friend Jelicka who was in the Israeli army."

"You joke, but you can't be too careful."

"I'm agreeing with you!"

"Good. And don't forget we're going shooting next weekend."

"Okay."

"Okay," she repeated. "'Love you, bye."

No matter what happened on this date, or even at work, I would always have my Muffs.

A giant aquarium filled with Puffer fish divided two sections of the upscale Boa, the steak house named for a snake, situated on the ground floor of a high-rise office tower at the west end of the Sunset Strip, and the aquamarine hue casts an unflattering glow on nearby diners.

The smell of seared sirloin wafting from the plates carried by the attractive, black-clad wait staff provokes hunger in the carnivorous clientele and makes it clear that, despite the cool-colored surroundings, the kitchen staff knows how to prepare a red hot steak. I could not wait for one of those plates to land in front of me.

My date, sitting opposite me at one of the restaurant's more intimate tables, sipped from a drink he'd started on before I arrived. Our menus were displayed in front of us, and I used mine to steal glances at him whenever his head was down. He was well dressed and attentive and looked surprisingly like his photos. I'd pegged him correctly as in his fifties. The actual number fifty he hadn't seen in years. Straight nose, dark brown eyes, a clearly-defined chin, and he was still in possession of most of his hair, which looked real from what I could tell. But without any visible strands of gray running through it, I suspected he must get some assistance from a colorist. He had lied about his height, but I wasn't going to hold that against him. Being five-nine, it's hard for me to find many guys, age-appropriate or not, who are taller than I am. So what's a couple of inches? There was only one thing I was totally not prepared for:

"So, Quuueeeeen, whahdjyoo doo pfor pfuhhhnn?" he asked.

What an accent. Though charming, it was almost impossible to penetrate. Hearing him speak had come as a complete surprise. One would think he might have mentioned, in one of his many emails, that he was from Venezuela. One would think knowing someone's country of origin would be relevant to a prospective date's decision to go out with that someone. This, most likely, was precisely why he hadn't mentioned this detail in any of those well-written messages he'd sent—messages, I suspected, that were written by somebody else. Not that any of this really mattered, such was the paucity of attractive, intelligent, age-appropriate men. I probably would have gone out with him anyway.

"What do I do for fun?" I repeated, making sure I'd heard him correctly. I hesitated, not wanting to go too far down the road of story-sharing before we got our order in. I was determined, regardless of how the evening developed, to get a good meal out of this, so the sooner I got my steak, the better.

"Let's see. Gosh, so many things… " I looked back at the menu, considering the NY Strip and how much pfuhhhnn that could be, but he pressed on without me.

"Djyoo lie doo tance? Djyoo lie doo go-honzee lon hyge?"

What's a—Oh, I get it—hike, long hike!

"Yes, I do like to hike. There are lots of good hiking trails in L.A., don't you think?"

He had a peculiar way of cocking his head to the right whenever I said something. Maybe it was because English was his second language and doing that helped him concentrate? Or maybe he was deaf in one ear? Not sure.

John—or more likely Juan, though I'll give him the benefit of the doubt and call him John—claimed to be a refugee from the Chavez regime who had fled his native country years ago with the family fortune, the sum of which remained as unclear as the reason for the head tilt.

"Oh, djyess." He smiled through too-white, too-even teeth.

Some of that fortune went to a cosmetic dentist, that's for sure.

Across the crowded dining room, I saw a man sitting alone. There was something familiar about him, just like there'd been something familiar about the guy at Firefly, but the way his body was positioned I was unable to get a good look. Probably a washed-up former child star or somebody I dated once. Or maybe

I've been around so long, everyone was starting to look familiar.

I turned back to John, watching his head tilt back into listening position, and said, "And I like to dance. I'm not very good, but I like it."

No need to tell him about the pole dancing—he'd only get ideas.

"Thass goood, Queen," he said, righting his head and taking a big gulp from his drink. "De higing iss berry good por zee-elth, but de tancing is beery good por zee-soll."

I nodded, still deciphering. "Oh—the soul, of course!" I said to the tilted head. "And health. Absolutely. Great for your health and your soul."

A waiter finally appeared to take our order. Metrosexual and wearing all black, except for a red tie, he rattled off a couple of specials, while John tilted his head to listen to the elaborate descriptions, only righting it again once the waiter left.

John didn't seem like a bad guy so, mixed assessment notwithstanding, I resolved, as part of the Quinn self-improvement campaign, to put all my criticisms aside. I was in a beautiful restaurant with an attractive—who cares if he was a little short?—man who seemed very interested in me. I would practice gratitude. Yes and thank you. There were, after all, so many truly horrible places I could be right now that it would be selfish of me not to be grateful. All that said, I decided to remain sober just to keep myself honest.

"Jhyehhsss," John said. "Zzee-art and sol har soo eempohr-tent. Ahm so appy daht dwee ahgree on daht." As he spoke, he lowered his voice so it sounded like the low rumble of thunder on a sex-laden summer night. "An tehll me, Queen, abow djyour tanhce. Djyoo lie doo doo zee tengo?" His eyebrows lifted and tilt went his head.

"Tango?" He'd asked the question so suggestively, I suddenly felt exposed. They say tango is the closest thing to sex with your clothes on, not that I had any first-hand experience. Pole dancing comes close, I guess—except that you're dancing with a pole, not a person.

"Si, si—tengo. Como los Ahrzhenteen. I ham tahncing de tengo pfor mehny, mehny jyeeehrs."

"I didn't realize people in Venezuala did Argentine tango," I said, trying to make a joke.

"Oh jyheesss, off corssse dey doo. De Venezuelan peeepowl hahrr no so particulahr when ees a goohd tance weer eet come from. I weel teesh you to tengo eef you lie."

What exactly did he mean by "If I lie?" Though I was game to tango in a general sense, it was becoming ever more clear that I wasn't about to try it with John. And with his suddenly too-obvious wooing, I was beginning to think I didn't even want to continue the conversation.

"Well, John," I said. "You must be very good if you can teach."

He gave me a seductive smile, his sparkling teeth catching some of the blue light. He was very smooth—too smooth. "Djyoo can call me Jojo. Ees whahd mohsse ahf deez people dey call me."

"Okay...Jojo."

The waiter returned and set down another drink in front of John. I hadn't even seen him order it, but it gave me a chance to think about how to redirect the conversation.

"I also like to read," I blurted out. "Not that I have a lot of time for it."

"Oh, jyyehsss? Djyoo lie doo reedee boogz?" He sipped his drink and resumed his head tilt.

Reedeeboogz? "Oh, books! Yes, very much I like to read dee books, I mean, the books. I'm even in a book club."

"Jyyehsss?" This seemed to enchant him for some reason. I decided it was probably best to avoid telling him we're called The Muffia. This would only give him ideas.

I just needed to keep him in his seat and the conversation away from topics that might get him riled because I'd be damned if I was going to leave before I got my dinner. I was hungry, and I'd already invested too much in this guy. Wow, Jelicka was right.

"I theenk hi haff eyrd of deez boogcluhbzz. Djyoo read a boog ahn djyoo gehdogehther doo deezcuss dees boog, jyehhss?"

"Mmmm, I think so, yes." Man, that accent was thick! "Every six weeks we get together, have a great meal, and talk about a book—other stuff, too. Actually mostly, it's the other stuff we talk about."

His head remained in the tilted position for a beat too long. Straightening, he downed his drink and scooted his chair closer. Apparently, John thought talking about books was an aphrodisiac.

"Tayhll mhe, Queeen, abhow dees boog cluhb."

Didn't I just do that? How many drinks had he consumed? He probably had one or two before I even arrived, which meant he was on his fourth. He seemed to be grinning bigger, making larger gestures, and raising his voice, and people were noticing.

I decided that maybe if I talked more—even if it meant repeating myself—he'd talk less. That way, I wouldn't have so much trouble understanding what he said, thereby conserving energy in case I needed to run, which hopefully wouldn't happen until after I ate my steak.

"Well," I began, "There are nine of us in the club—all women and…"

"Hall weemens? Oh, thees hi theenk ees bfeery eenteresding, jyhess?" He slapped the table, startling the young hippieish couple at the table a few feet away.

OK, it really wasn't that interesting. There are some 300,000 book clubs in the U.S., supposedly, and most are made up of women. In any event, he certainly didn't need to slap the table for emphasis.

"It is interesting." I tried to keep my tone dry and clinical, as if I were being interviewed for the job of librarian. "We've read thirty or forty books so far. Of course, I've always enjoyed reading, but being able to talk about a particular book with a group of smart friends has taken it to a whole new level."

"And theess weemens are lyga-djyoo, Queen? Sehxsy and phowerfool?"

It was kind of cool he thought this; that is, if he thought this. But the motivation for these questions was so obviously not about books, that anything he said on the topic was suspect.

"Well, you know, we're just reading books." I tried laughing it off.

"Whahd boogs haff you rhaid een djyoor booog cluhb?" His head really tilted this time. Where was my steak, already?

"Let's see… We just read a book called The Glass Castle."

"Mmmmm…Dee Glahss Cassell." He seemed to savor the title as he sat back in his chair and closed his eyes. The alcohol was clearly getting to him because his head remained tilted. He was less and less attractive, and I was about to tell him I had a client emergency with Jennifer Aniston, steak be damned, when his eyes popped open and he attempted to focus, his head now swaying.

"Ees a nyhss image, doan djyoo theenk, Queen? Zee cassell mayde ahf glahss."

"Yes, I guess it is a nice image." Help! "Anyway, it's a memoir and goes back to when the author was four and her pink tutu caught on fire. Then there was how she fell out of the family car on the freeway, how she shot her neighbor—he was this freaky twelve-year-old white trash rapist—and how her mother would send her to the bars to search for her father, who was certifiable, and how he pimped her and her siblings to get money out of people—Dammit, I should have avoided using the word 'pimp'— but mostly, the book is a non-stop road trip with the insane parents dragging the author and her three brothers and sisters from one poor white trash town to another, whenever the bill collectors were about to find them or when Dad got another cockamamie idea to go somewhere and mine for gold or whatever; and well, suffice it to say, we all decided that the 'glass castle' represented a sort of holographic, no there-there, yearning of Jeannette's failed father that he hangs over the family convincing them to buy into his crazy dream, which somehow they do."

I looked at John. My overwhelming amount of words, delivered speedily as they had been, was having the desired effect. He looked as though he might keel over. So I pressed on, hoping I might actually make it happen.

"And you want to know the really amazing thing? She survived! Jeannette is now a very successful writer living on Park Avenue with a weekend house in the country. Meanwhile, her mother is homeless on the streets of New York! That's right, mmm hmmm. And she wants to be; can you believe it? Her mother is a professional dumpster diver who's made it her mission to rescue stuff from landfills. So in the book, Jeanette asks her mother what she can do to help—you know, because what daughter wants to see her mom dumpster diving?—and you know what her mother says? 'An electrolysis treatment would be nice.' That's what she says, an electrolysis treatment! So that just tells you her mom really was crazy, or maybe she just never lost her sense of humor. Anyway, it's incredible that she made it through."

John was speechless, and I wanted to keep it that way; speechless and on his side of the table. Sadly, it didn't last.

"An djyoo lyga dees boog?" He suddenly lifted his head, looking baffled.

"Oh, djyess," I said. "I lie dees boog pfery, pfery much."

His eyes narrowed, but he was so far gone, I don't think he

trusted what he was hearing. "Hi thaynk I prayfair dose boogs dat haff an appy hainding, doan djyoo?"

I saw his hand moving toward mine across the table, and I quickly picked up my water glass. "Not always. Books are as different as people, don't you think? Sometimes I prefer to be with one person over another, just like sometimes I'd rather read a thriller instead of chick lit. And sometimes I like to read memoirs just to see the kind of crap people get themselves out of."

"Djyess, I see djyoor poyne. Boogzann peepohl harr deeferen, djyoor righ." He looked at me with great intensity, as if deciding now was the time. Wait—the food still hadn't come. Where was it?

His voice went still deeper when he said, "Een zee sayme wahy, to me a boog eez lyge a woohman. Eeesch woohman eeza ole nyew worhl waiding doo be essplore, an eesch pooosee ays deeferen from dee ohthers. Eeesh whan eez waiding to be deeskohfver."

I think he just said pussy. Yes, he did. He said 'a pussy is like a book.' Whaaaht? Maybe people who seek romance online should expect this kind of thing, but it was our first date and he's talking about pussies?

Instead of reacting, I pretended not to understand while I determined that it was probably best to abandon my steak and leave.

"Whaahdjyoo theengk?" He moved even closer, and I could feel his breath—hot and clammy and smelling of whisky. Seeing John's alcohol-infused eyes, I could no longer deny what I'd been thinking for the past half hour: The guy was a creep—an opportunistic, smarmy, lying, short, hard to understand, prick. I could practice gratitude about a lot of things, but John was not one of them. Practicing gratitude is relative anyway. Sure, I was grateful he wasn't raping me, but that had more to do with the fact we were in public in America than anything else. If this were Venezuela, I probably would have been raped by now and left for dead.

I opened my mouth to respond, only to close it upon seeing our waiter who was finally heading our way with what had to be our meals. Profuse with apology, he gently placed the plates in front of us—the perfectly prepared steaks, the artistically displayed frites with the decorative seasonings, and a mélange of al dente, locally-sourced sustainable vegetables. Clearly, I was not so distressed that I was unable to appreciate the mouth-watering aspects of Boa's gustatory presentation. This much I truly could be grateful for.

"Will there be anything else?" asked the waiter.

"Yes. I'll have this to-go. Please."

The waiter blinked and glanced at my inebriated date. Surmising there would be little resistance, he picked up my plate and did a quick pivot away from the table.

Collecting my purse, I stood and quelled the disgust I felt. "Thank you, Jo-Jo. But next time you ask a woman out, I think you should let her know what she's getting into. It would save you both a lot of time."

He shrugged like he'd been through this before; perhaps he even expected it.

Ordinarily, I might feel guilty about sticking a guy with the check, but no such feelings arose. He'd lied, he'd been rude, he'd gotten drunk, and he'd made an obviously unwanted pass. My conscience was clear.

The Muffs were right: Saturday nights are not the best for first dates. But, despite this setback, I was not going to give up. I'd chalk it up to "experience" and press on, starting with that webinar on online dating success I signed up for.

Walking past the bar, in pursuit of the waiter with my steak, my eyes drifted across the faces—young hotties of both sexes, middle-aged tourists, and old farts with twenty-something babes fawning over them. They all looked so happy. Was there any real love on display, or was everyone just playing the game? Suddenly

I felt very old going home alone—again. Well, at least I had my steak, and for that I was grateful.

My gaze continued to drift over all the happy people and then—there was that guy again. How the hell did I know him? He didn't just remind me of the guy I'd seen at Firefly, he was the guy I'd seen at Firefly. He was also the guy sitting in the main dining room earlier. And like before, he was facing away from the direction most everyone else was facing. Was he trying to avoid being seen? If so, by whom? Could it be me?

"Enjoy," said the waiter, handing me my meal, all wrapped up in a shiny black bag.

I thanked him, glancing back at the table where John was still seated. He was leering at the poor hippie girl at the next table who stood just in time to avoid having him fall on her. Wow. Some people really don't get it. But again, the human mind can rationalize almost anything.

I continued toward the front door and once more looked around for the man I recognized at the bar earlier, but it appeared he'd left. And as I exited the restaurant and walked to my car, I hoped the entire evening would turn out to be one big bad dream.

CHAPTER 14

"SO WHAT happened?" It was Madelyn, early the next morning, calling to check in.

If it were someone else, the caller's motive might have been schadenfreude—that is to say, she might have been hoping to find me miserable so she could wallow in my misfortune. But Maddie wasn't like that. Anyway, we Muffs saved our schadenfreude for our enemies.

"Not worth discussing," I said.

"So it was *that* good." She sounded bemused. "Want to talk about it?"

"Some day. Right now, I wouldn't know where to start."

"You didn't sleep with him, did you?"

"Hell, no; nor would I ever sleep with any guy I met on the Internet on the first date, let alone the lying, incomprehensible, alcoholic freak from last night who gets his teeth over-Zoomed."

"Is that even possible?"

"They might have been painted. I'm telling you, his teeth glowed."

"Oh, well. They say it's only a mistake if you don't learn from it."

"Believe me, I learned something all right: not enough due diligence. The whole thing could have been avoided. And I should have insisted we talk on the phone, but I let him convince me it was more romantic to just meet."

She let out a long breath. "I want to tell you something, and it's the only thing I'm going to say on the subject unless you ask—"

"I'm listening."

"It sounds like this guy definitely had more than his share of issues, but everybody has something wrong with them. So if you want somebody, you're going to need to decide what set of baggage you want to deal with. Like how my crazy Scot insists on calling me Bonnie Lass, and he's always saying 'jolly good' this and 'jolly' that. The first few times it was cute, but now it makes me cringe. The thing is, I know there's a really good guy in there, so I'm trying not to let it bother me."

"I'd take 'jolly good' over the Venezuelan pussy monster any day."

"He's Venezuelan?"

"A Venezuelan who likens books to pussies."

"As in...?"

"As in not cats. 'So many poossies in de worhl and eeesh whan is deeferen, wayding doo bee deeskhover.' "

"Not much you can do with that." She laughed, no doubt at my perfect imitation of John/Juan's accent. "But speaking of books, you need to pick one, Quinn, right *now*. If you don't, I'm going to hang up and drive to the last brick and mortar book store in the San Fernando Valley right now and pick one for you."

"I'm sorry, I *have* been thinking about it. With millions of books coming out every year, you'd think I'd be able to find one."

"Yes, you *would* think. Just choose already; what's the worst that can happen? Anything will be better than that date you went on."

"When will there be good news?"

"What's that got to do with anything? It would be good

news for all of us if you chose a book, I'll tell you that much."

"That's my book pick: *When Will There Be Good News?* It's by Kate Atkinson. I read it a couple of years ago, and it's really good."

"Sounds bleak."

"She's Scottish, like your boyfriend, what's his-name?"

"Rory."

She'd already told the Muffs his name, of course, but in my defense, she'd equivocated so many times—was still equivocating—that I hadn't wanted to commit his name to memory. Plus, the romantic in me still saw her with Udi, or even Cullen—the adorable writer she met while shopping for vibrators. If I had gone to Babeland with her that day as I was supposed to, it might have been me who'd struck up a conversation with the charming Cullen, and I wouldn't be searching for love on the Internet. But no, I hadn't joined her that afternoon because I chose instead to go on a lousy date with a wannabe actor.

"Rory, right. Jolly good, then," I teased. "By the way, lass, if you were thinking of doing your book shopping at Barnes and Noble, I dinna think they'll have it."

"Well, I don't read electronic anymore," she said, choosing to ignore my attempt at a Scottish accent. "Reading's less satisfying. I guess I'll have to order it from Amazombie. Damn, I wanted to buy something *today.*"

"How 'bout a latte?"

A few hours later, Madelyn and I pulled into a parking spot on Montana Avenue in Santa Monica. She had secured an afternoon of quality, age-appropriate activity for Lila while, at the same time, bowing out of Rory's hurling competition. I didn't probe too deeply into the nature of what hurling was, beyond determining that Rory's brand of this activity had nothing to do with vomiting and everything to do with Gaelic pride. From what I could tell, it was an Irish sport played by some Scots involving sticks with sharp edges, a hard ball, and the possibility of grievous bodily injury. No wonder she didn't care to watch.

Lined with shops and cafes, Montana Avenue borders some of the most expensive real estate in L.A., and it's one of the destination streets scattered around our megalopolis where a girl can do some serious damage with her credit cards. It's also prime people watching territory, attracting both those living in the nearby expensive homes as well as people like us—those whom marketers refer to as "aspirational," who are also the type to make any shopping street a destination on a weekend afternoon.

"I hope you'll keep this between us, which means don't tell Jelicka," Maddie said as she fed the meter for her parked Prius. "But I have to get this off my chest."

"Okay."

"You know when you called me from Japan after you thought you saw Udi at the airport?"

"Yes." Seriously, did she think I'd forget?

She looked ahead, down the block, and pulled me under the awning of Planet Blue. "It's not that I didn't believe you. I'm willing to concede that the events surrounding Udi's—let's just call it collapse—were definitely odd. But the thing is, I don't see what there is to do about it now."

"I know. I realized that after I cooled down and was on the plane, and I'm sorry. All I did was upset you, and myself—aside from waking you up, of course."

She waved her hand dismissively. "Doesn't matter. I'm the one who should be sorry; I sort of lost it on you."

"No worries." And no point laying blame.

"You want to know what's really screwed up?" She took a deep breath and released it slowly. "If you hadn't told me you saw Udi, and I found out later somehow, I would have been upset by that." She smiled wistfully. "It's like seeing your friend's husband with another woman, and you're not sure if you should tell her, you know? Awkward."

"I just thought you'd want to know, I guess. Because I'd want to know."

"Sorry I took your head off."

"Stop, it's fine. I made the plane."

She peered into the window of a high-end eyeglass store. "Did you, you know, do anything about it?"

"You mean beyond telling you I saw him? No. There was really nothing to do."

"That's the thing I keep coming back to," she said. "Even if one of us tried to get somebody to listen, who would believe us?"

"Maybe in this age of picking up cellphone conversations and monitoring everybody's every move, someone would believe us. Who knows? It could just be a matter of going back through cellphone records, finding where Udi called you, track his number, and see who else he called; then they track all the people whose numbers he called, particularly those who might be from countries on U.S. watch lists."

Maddie smirked. "What movie is that plotline from?"

She wasn't far off. One of the dangers of working in the entertainment business is that the line between life and filmed entertainment blurs to the point of singularity. But in this case, it wasn't a movie, unfortunately.

"I'm talking headlines. The New York Times and Huff Po. This stuff is really happening. I think that's how they caught the blind sheik; one of those ISIL guys anyway."

She looked up. "A drone could be capturing our meeting and listening in with high-tech sonar monitoring equipment at this very moment."

The only visible thing in the sky was a plane high overhead, barely audible. Otherwise, it was a typically gorgeous, clear Southern California day with a few cumulus clouds spotting the blue.

"Maybe we can't see them," I said. "They're shrouded in the cloak of invisibility."

"You're mashing up your blockbuster flicks."

"Why not? Everyone else does. That's how they come up with the next one."

She waved skyward. "Hello up there! We're going to eat now."

"Yeah, we'll let you know what we had when we come back out."

She turned to me and said quietly, "I think about him a lot."

"I know." Standing on the sidewalk, I put my arm around her shoulders, and we stood there for a few minutes saying nothing.

Finally, she shook her head and collected herself. "So, what's it going to be, Quinn?"

I glanced toward the west end of Montana where Babalu served local, yummy fare. Doing a 180, I then faced east and the eponymous mainstay, Cafe Montana, with its usual Sunday brunch crowd out front waiting. As I began to turn back to her, I spotted a familiar face. He was not too far from us, maybe 200 feet away on the sidewalk. It was the same guy I'd seen the night before at Boa and the same guy who'd been at Firefly. This time, he wore a baseball cap, but it was the same guy. The creep factor suddenly dialed up inside me big time. This was no longer any kind of coincidence.

"Don't look right away, but there's a guy on the sidewalk over there with a Yankees cap on."

"Oh, yeah—think it's Udi?" She was jibing me. "Or...what if it's someone from the Department of Homeland Security who overheard our conversation when you were in Japan and now he's looking to make contact."

"This is no joke, Maddie. I've seen the guy several times recently—he was at Firefly last week when we were there. He was also at the restaurant last night, and now he's here. He's got to be following me."

Sensing my angst, Maddie quickly dropped the attitude. She focused her gaze up the street to where "Yankees" was still standing. "I can't really see his features from here, but I can tell it's not Udi."

"No, it's not Udi."

"Is it possible you and Paige both have stalkers?"

I took a moment to reflect on the events of the last couple of weeks. "I may have even seen him even before Firefly, but I can't remember where."

Maddie's mantle of the pre-possessed attorney-mediator had been restored. "And you have no idea who it is?

"None."

"I just don't think it's possible that more than one Muff has a stalker."

"We're The Muffia," I said. "I'm surprised we don't all have one."

She smiled. "Good point."

"How is Paige anyway? Have you seen her? Did anyone ever find out what happened?"

Maddie shook her head. "Lauren saw her, and Sarah, too, I think. Apparently, she has a massive shiner, poor thing. And she definitely put a restraining order on the guy."

"Really? Yikes."

"Soon he'll be tormenting women at some other tennis club, though Paige should keep her eyes open; he could be back. Restraining orders get broken all the time."

"Why don't we go see her? She's probably feeling lousy, like we abandoned her," I said.

"We'll call her later. Come on, let's eat." She turned me

around. "Don't look back. If he is a stalker, you don't want to let him know you know he's there, right?"

"Right."

And with that, we headed toward Babalu without so much as one backward glance.

"If somebody *were* following you," Maddie said, picking up a raisin pumpernickel roll from the basket of artisanal breads, "let's figure out who might do that and what the reason would be." She slathered butter onto the roll. "Other than your beauty, of course, or your pole dancing skills, celebrity access—perhaps even your connection to me and Udi, international man of mystery."

I glanced out Babalu's plate glass window for the third time since we'd sat down, worried I'd see the man in the Yankees cap hovering nearby. "You joke, but I'm not making this up."

"I didn't say you were." She was about to take a bite of her buttered roll. "Do you think he has something to do with the pictures that were sent to your boss? And if so, who hired him?"

The questions didn't surprise me; it's not like I hadn't been wondering about these things myself. In fact, the only times I hadn't been thinking about Picturegate was when I was pole dancing and out on my lousy date. I slurped a spoonful of cream of asparagus soup, savoring the flavor.

"The answer is 'He might have something to do with the pictures,' " I said. "And there are three possibilities as to who could have hired him. The first is Talent Partners—they could be having me followed to find out if I really am the insane lunatic they see in the pictures; or maybe their attorney told them they needed additional proof of crazy behavior before firing me in order to avoid a lawsuit."

"Possibly," said Maddie, chewing. "It would depend on the termination clause in your contract. Do you remember the terms?"

I shook my head. "What's the point in understanding an employment contract when questioning the terms means they won't hire you? They can put whatever they want in those contracts, unless the prospective employee has some sort of superior negotiating ability, which I obviously didn't have."

She shrugged. "You might take a look anyway. But, I don't know, I doubt they'd have you followed."

"Okay, I'll check just to be sure."

"It's too bad employment isn't my area of expertise, or I'd volunteer to mediate."

Madelyn was always looking for opportunities to resolve conflict. She mediated so rarely, she didn't care any more if somebody thought she was biased, which she would clearly be in this case, given she was my friend.

"The second possibility as to who hired him is Titania. She's having me followed, hoping to get me in another compromising position to strengthen her case."

"Mmmm…" Maddie shook her head and dabbed some chimichurri sauce from her lip. "I don't think she'd jeopardize her career by risking exposure now. Unless she's stupid, she's already done the damage she set out to do."

"She could always do more." I glanced out the front window again. No Yankees.

"By the way," Maddie said, "what did you do with the button you found—the one with Titania's picture on it kissing the guy? Oops— I hope that wasn't a secret. Lauren told me."

I wondered if Lauren had also told her about the private investigator. I decided to play that close to the chest for now.

"No secret. And the answer is nothing yet. Outwardly, Titania doesn't seem to know the button's missing, and Jamie's been quiet on the subject of Picturegate since a couple days after she brought it up. I'm hoping she's forgotten."

"Not if what you've been telling us about her for the past three years is any indication. She doesn't sound like a woman who forgets much."

"True. I was thinking I might leave the button where Jamie could find it, but in a place that won't look like it was planted. The trouble is if Jamie finds it, it has to be where Titania left it. Otherwise, Titania will know somebody else was snooping in her desk, took the button, and planted it for Jamie to find. And if that happens, she's going to know right away that that snooper was me."

Despite my enervating situation, the asparagus soup was delicious. I began to slurp some more.

"Mmmmm," said Maddie pensively. "You have a point—maybe you should wait until Jamie brings it up again. When she does—'desperate situations call for desperate measures,' and all that."

"Desperate measures," I repeated, musing about what those might be.

"What's the third reason?"

I sat back in the chair. "Steven."

Maddie stopped chewing. "Why would Steven have you followed? You said it was all over with him. Oh, Quinny, please don't say you've fallen off the wagon."

"No, no, I haven't. Not really. I've refused to see him, and that's why it could be him. I haven't returned any of his calls since—gosh, I have to think about this— the day after the day after I got back from Japan."

"What happened the day after you got back?" She gave me a hard appraising stare. "You slept with him, didn't you?"

"I'm weak."

She rolled her eyes.

"But since then, I've been extremely good."

"He did seem obsessed with you," Maddie agreed. "Maybe

you should call him and ask if he's having you followed. The direct approach is usually best."

"I would, but whenever I'm on the phone with him, he always talks me back into seeing him. I just...if I could get myself interested in someone else, it would be a lot better."

"Quinn, listen; that's the past. You're changing your life now. You're meeting other men, having a good time—mostly. Forget about the Venezuelan. All you need to do is ask Steven if he's having you followed."

I pushed my soup bowl away, determining she was right. "Can I borrow your phone?"

"Why do you need my phone?"

"Steven won't recognize your number."

"My number's blocked."

"Even better. Hand it over."

Maddie frowned but fished her iPhone out of her bag. I dialed Steven's number and put the phone to my ear. It rang once, twice, three times—then there was a click, followed by his recorded message. What a nice voice he had.

"Didn't pick up." I hit "end" and handed the phone back to her. "I'll try later."

"Don't forget. Confronting him directly might put an end to the whole thing."

"If he tells the truth. But he's been carrying on an affair with me for two years, so we already know he's a gifted liar."

Maddie, mid-chew, let out a mmmm in agreement.

An idea struck. "I know..."

"Uh-oh, I'm not sure I'm going to like this." She put her fork down and picked up a third roll, which seemed very out of character.

"Are you extra hungry or something? I don't think I've ever seen you eat this much."

"I know, it's terrible. Peri-menopause. I need to get it under control, too; I can't afford a whole new wardrobe."

"So give me the roll."

Maddie stared at me blankly.

"I'm peri-menopausal, too, but it doesn't make me hungry, just sharp-tongued. Give it to me, Madelyn," I repeated firmly.

A couple of seconds went by before she dropped the roll into my outstretched hand, and I put the whole breadbasket out of her reach.

"Thanks."

"No problem. So here's my idea: what if I follow Titania one day when she leaves work? If I catch her with a guy and get a really good bunch of pictures to show Jamie… "

"I wouldn't recommend it," said Maddie. "If you're close enough to get the picture, she'd see you. No, if you were going to follow her, the only way to do it is to pay someone else to do it; like someone did with Yankees. But that gets expensive."

I glanced out Babalu's front window again, searching for the man I suspected was following me. "Maybe I should just ask Yankees how much he charges."

"I wouldn't give it away that you know you're being followed. Not yet anyway. You might still need to play that card, er... button."

"Good point. Okay, skip that idea. You're so smart, Maddie."

"Glad I could help. The truth is, other peoples' problems are always so much more manageable than my own. Speaking of which, what do you think about Lila wanting to get her pubes waxed?"

CHAPTER 15

WHEN I started pole dancing, most of the Muffs raised their eyebrows. For one thing, they'd never known me to exercise. For another, they thought pole dancing was only for women who worked in strip clubs or wanted to perform lap dances for their boyfriends. Though this was untrue, no amount of wind expended on my part had been able to change their minds.

After meeting K-Love at a client's book signing and attending an introductory session at S-Factor in Encino, I'd been coming to class for about ten months—granted, sporadically—and I was convinced that even if it *was* a guy who motivated a girl to try pole dancing, class is too physically challenging for it to be only about pleasing men. Most of the women who dance—some of whom are gay—are doing it for exercise and to get in touch with themselves.

That was my reason, anyway. Sometimes, working for "The Man," can leave a person feeling disconnected from everything that matters. Being in a class led by K-Love helps me reconnect.

And so it was, after another busy day at work, one day closer to D-day on Picturegate and still no sign of the private investigator who was supposed to help, I left early for the drive to S-Factor for some reconnecting. From the first moment Nicki

Minaj let loose of her voice, I let go of my angst. I even felt the lines on my face smooth away; my only thoughts were of breathing and releasing.

And, per usual, it worked. When class ended with deep stretches to John Legend singing "Save Room," I felt wonderful, as I always do, and resolved, as I always do, to get there more often. Why is it we humans don't always do what we need to do to stay healthy?

As I left the dance studio, pushing open the glass door and stepping into the evening, I had a new outlook and faced a new beginning. It may be cornball talk but, with every passing moment, you really do have a chance to turn it all around. Everything was going to work itself out; I was sure of it, and I was *not* going to worry about the future. After all, what did worry get me except stress? And stress kills, right? If I lose my job—I'll get a new job. And looking for guys—? *Puh.* I'll eventually meet someone to spend the rest of my life with, and hey, it might even be a dog, and that might be perfect. Might? No, it *would* be perfect, if that's what happened.

As all these thoughts ran through my head, I noticed a man sitting on a low wall in front of Katsu-ya, the Japanese restaurant adjacent to S-Factor. His face was pointed down, his eyes focused on his phone, but big relief—he wasn't *Yankees.* Just thinking about the man in the baseball cap made me tense, threatened to undo all the good I'd just worked so hard to achieve. I exhaled the thought away. *Yes, yes, yes...*

So engrossed was the guy in his phone, he didn't even look up as I approached, not that he should have, but I guess the vain part of me wanted somebody to notice how radiant I felt. Once again I had to kick myself because I'd just spent an hour and a half re-learning that *I* was the only one who had to notice how radiant I felt. *Sheesh, it was hard getting these lessons to stick.*

Why should I care if he notices? He wasn't even my type;

I'd passed up a few of his ilk on *NowLove*, superficial though that was of me. Khakis and a white oxford cloth shirt, brown loafers, and matching belt—he looked like a corporate type on casual Friday. Only his body seemed bigger and blockier—like he worked out too much to have a corporate job. His hair, what there was of it, was cut very short, so I figured he might be ex-military, though those loafers looked too expensive for the pay grade.

As I walked past him, heading for the parking lot, he glanced up suddenly. "Quinn Cunningham?"

I stopped, turned, and found myself looking down into a pair of startling blue eyes that penetrated me at a glance and put me in mind of an airport scanner; not a person, but the actual machine that reveals all.

"I didn't mean to startle you, Ma'am," he said in a voice void of emotion but not the least bit threatening. "My name's Frank Sexton. I'm with Source Security."

He knew better than to assume I'd take his word for it. "Please have a look."

His eyes flashed to his phone. He moved a couple of fingers over the screen and stood, extending the phone toward me.

Clasping the phone, I scrolled down over the thread—an email from Lauren, followed by one from George to Source Security's CEO, then on to the head of the HR department, and finally, the assignment of "Frank Sexton." My name appeared throughout.

"I was wondering when you'd show up. It would have been nice had someone let me know," I said, handing the phone back.

"I believe you were informed," Frank said calmly, though his eyes remained disturbingly active as he surveyed the courtyard and surrounding environment. He closed the phone and clipped it to his belt.

Don't take his word for it, Quinn. Powering up my iPhone, I discovered that Lauren had sent me a text during class spelling everything out while, at the same time, intelligently adhering to the practicalities of potential phone hacking—not that anyone would care enough about my little problem to hack my phone. Suffice it to say that leaving aside the cryptic nature of the text, she'd given me enough information to make me feel confident that Frank Sexton—though probably not his real name—was not a serial killer.

"Nothing like waiting 'til the last minute."

"It's safer that way." Frank stood and gestured to Katsu-ya's entrance. "I thought we might go inside and have a brief discussion about your situation."

I hesitated. A voice came from behind me. "Everything okay?"

I turned to see K-Love standing just outside the door to S-Factor. Everything *was* okay; the new leaf I'd turned over in class was still facing up.

"Everything's good, K," I said. "Thanks."

Ten minutes later, Frank Sexton and I were seated at Katsu-ya's sushi bar—Frank with water in front of him, me with a hot Saki. He hadn't cracked a smile, but all still felt pretty good in my post-pole world, even after getting Frank up to speed on *Yankees* and Picturegate.

"Don't do anything to draw attention to yourself," Frank said calmly. "But do you see the man who's been following you?"

Hmm, the only way I'd be able to answer that question is if I turned around and looked around the restaurant, which would surely draw attention to myself. Suddenly having a private investigator seemed like an overreaction. "Not at the moment," I said. "Mr. Sexton, I feel a little silly… "

"Call me Frank. Can you tell me why you feel silly?"

"I guess it's because this whole thing could be a big misunderstanding."

"Could you explain what you mean by 'this whole thing?'"

Frank was cordial and professional, though lacking in a certain charm one might want in a private investigator—especially in light of all the interesting, sexy, and brave private investigators in movies and T.V. whom I grew up watching. Magnum P.I. he was not. And yet, he had a lot going on in those eyes. He appeared ageless and might have been anywhere from thirty-five to fifty-five.

"What I mean is that I might have leapt to the conclusion that a man I've seen several times in a few different places is actually following me. It could just be coincidence."

"So you do *not* believe someone is following you?" He glanced past me, his eyes observing, taking in the details of his environment. It was probably a habit he had, a handy vestige of his days in the military. *These corporate espionage guys don't fool around.*

I took a breath. "No, I don't *not* believe someone is following me."

Those piercing blue eyes narrowed. "That sentence contained three negatives. Are you aware of that, Ms. Cunningham? It makes the determination of what it is you do mean to say very difficult."

Skip the cordial, professional description; the guy was anal. "I'm sorry," I said. "What I meant was, I have reason to believe someone's following me, but I don't know for sure."

Frank was appropriately named, even if it was a put-on, and his frankness was disconcerting—his questions those of an automaton programmed ahead of time. I didn't know any Marine Drill Sergeants personally, but I had the notion that when one of them retired to the public sector, he'd be a lot like Frank

Sexton—by the book, upright, and more than a little uptight.

He pulled out a little notebook, which fit perfectly into his shirt pocket, and I watched as he jotted something down. "In preparation for our meeting this evening, I have been going through data I had access to regarding your online presence and digital footprint... "

Maybe I should have been upset about Frank probing my data but, with all the online spying these days, it was hardly a surprise. I've Googled myself, of course, and been less than impressed with what came back. But I was actually very interested to learn what a skilled hacker might find; all that stuff I might want to keep private if I had the choice. I still didn't think there'd be much of interest. What would anyone do with my Zappos shoe order history other than determine I like shoes? They'd send me targeted shoe ads, which are annoying and probably result in my never going to their websites. Did they care I had 764 friends on Facebook? Maybe if one of them was on the terrorist watch list, which I hoped wasn't the case. I realized, to my chagrin, that Frank must have also found out about *NowLove*. Ugh. Well, I thought, hopefully he can't read the direct messages. That would be embarrassing.

I smiled, sipping my Saki, which was going down very easily. "Find anything interesting?"

"There was nothing in your dossier that suggested you could be the target of unwanted surveillance."

"I have a *dossier*?"

"File, dossier—the terms are interchangeable."

"I prefer having a dossier. It makes me feel like I'm in a John Le Carré novel," I said, feeling wistful.

"Good writer," said Frank, revealing a sliver of personality.

"So they say. These days, my reading material is limited to talent contracts and whatever we're reading in book club. The

Muffs aren't much for thrillers."

"The Muffs?" his eyebrows shot up.

"Our book club is called The Muffia, and hence, we members are the Muffs. Lauren—George's wife—is a Muff. I'm surprised she didn't tell you."

Frank's face, though tanned, turned a shade of pink. Straight-laced as he was, he was starting to grow on me. If I got him to blush, I wondered if I might get him to smile.

"Anyway, we don't usually read thrillers, but I did just pick a police procedural for our next meeting. It's Scottish, though, and pretty literary as police procedurals go."

He was assessing, constantly assessing—me and everything else. But what was he getting from all that assessing? *Probably make a helluva TSA agent.*

I decided to shift gears. "Is your real name Frank?"

The expression didn't change. "Yes."

"But if it were really John or Kevin, would you tell me?"

"My name is unimportant," he said laconically.

Well, that shut that down, I thought. *Okay, I'll just sit here.*

After a couple of seconds, Frank cleared his throat. "Now—I'm familiar with your position as a talent agent, which we'll come back to, but I'd like to ask about your hobbies outside of work. Pole dancing, for example. It does not fit with the rest of your profile."

He glanced up and our eyes met. I felt a little jolt. *What was that?*

"Funny you say that, Frank. That's kind of why I started taking class. I needed to get out of my rut." He jotted something down. "Do you know what it's like to be stuck in a rut, Frank?"

I had the growing awareness that I wanted to flirt with the guy. But it was probably just the Saki, I told myself. And maybe the pole dancing. I looked around the restaurant, thinking *Yankees* might have appeared. I didn't see him.

"Ms. Cunningham, this will go faster if you allow me to ask the questions. I am here at the request of the Busch family, with whom I have been working for several years. I know my job, and I want to help find out who might be trying to sabotage you so you can retain your position and go on living your life."

That stream of words left me speechless. Beyond that, however, the content of what he'd said made me feel safe. I felt like I had my very own someone to watch over me, short-lived as it would be. It might even be better than a boyfriend, I thought. In light of this, I decided to go along with his program.

So I put down my Saki cup and began filling in the details. I probed the minutia on the guy in the Yankees cap—when I'd first seen him and where. I told him about Jamie and Titania and the picture button I'd found, as well as my suspicions that Titania wasn't gay. I admitted to him that I'd been having an affair with a married man, and that I'd broken it off for good after a few failed attempts. It was important to me that Frank knew how I'd gotten involved with Steven in the first place—that he hadn't told me he was married and, by the time I found out, he had me hooked. I told him about Steven's promises, which all turned out to be idle, and other sordid details. I wanted him to know I was repentant. Meanwhile, I couldn't tell what he was thinking. His eyes were focused on his little pad as he took it all down, his face unmoving.

At last he asked me about the pictures on Jamie's phone. He took me back to that day at Narita—a day I'd thought about many times since Jamie first confronted me. Soon I was painting the scene for him: I was calling Madelyn, listening to her reaction, then running for the plane, falling, the heel of my shoe breaking off, the *Hello Kitty* girls' terrified faces, the freckled guy handing me my—

Suddenly, I realized. "Freckles is *Yankees*!" I exclaimed.

"What are you saying?" Frank said.

"That's where I'd seen him before—the guy who's been following me. Now I know he *is* following me. It's the same guy—the freckled man who handed me my shoe is *Yankees*." *But wait—that would mean he followed me from Japan?!*

Excited about what all this might mean, I was disappointed to see Frank was unfazed by these revelations. He just continued jotting notes. No matter what I said, he accepted everything with no change in reaction.

"What do you think this means?" I asked before clarifying. "And what I mean by 'this' is: what do you think this sequence of events means, given that the man I've been seeing all over L.A. is also the man I saw at Narita and is probably also the one who took those ridiculous compromising pictures?"

"I don't think anything at this juncture, Ms. Cunningham." Frank glanced up at me, his face still arranged in a serious expression. "But you have given me a lot to work with." He almost smiled, but not quite.

He stood, placing the perfectly-sized note pad back in his shirt pocket and tossing a couple of folded bills on the table. "I'll be in touch."

"When will that be?" I asked. "And can you call me Quinn? You know there's not much time to figure out what's happening before… "

He held up his hand, presumably to silence me. "When you see me again, you don't know me, understand? Wait until I approach you."

"But what if I need to talk to you?"

"Trust that I'm doing my job." He took a last scan of Katsuya. "And wait five minutes before leaving."

So much for that someone-to-watch-over-me thing.

CHAPTER 16

*I*F MY failed date with John had proved anything, it was that I was lacking certain key bits of information necessary for achieving online dating success. Clearly, there was something I'd overlooked.

So, with that virgin online dating experience under my belt, and a glass of wine in my hand, I logged on for my free instructional webinar put on by *NowLove*, which promised to answer questions on topics ranging from: "Mistakes Made in Your Dating Profile" to "The Pitfalls of Taking Your Online Relationship Offline." Having made mistakes, and fallen in pits on my first date with John, taking the webinar would presumably keep such a thing from happening again. The only aspect of *that* date I cared to repeat was the quality of the meal.

Signing in late for the appointed start, I could see from the number of names listed on the left side of my computer screen that there were twenty of us in attendance, though more could be watching or simply listening without declaring themselves. The webinar format was notorious for encouraging voyeurism.

The leader of the webinar, someone named Wilder whose image moved in a pixilated fashion in the center of the screen, appeared to be in his late thirties. By the time I logged in, he was already giving tips on how to make sure one's online profile grabs the attention of a future mate—an inexact science, to be sure.

On the bottom right of the screen, there was a box with the prompt: "Type a question for Wilder," which presumably he would answer. But what seemed to be happening in that box, while Wilder was yammering on, was that several webinar participants were having their own sideline chat without any input from the webinar leader.

"So when you compose your profile," Wilder was saying, "if you want people to know *you*—and, of course, that is what you want—and you're not the type who likes going down blind alleys—*who does?*—it's best to be clear about who you are and what you want to find in a mate."

Well, my profile's good there, I mused. If anything, I'd been altogether too honest about what I wouldn't put up with and what I wanted in a man. In fact, I'd been so honest, it was shocking that anyone had responded at all, though as Vicki pointed out, most guys just see a decent looking picture and wink. They don't read lest they learn something they might have to pretend they didn't know.

"I recommend spending some time going through the profiles we've posted for suggestions," Wilder yammered on. "You can find those by going up to the menu bar under 'Frequently Asked Questions.' Scroll down to 'Profiles'; then go to 'Sample Profiles – Do's and Don't's.' "

Noting where to find the profiles, should I later need to consult them, I continued to read the posts coming in from the other participants as they appeared in the message box.

Someone was typing a question. *Ding*, the message appeared:

Message from Ospiritus12: Is there any way to tell if someone is a waste of space before you agree to meet them? Are there clues in the profile?

Good question, Ospiritus—I would have liked to have the answer to that one *before* my failed date with John. Though it would probably depend on what one was looking for. In my case, a guy who copped to playing Roxy Music and R.E.M. daily, thirty years after their 80s heyday, was a huge indicator that dating him wasn't going to work. Bryan Ferry, okay fine, in moderation, but daily Michael Stipe listening was a sure-fire romance killer.

Other people were now typing into the box, and my computer dinged twice in succession:

> Message from Sunny10Summer: Yeah, it's really hard to tell with some profiles what you're going to get, and so many people lie.

> Message from ChemEng$!: I have precisely stated I am looking for a woman with at least a Master's Degree, and my box is filled with bimbos.

Struck a nerve with that one, Ospiritus. And yeah, *Sunny10Summer*, people *do* lie, incredible as that is to believe. Sorry *ChemEng$!*, but with that handle, you asked for it. Even the bimbos can tell you're a, *duh*, chemical engineer who wants people—read: *women*—to think you have money, exclamation mark. Who's the bimbo now? A scientist who completely disregards predictability!

Several minutes went by with Wilder seemingly ignoring the posts, but finally he responded.

"All right," he said, his lips moving completely out of synch with the audio output. "It sounds like some of you may be frustrated with profiles not accurately reflecting the members who write them, and that the members you're getting matched up with by *NowLove* don't fit with what you are looking for. And

I'm sorry about that. We do our best at *NowLove* to take every-one's wishes into account, but sometimes… "

Wilder's saccharine sympathy for all of us sad daters bordered on irritating.

"It *can* be a frustrating process, I realize that," he went on cheerily. "But don't let the frustration ruin what is actually a really fun exploration. After all, you are looking for your *perfect* match; there's only one, and it probably isn't going to happen right away, so have fun while you search!"

Ha! Name something fun about it.

"*Ospiritus*, and I suspect many others, would like to know if there's a way to spot clues in a profile so as not to waste time pursuing someone who's not suitable. The answer is 'yes,' there is!"

I listened as he droned on, not saying much in the way of useable information— "send a message asking a question about something a potential match says in his profile," and "see how much your potential match knows about a topic that interests you."

Meanwhile, things were getting interesting in the blogversation.

Ding—

> Message from Toweloneon: This site has to many chiks lookin for a free meal.

Spelling really is so important. Ding—

> Message from SittinPretty: Seems like most guys just want to get in your pants.

Nothing new there, people. Ding—

Whoa, where did that come from—truth detecting algorithms? That would sure cut down on the blind alleys.

I waited for somebody to type a response in the message
box, but the cursor didn't move. Was there no mathematician to
cream over on this webinar who could provide this algorithmic
solution? Surely if the technology existed, *NowLove* should use
it. Meanwhile, Wilder was still not offering anything very
helpful.

Rocknrack was typing again.

Ding—

Wow, wouldn't that be cool—a positive use for all that personal surveillance data—one that helps the little guy find love
without getting ripped off or murdered.

Wilder suddenly stopped spewing pablum. Apparently, *RocknRack* had his attention. "I'll come back to this topic," he said
quickly. "*Rocknrack* has posted an interesting question, but I'm
sorry to say, *NowLove* does not have the technology to delete
sections of customers' profiles that are factually inaccurate. We
allow our members to put their best foot forward and present
themselves as the person they wish…"

Ding—

<u>Message from Rocknrack</u>: You encourage people to lie. It's a scam.

"That said," Wilder continued, out of synch, "we continue to strive to make our site and services better attuned to the needs of our customers. But thank you for that question, *RocknRack*. So going back, if a profile leaves out some things you'd like to know about a potential match, the best way to address this is to message the person you're interested in getting to know better and ask."

Ding—

<u>Message from Rocknrack</u>: If Facebook knows what drugstore we go to and what we just bought off eBay, there has to be a way for NowLove to expose a guy who claims to be 30 and single when he's actually 45 and married.

"Unfortunately, *Rocknrack*, we're barred from doing that kind of surveillance on our members," Wilder said as *Rocknrack* typed some more.

Ding—

<u>Message from Rocknrack</u>: That's a load of crap. Is it because everybody on your site, including you, is a freakin' liar? You'd think your management would be interested in customer satisfaction. NowLove might find itself with a class-action NowLawsuit.

"Here at *NowLove*," Wilder said, as he tried to manage the escalating vitriol coming from *RocknRack* while simultaneously punching in a number on his phone—an effort, most likely, aimed at blocking *RocknRack* from further comments— "we like to believe that...

Ding—

Message from Rocknrack: A good friend of mine went on a date Saturday night with a total loser who she would not have gone on a date with if she'd known certain things that a "smart system" would have revealed. She ended up at a fancy steak house with a guy who could barely speak English, and he immediately starts talking about women's vaginas!"

Whaaaht? How did RocknRack know that?

"We like to believe our members can talk amongst themselves and make intelligent choices," Wilder persisted.

Meanwhile, *Rocknrack* kept on writing. Whoever he or she was, *Rocknrack* had just described my date with John, though countless other bad dates had probably gone the same way mine had. Did I know this person?

I started typing.

Ding—

Message from Miss_Quinn: W-h-o-a-r-e-y-o-u?"

I was pretty sure *RocknRack* was referring to my date with John, and the only way whomever it is would know about it is if she was a member of the Muffia. *But which Muff?*

Ding—

Message from Miss_Quinn: Are you a member of the Muffia?

Ding—

> Message from Rocknrack: Butt out, Miss_Quinn. I'm doing this
> for you.

Okay, one question answered. *Now which Muff?*
Wilder was on the phone with his mic off on the webinar,
but now other people were responding to the thread between
RocknRack and me.

Ding—

> Message from Toweloneon: What's the Muffia? Is that another
> dating site? Or another Ashley Madison?

Ding—

> Message from Robert 87650: Sounds kind of fun.

Ding—

> Message from SittinPretty: The Muffia is a lesbian porn
> site!

I couldn't let that comment go by without setting *SittinPretty*
straight.

Ding—
> Message from Miss_Quinn: The Muffia is a book club.

Ding—

> Message from Rocknrack: It's not lesbian porn, and it's not

Ding—

Ding—

Ding—

Ding—

The computer kept dinging with messages appearing in quick succession, randomly replying to one message or another, in no coherent order, having to do with pornography, dating a lesbian, how to keep from dating a lesbian, joining The Muffia, book recommendations, and other topics. The webinar was fast turning into a free-for-all, and Wilder's loss of control was evident. Given the quality of my computer's Retina display, I could make out the perspiration on his brow.

The box onscreen, where the questions and answers were displayed, started to glitch. *Saw that one coming.*

"We seem to be having some difficulty with the message and response features of the webinar," Wilder said, his eyes repeatedly shifting from the camera lens—presumably to facilitate the glitching. "But feel free to continue submitting your questions and… "

The constant dinging ended, along with the message box going completely blank.

When Wilder found the lens again, his expression had changed. "…we'll do our best to get to most of them," he said, all happy-faced. Clearly, *NowLove* had turned us off. *So much for member input.* "Now," he continued, "where were we?"

Nowhere. I logged off and considered, for a moment, which of the Muffs was most likely to put herself out there on the topic of dating site abuse. I assessed each in turn: Vicki was my online dating go-to person, the one who was intimately involved, but she and I had talked about this already, and I didn't see her as the culprit. Madelyn might hold the opinions *RocknRack* expressed, but she wouldn't behave the way *RocknRack* had. It wasn't Sarah's style, nor Kiki's, and it definitely wasn't Lauren's. Jelicka wasn't good with computers, so I doubted she'd be able to figure out the webinar function. And though I could imagine Paige doing something like this, she had been out of the Muff loop of late, and I didn't think she'd make her presence known this way. That left...

"Rachel, it's Quinn."

"Hey, Quinn. What's going on?" Her tone revealed nothing.

"Are you *Rocknrack*?"

"Am I what?" She feigned innocence. "What's a...?"

"You know what I'm talking about. *NowLove*?" I was more curious than anything else. "I'm not mad at you," I added.

There was a pause. Finally, she sighed.

"Websites charge a lot of money, and it pisses me off. They should do more for their customers. Did you know there are computer algorithms now that can tell online shoppers when stuff for sale has been stolen?"

"Really? No... "

"Yes, there are. And if they can do that, they can tell female shoppers when a guy is already married, don't you think? Or when he's a conniving, lying, duplicitous dick."

"I'd settle for knowing even one of those things," I said. "But Rachel... "

"We're better than that, Quinn!" She was ranting. "We deserve better. I mean, I know you want to be with somebody;

we all want to be with somebody who loves us. Who doesn't?"

It seemed to me now that her last break-up had been more devastating than she'd let on at book club.

"It's a scam!" she shrieked. "I mean, Maddie told me about that creep you went out with. If you want to go out with somebody so badly, let us find you someone."

"You know what, Rachel?" I said, calmly, trying to talk her down. "I get your point, but there's no reason for you to lose it on *NowLove.com.*"

She just kept going. "Did you know that *ItsJustLunch* sends friends of friends of friends of management to go on fake "dates" just so they don't get sued by all the lonely women who've signed up believing the ads! It's true; check "The Haggler!"

Notwithstanding the fact I didn't know who The Haggler was, it was quite clear Rachel felt wronged by the dating industry. Or maybe it was just men she had a problem with. But since my date with John, I had a different perspective on the whole process. Like the virgin who just wants to get the first time over with, now that I'd been officially deflowered of my first-timer online dater status, I was okay with whatever course my dating life took and however long it took.

The culmination of my soul-searching and self-analysis at this pivotal moment in my life, with my career threatened by persons unknown, was that finding a partner wasn't worth worrying about—certainly not worth spending hours online looking. If it was meant to be, it would happen eventually. But the process of being online and having exchanges with a few guys had yielded one giant benefit: I no longer felt that Steven was the only man for me; I felt cured of him and almost hopeful. That alone had been worth the price of admission.

"You don't have to find me anybody," I said. "I'm good. I realized that yesterday. If I meet someone, great; if I don't, I'm not going to force it."

"Okay, good. I'm probably not the best person to help with dating advice anyway."

"Are you giving me the reason behind your 'Nude Men Without Faces' series?" I asked. "I never would have guessed. But if selling out is any indication, you've struck a nerve."

"Yeah, lucked out there." She laughed, one big, ironic outburst.

"You want to talk about it?" I asked. "You haven't given us many of the details about your last breakup. I'm happy to listen. Unless, of course, you need to remain pissed off and miserable for the sake of 'Nude Men Without Faces II.' "

She laughed again. "He's not worth discussing. But thanks anyway."

"Well, if you ever want to, I promise it will stay between us." I waited another beat to see if she'd change her mind, then thanked her again for looking out for me. One thing I could always count on was a Muff watching another Muff's back.

CHAPTER 17

*F*OUR DAYS later, with still no update from Frank—*where-the-bleep-was-he?*—Sexton, I joined Jelicka, Maddie, and Rachel on a drive to Jelicka's favorite shooting range up the coast in Oxnard. Paige had also been invited—Jelicka telling her that having a stalker mandated knowing how to protect herself—but she claimed to have a previous commitment, which Jel took to mean her plastic surgery scars hadn't healed.

The plan, as Jelicka described it, was to go to the firing range and shoot at paper cut outs of "evil, horrible, terrible" men, aiming for their hearts, so that we'd be prepared if ever we were confronted by the real thing. According to her, one afternoon spent with her, and we'd all know how to shut such a guy down. Of course, Jelicka was the only one of us who owned a gun, so I don't know how ready we'd be, but at least she felt she was giving us the mental ammunition to defend ourselves.

On our way back to L.A., after shooting up a box or two of ammo, we planned to stop at Kiki's to see just how we might help with the problem occupants in the house next door. Jel was hoping that if we were riled up enough, we might storm the place and catch the neighbors in the act of shooting porn. *Not gonna happen*, I thought. Not with me, anyway. The last thing I needed was more compromising pictures.

Oxnard is a small seaside city with agricultural roots—it's

known for the freshest strawberries on the south central coast. If you've ever had reason to be driving the north-south route in the westernmost part of California north of L.A. known as "The 101"—we Californians being notorious for putting a "the" in front of any freeway number—you'll likely have seen the miles and miles of strawberry fields that stretch across Ventura County. And if you drive through at harvest time, you can see hundreds of migrant workers, many of whom are illegal, out in the fields picking them.

Personally, I have no problem with this—people want strawberries, farmers grow strawberries. When the strawberries need to be picked, the only folks who'll pick them for what the strawberry farmer will pay are illegal immigrants. What's a farmer to do?

We need undocumented workers in America, no matter what Texas says. That's why I find it ironic that the state of Texas, with all its bluster about shutting down immigration, sends its prize football team, the Dallas Cowboys, to Oxnard, California, the heart of illegal immigrant strawberry picking for summer training.

Oxnard is also home to an inordinate amount of shooting ranges per capita. With a population of 200,000 as of the last census, there are five shooting ranges within city limits. Perhaps not as many as in, say, Oklahoma City, but it's still one shooting range per 40,000 people. Compare that to the city of Los Angeles where the population is almost four million and the total number of shooting ranges numbers sixteen; that's 250,000 people per shooting range. People can say L.A. has a high crime rate, but chances are Angelenos aren't learning how to shoot a gun in L.A. At least *we* weren't. We were on our way to Oxnard, an hour north past the strawberries, the migrant workers, and the outlet center at Camarillo to get to Shooter's Paradise. It was a dive of a place through a small, desolate warehouse district and down a back alley lined with abandoned pickups—trucks, that is, not hookers—though a few of *those* might have been nearby, too.

You might ask why, given all the mass shootings that have taken place in schools, movie theatres, and shopping malls in recent years, members of The Muffia—a sophisticated (arguably) group of women who should know better—were going to a shooting range when we might be fighting to get guns off the streets. So let me address that.

We *are* working to get guns off the streets. It's not just political, but when you see some of the people who hang out on the streets of Southern California, you don't want them anywhere near a gun; they can't even walk straight. So the Muffs go to rallies and send money to lobby for greater background checks and mental health reform. We have been known to argue with many a blithe and blind espouser of Second Amendment hyperbole.

The second thing is, getting comfortable with guns—granted, this might never be possible—comes under the heading of common sense capability, right up there with knowing how to swim, drive a stick shift, and ride a horse. Now numbering in the billions, guns are not going to be wiped from the face of the earth unless there really is an apocalypse, in which case all of us—believers and non-believers alike—will get wiped out just like T-Rex and the Brachiosaurus. Knowing how to use a gun does not make a Muff an NRA member.

The third reason we were headed to Oxnard is, well, Jelicka finally wore us down with promises of a group ammo discount from her buddies at Shooter's Paradise, along with a cushy drive up in her Audi A8—the one luxury item she'd held onto in her divorce settlement—and a box of red-velvet cupcakes from Sprinkles.

"What's going on with the Titty-tranny?" said Jelicka, once

we were on our way.

"Who?" asked Rachel.

"That little two-timing, bisexual Slovakian conniver."

"She's from Moldova," I corrected.

"Still—former Soviet bloc borscht eaters. They're all the same."

"Come on, you eat borscht," Maddie said.

"All the time; that's how I know," Jelicka retorted.

Maddie, sitting in the front, turned around to look at me. "Did you leave that picture button you found somewhere Jamie could find it yet?"

"There are problems with that," I said. "*I* know it's Titania in the picture, but it was taken at such an angle that reasonable minds might legitimately differ. And Jamie, with her unreasonable mind, well, who knows what she'd say? I need more proof."

"I think you should get Titania alone and confront her. Say you have more on her than you do, and watch her body language," said Rachel. "Maybe she won't have time to come up with some lame excuse, you know?"

"I agree," said Jelicka.

"Just be careful," Maddie chimed in. "I've been thinking about it, and it could backfire if she calls your bluff."

Jelicka was undaunted. "You want her on notice and worried about her own job. Tell her you suspect she's keeping secrets from Jamie, and you know what they are."

"Yeah, that'll get her," Rachel agreed.

I gazed wistfully as we drove by the Camarillo Outlet center, wishing I had five-hundred bucks to drop on clothes. A little retail therapy never hurt anyone—until the bill arrived. *Where was Frank Sexton, and what had he found out so far?* That's what I really wanted.

"You're not acting all that concerned," said Jelicka. "What aren't you telling us?"

There's not much that goes unnoticed with these women. I decided it couldn't hurt to tell them.

"Well, in an interesting turn of events, there's somebody helping me—or at least I thought there was. There isn't much time left to prove to Jamie that the damaging pictures will be contained. Whoever sent them is out to get me fired and ruin my reputation, but he or she is waiting for something—who knows what? —before they make good on the threat and put the pics online. So if we can find out who sent them and why, we might be able to keep that from happening."

"It *is* you in the pictures," Rachel verified.

"Unfortunately, yes. But no *Hello Kitty* girl was ever in any danger."

"God forbid the world loses any *Hello Kitty* fans," said Jelicka.

"If you want, I could arrange for one of the guys who pose for me to make a pass at Titania," Rachel offered. "You might get some more pictures of her you can use."

I kind of liked that idea, especially if Frank didn't come up with anything soon. "I'll let you know," I told her.

"So who's helping you?" Maddie asked.

I couldn't remember if I'd promised Lauren that I wouldn't tell any of the Muffs about Frank or just about the free ticket to her Alzheimer's benefit.

"It better not be 'married guy,' " Jelicka said.

"Don't worry. Steven and I are completely done this time. By the way, Maddie, he claimed he didn't know anything about someone following me."

"What are you guys talking about?" Rachel asked.

I filled her in, and Jelicka doubled down on the need for self-protection.

"Are you going to tell us about this helper?" repeated Maddie.

I decided Lauren had meant the ticket and so plowed ahead with the explanation. "He's this undercover guy from George's dad's company who's on loan until we figure out why someone's trying to sabotage me. But like I said, there isn't much time."

"Really? A private investigator?" Jelicka was thrilled. "Do you think he'd talk to me about his experiences? Because you know, that's one of the areas I'm considering going into."

"I can ask," I said. "He might—but probably not until this is over."

"What's he like?" asked Maddie. "Must be kind of weird having someone following you."

"Yeah, how is that?" Jelicka asked, checking the rearview mirrors.

"I don't really know what it's like," I said. "To tell you the truth, I might have imagined the whole thing. He accosted me at the dance studio after class one evening, and since then, he hasn't really 'reported in' or whatever it's called."

Jelicka checked her rearview again. "So you think he's following you now?"

"I don't think he's following *me*; I think he's supposed to be following the people who might be trying to get me fired. But it feels kind of nice knowing there's somebody out there watching over me, you know?"

"That does sound nice," said Maddie.

Rachel groaned. "Please...if being looked after means having a guy who takes your money and spends most of his days watching porn, I think we're better off without one."

"They don't all watch porn," Maddie pointed out.

As I'd suspected, and what had been made clear during the webinar, Rachel's last couple of break-ups—first the gaffer and, after him, the rebound Greek—had been ugly, but she hadn't said just *how* ugly. She'd been with women, but bottom line, she preferred men. She liked the cock. But now, having made the choice, she was embittered by her bad relationships and was taking it out on all men in her work. What was good and bad was that she'd found success (good) for her latest series of paintings depicting naked men with no faces, but she'd also found validation for some pretty negative feelings (bad). I wanted to tell her, "You'll get over these guys," or "This too will pass," or some other tired bromide people say at times like this when they don't know what else to say. But I said nothing. She knew I was there if she wanted to talk.

In the end, most of us have been through bad break-ups and heartache, yet we usually recover and try again for love. What else can we do? I put my hand over hers and gave it a squeeze. I think she got it.

Jelicka stood at the front of the shooting stall, earmuffed and begoggled, her gun arm extended toward the target. "Your stance can either be open or like this."

She shifted easily from facing the paper target with her body—her legs parted slightly wider than her hips, straight but not locked—to having her right foot positioned behind the left with her left side facing the target. For Maddie and me, this was a review; I'd seen both stances on a previous visit to Shooter's Paradise. For Rachel, it was brand new."

"I prefer this stance myself," Jelicka said. "It just feels more solid, especially if your gun has a kick on discharge."

Rachel seemed twitchy. "You okay?" I asked her as quietly as I could, given our earmuffs and the sound of guns going off in the neighboring stalls.

"Oh, yeah." Her eyes glowed through the scratched lenses of her goggles. "I think I'm going to enjoy this."

I smiled. "Easy, pardner."

For Rachel, this could go one of two ways, I thought. Either shooting at drawings of men on paper targets would help her banish the demons and give her new and better ideas of things to paint, or she could become totally unhinged.

Meanwhile, Jelicka continued with her instructions. "You can hold the gun in one hand, but I recommend supporting the shooting hand with the non-shooting one like this. Being women we're—*duh*—not as physically strong as the other sex."

She suddenly changed her tone to that of a non-threatening Southerner: "I do declare, women are delicate flowers, meant to—*shit*." She clutched her hand.

"What is it?" Maddie asked.

"Broke a nail," said Jelicka. "Ouch—down to the quick, too." She examined the damage. "Screw it."

She faced the target—a life-sized drawing of a mustachioed man wearing a balaclava and holding his victim in a headlock—released the safety and let go two rounds from her Glock. She then put the safety back on, placed the gun down, and flipped a switch that brought the paper target closer so we could examine the damage.

"Oh my goodness, look at that—the delicate flower killed the big, bad rapist," Jelicka said, admiring her handiwork.

The guy, had he been real, would most certainly have been dead. She'd nailed him twice, right between the eyes.

"I hope my aim is better than the first time we did this," Maddie said. "This flower had no power."

Jelicka picked the gun up again and sent the target out a few feet. "Don't worry, you'll get it. How do we get to Carnegie Hall, ladies?"

"Practice, practice, practice!" the rest of us said in unison, causing a couple of the tattooed guys in the next stall to glance over. All of us were wearing fitted jeans designed to flatter. Rachel was even showing some skin at the belly. The poor boys; we must have been distracting them from making a bullseye.

"I still can't believe I let you talk me into going to Nissim's house to look for evidence and you pulled out that gun. *That gun*," Maddie continued.

All of us had heard about Jelicka and Maddie's illegal search of Udi's friend's house after Udi had "died." They'd turned up nothing, and the escapade could have landed them in jail—or even dead—had Nissim not been so forgiving.

"I want to try," Rachel said.

"Let's do it," said Jelicka. She placed the Glock on the shelf and maneuvered Rachel into position at the front of the stall facing the rapist. Rachel claimed never to have shot a pistol in her life, but you'd never have guessed. She assumed the stance and positioned the gun like a seasoned pro. Surprisingly, most of her shots found the target—or at least the paper the target was on.

After she'd fired out the clip, she stood taller. That's the strange thing about guns. Even if you hate them, or are scared of them and think they should all be banned for fear they could end up in the hands of a psyche patient off his meds, holding and firing one gives a person a sense of power and control in a world where we truly have very little of either. But the power isn't real, and we'd be wise to remember that.

We took turns, and Jelicka was positively in her element. She *could* become a P.I., I thought—that is, if she could put up with the classroom part of earning the degree. And if she couldn't hack that part, she could probably make money teaching marksmanship to Beverly Hills housewives. She'd been one herself.

I found myself wondering what kind of a shot Frank Sexton was. We hadn't talked much that night about his background, only my own. A wave of panic hit me. I was running out of time. Where *was* Frank Sexton? He should have found something out by now—if not about the pictures, surely about *Yankees*. I wanted to call him to get an update, but he hadn't given me his number, which I took to mean he didn't want me to have it. That wasn't how he worked. He told me he'd 'be in touch' when he had something. I decided I'd call Lauren later and see if she could find out what was going on.

After my third time up to shoot, and a fair-to-middling showing with two shots through the head of the paper rapist and a few others going way wild, dinging into the depths of the range, I flipped the safety on and put the Glock back on the shelf to give another Muff a turn.

I was backing out of the stall, out of the way of my friends, when I glanced over to where the tattooed guys were still checking us out. The more heavily tatted guy gave me his thumbs-up in approval. I gave them a polite tip of my head, but offered not a trace of encouragement.

Glancing beyond them, I spotted Frank Sexton. He was dressed like a member of the Special Forces Unit in *The Bourne Identity*. He stepped back from his stall, his handgun clipped to his holster and a badge flipped open on his belt. Our eyes met, and I felt my jaw drop open.

He began walking toward me and, as he passed, he gave me a barely perceptible nod. I almost said something before remembering he told me not to. I hesitated. *Should I do it anyway?* With only a few days until the pictures went public and Jamie fired me, shouldn't he have told me what was going on by now? *Yes, he should have.*

I said nothing. Oh, but *man*, he looked sexy rigged up like he was.

Wait—did he really? I had to remind myself he wasn't my type. All this exposure to the violent underbelly could not possibly be good for me.

I glanced over at the Muffs and found Maddie watching me curiously. I gestured toward Frank retreating toward the exit and mouthed the word "hot," giving her the thumbs-up sign. She had just enough time to glance over her shoulder and take in

Frank's back as he opened the door out of the range and disappeared through it. Turning back to me, she shrugged and gave me the thumbs-up sign in return, but it wasn't the corroboration I was seeking.

Disconcerting as it had been seeing my erstwhile Private Investigator, and the conflicting feelings that doing so summoned in me, his presence restored my sense of security—false though it might be.

"Anyone else?" Jelicka asked, bringing me back to my senses. "Last call."

I shook my head, and Rachel ran her finger like a knife across her neck. We'd all had enough and were ready to eat. Kiki had promised us lunch and libation while we scoped out the libidinous neighbors. Shooting apparently works up an appetite.

Jelicka ejected the gun magazine for the last time, emptying the remaining bullets into her pocket. Flipping the wall switch, she brought the paper target within reach and pulled it from the clips. We stared at the bullet-riddled drawing of the rapist and his female victim.

"We nailed that sucker," said Jelicka. "He's either so dead his mother won't recognize him, or he'll wish he never went into that house for the rest of his castrated, crippled, blind life. But next time, ladies, let's make more of an effort not to shoot his victim."

An hour later, decamped from Shooters Paradise, the four of us were ensconced on Kiki's patio where we had an obscured view of the notorious house next door. Kiki shuttled back and forth from the kitchen with platters of cheese, crackers, crudité and garlic shrimp, all of which was now laid out on the outdoor dining table around which we sat. The tasty crustaceans were almost gone, having been snatched up like gift bags at a charity lunch.

From where we sat drinking Sangria and munching, we could make out most of the neck and head of the atrocious cement giraffe we'd seen in the pictures sticking his head over the eight-foot high stucco wall. The long-necked waste of statuary materials was ugly in so many ways, and Jelicka might have used it for continued target practice had her Glock not been safely stowed in the A8. Instead, she poured the last of the Sangria as Rachel explained her own choice of artistic subject matter.

"The 'Nude Men Without Faces' series was inspired by the lack of spirituality I find in men today—not even just the good-looking ones," she was saying. "They're not spiritual, but it's like they're trying to promote their own godliness, almost as if they have become their own Gods and, therefore, only worship, guess who—? Themselves."

There was some mmm-ing in acknowledgment as Kiki returned with a full pitcher of Sangria, along with a tiny pot of Tiger Balm for Maddie's trigger finger, which had suffered minor strain from excessive gun firing. I worried that Kiki, being the most religious of all of us, might object to any discussion of G-O-D, but she just sat there gently rubbing the tiger balm into Maddie's finger while the warm, early Encino evening embraced us all.

Kiki's own recent crisis of faith—which involved a lot of soul searching having to do with her being a lapsed Catholic married to a secular Jew—had apparently left her less beholden to any one dogma and more accepting of other perspectives, no matter how crazy.

Rachel continued, "So all this need for worshipping sort of presents a problem for us ordinary women when ordinary men want to be worshipped as if they're real Gods—not that a God is even real."

Kiki put the lid on the tiger balm. "As real as you want to make Him."

"*Mmmm,*" said Maddie, ruminating. "It's hard being mortal."

"Saul's doing a pretty good job," said Kiki.

At least one of us was in love.

"We can't possibly accomplish *multiple* man-God worship in any viable way today even if we wanted to. If every man wants to be a God...?" Rachel shook her head. "Think about it; at your agency, Quinn—do you bow down to acknowledge every manifestly-huge ego walking around the place?"

I'd lost the thread of what it was we were talking about. I shrugged, holding up my hands in surrender.

"Right, because it can't be done," Rachel plowed on. "So, to answer your question, Maddie, what I'm saying in the paintings is the faces can't be displayed because they belong to the soulless and interchangeable, thus cannot be worshipped; they are, in fact, unworshipable."

"Wow," said Jelicka. "Did you make that up?"

"I *read*, Jel."

"You must have gotten that from some militant feminist magazine," said Kiki.

"What I'm saying is the 'everybody is a star' syndrome is backfiring," ranted Rachel. "Sure, anyone today can lay down music tracks in their garage using fake instruments, stealing other artists' work and manipulating the sound. Anyone can put her 'art' online where, if it feeds into some zeitgeist-y movement, it will get discovered and the 'artist' moves into the mainstream. But even though there's a bigger potential audience, it gets diluted because there are so many of these people. Other people rip off the first group, then the fat cats come in to monetize anything that is truly good, and they take it and get away with outright theft! I'm better off than most of these artists because my work is kind of hard to steal, you know? I work on huge canvases—you can't just download them."

"I'm a little confused," I said, looking at the others, a couple of whom had gone slack-jawed. "What are we talking about?"

"Not everyone can be a star," said Rachel. It was true but, at that moment, it appeared as though she'd lost all of us.

"*Shhhh,*" whispered Kiki, just in time to save us from further confusion. She quietly walked closer to the wall that separated her house from the house next door. Jelicka finished pouring herself more Sangria, and we joined Kiki to listen.

Snippets of sentences drifted over—innocuous words like house, exterior, kitchen. Nothing they were saying immediately suggested nefarious activity. From their conversation, they might have been talking about upcoming renovations.

A different voice was audible now; somebody new had come onto the patio.

"That's the owner," Kiki whispered when she heard him.

The speaker was male, and I pegged his accent as being from somewhere in Eastern Europe. He spoke loudly, peppering his conversation with terms like "tracking shot," "kino," and "video monitor," which told us the subject of their conversation was not home improvement.

"They *are* making porno," said Jelicka.

"Sounds like they're planning to anyway." That's our Maddie— never one to accuse too hastily.

"I told you!" Kiki said as she directed us back to the table. "I really don't want Troy hearing or seeing any of this."

"So far it's just film moves they're talking about, not sex moves," Jelicka quipped.

Kiki held her finger to her lips and vehemently *shhhd* her.

"Don't you think he knows what's going on?" asked Rachel. "I mean, he knows about sex, right?"

Jelicka took a big gulp of Sangria. "More to the point—don't you think he's watched it on the Internet?"

"No," said Kiki with a trace of defiance. "Definitely not. We have Net Nanny."

"How old is Troy now?" I asked.

"Just turned fourteen," said Kiki.

Rachel glanced away and under her breath mumbled, "Yeah, good luck with that."

"Net Nanny?" Jelicka chortled. "No matter what kind of nanny, when it comes to making movies, you always want the biggest piece of *gross*, never *net*." She hesitated for a second. "*Gross Nanny* sounds kind of interesting, though. Could be a sequel to *Bridesmaids*." She knocked back another gulp.

"It's software. He can't access certain websites," Kiki said, deadpan.

"As far as you can tell," Jelicka said pointedly. Clearly, she knew nothing about parental control software, but I could also see that Kiki was in denial about what Troy, and for that matter, *all* kids these days knew.

Trying to be supportive, Maddie put her hand over Kiki's. "It's possible he really doesn't know. But at some point, sooner rather than later, you and Saul are going to need to talk to him. Might as well not put it off too long, just in case he *is* listening to what's going on over there."

"Parental controls are a lost cause anyway," said Rachel. "His friends will just show him on their stupid smart phones."

"Life is so complicated," Kiki said, dispirited. "I realize people have worried about their children since humans started having children, but these days it seems impossible to keep things from them."

"I have a similar problem with Lila," said Maddie. "Some of the popular girls at her school are getting their pubes waxed, so now *she* wants to. I didn't get my *legs* waxed 'til I was thirty, so there's no way I'm letting her do it!"

"Why? What's the problem with it?" Jelicka asked.

"Are you really asking that, Jelicka?" Kiki inquired.

"Well...yes." She seemed truly mystified.

"I'm glad you didn't cave," I said, Maddie having decided after talking it through that day at Babalu.

"*My* big objection with it," said Rachel, "is that she probably wants to do it so the boys will notice, which is a horrible reason."

"Why would boys be looking at Lila's pubes in the first place?" asked Kiki appalled.

"They're not," said Maddie. "She doesn't even have enough down there to wax. For all I know, the mean girls aren't getting waxed, either, and they made the whole thing up to make the not-so-popular girls feel bad."

"I hate bullies," Kiki said.

Jelicka snorted in semi-drunken amusement. "Why bother anyway? No man notices, unless it's a full-on Brazilian with vajazzling—no straight man, anyway."

I wondered what sort of sampling of the male population Jelicka had used to reach this conclusion. We really needed to talk to her about her drinking.

"Regardless, it's a bad precedent to set." Rachel sounded annoyed again. "I mean, if she's living to please boys now, what hope is there?"

The Muffs should also talk to Rachel about her growing militancy.

"It's just peer pressure," Maddie said. "But enough. We need to brainstorm about how we can help Kiki close down the porn palace. Right?"

There was general agreement among those assembled.

"Okay, good. Ideas? Maybe we start by each of us asking ourselves the question: What would we do if there was such a house next door to us?"

There was a pause while we pondered the question.

"Watch?" said Jelicka.

Kiki and Maddie threw her a look.

"Oh, come on, I'm *kidding*," she protested. "Taking all this too seriously is not going to get rid of them."

Though I agreed there was some prurient value in watching, it was also true that Jelicka's comment wasn't helpful; and we were there, after all, to get rid of the prosecutable pornographers.

Kiki seemed to be losing patience with us, as she'd lost patience with the people in the house.

"Okay, we'll focus now," said Rachel, staring at Jelicka.

Jelicka sighed. "I'm sorry, I'll stop. Does anybody remember right after Roscoe took up with the older woman, when I was thinking about going into the growth field of mature porn?"

We *mmm'd* and nodded, very glad she hadn't pursued that career path, but unsure of its relevance to Kiki's problem.

"Well, I did some research—even went to a shoot."

"At a private residence?" Kiki asked.

Jelicka shook her head. "A warehouse in Chatsworth. But still, everyone downplayed what they were doing there. You'd never know they were shooting porn from the way they dressed when they weren't on set. They told me they never made a big show of it because they'd only get harassed."

"Makes sense," Rachel said, looking at Kiki. "You probably can't tell that the people going in and out of that house are in the porn business, can you? And since this is a residential neighborhood, they'll be extra careful about not getting exposed."

"Ha-ha," Kiki said sardonically. "Just because they aren't getting out of their cars wearing thongs doesn't make them any less visible. Believe me, I can tell."

"What I'm saying," said Jelicka, "and what I think Rachel is suggesting—correct me if I'm wrong, Rachel—is that if we were to hang around the house wearing very provocative clothes, like she said she could, and we pretended we were involved with the movie getting shot inside, maybe more neighbors would complain to the city and eventually shut the place down."

Kiki frowned. "Maddie—did you find out anything from your friend in the film office?"

"Maddie inhaled sharply. "You're not going to like it."

Kiki wailed. "Pleeeeze, don't tell me that."

"What I discovered is it's not necessarily illegal to shoot a movie, including a smutty one, inside your own house. The thing is, if you plan on selling the film or using it for any commercial purpose, you need a permit. Getting that permit is, unfortunately for you, pretty easy—even for porn, as long as certain restrictions are met having to do with parking, noise, security guard—stuff like that—with porn having the additional requirement that the shooting of sex scenes has to be concealed from the public."

"Are you freaking *kidding* me?" Kiki was about to go ballistic.

"Define 'concealed,' " Jelicka chortled with Rachel adding, "Right, and 'public.' Neighbors and cement animals don't count."

"Yeah, you can shoot porn anywhere these days," Jelicka went on. "Don't forget all the selfies the politicians sent around before Snap Chat."

The two of them found all this hysterically funny and continued on about recent public sex scandals, political implosions, and the like, forcing Maddie to top them. "The good news is," she spoke over them, "my friend also told me that your neighbors did *not* pull a permit, which means that unless whatever they're shooting is for their own use… "

"Yeah, right," said Jelicka. "Who rents Kinos and does tracking shots for home videos?"

"Homosexual Republican Senators?" giggled Rachel.

"...it's illegal to shoot in that house," Maddie finished.

"So they're probably thinking that since they're keeping it small, with bare bones personnel and equipment, they can get away without a permit," I said. "If no one notices, they can't get caught."

"Exactly," said Maddie. "But they're thinking *wrong*."

My mobile vibrated, making me jump. Caller I.D. showed it was Steven—and Rachel, regaining her composure, peered over to see. "Do not take that call," she said. I hit *Dismiss*.

"If somebody does notice," Maddie continued, "and they get caught, the fines are pretty steep."

"And we have noticed," Rachel said.

"Right." Maddie stabbed the last garlic shrimp. "We have noticed."

Kiki was smiling. "I'm feeling better about this, you guys."

"So all we have to do is catch them," I said warily, "which shows we noticed."

"That's it," Maddie said. "And that's not all that easy. Let's say Kiki thinks her neighbors are in the midst of shooting and she calls the cops. They can't just storm through the house and catch the pornographers in the act. They have to enter the premises legally, which basically means they have to be invited in, which isn't going to happen. The only other way is for Kiki to work with the cops to build enough probable cause to get a warrant and force entry."

"I *was* feeling better," Kiki said, returning to her state of frustration.

"This sucks," said Jelicka. "Our tax dollars, hard at work."

Rachel chimed in. "You'd think Kiki's rights as a quiet, law-abiding citizen would trump what is clearly a violation of zoning laws."

"Come on, Maddie. There has to be something we can do," I said.

Maddie thought for a couple of seconds. "My friend in the film office said that sometimes the vice squad will investigate, and they can be very good at blending in—they'll get invited inside, observe film equipment moving in and out, meet the actors, etc. But with this being a private home, anyone who's not supposed to be hanging around will be noticed immediately. And if the film equipment gets unloaded inside a closed garage with all the windows blacked out, it might be impossible to prove what they're doing, even though you see what are obviously actors, actresses, and other film-related people and equipment coming and going."

Kiki sighed again, disconsolately, and the rest of us did what we could to bolster her sagging spirits. Despite Maddie's gloomy prognostications, we came up with a plan to rendezvous on a night when Kiki was certain they were shooting and we'd spring a *coup de main*. The fine points still needed to be worked out, but basics were set, and I planned on asking Frank Sexton for help. Certainly Lauren wouldn't mind if he did a little extra extracurricular "work" for Kiki, given that doing so would still fall under the general heading of "helping The Muffia."

First, however, I wanted to yell at Mr. Frank Sexton for keeping me out of the loop about what was going on with Picturegate. I didn't buy that he had nothing to report. He *had* to have *some*thing to tell me. Meanwhile, time was not my friend, and I had nothing but a picture button to suggest that at least one person I knew wasn't playing fair.

CHAPTER 18

CONSIDERING FRANK Sexton had shown up at S-Factor and Shooter's Paradise without advance warning, it wasn't far-fetched to conclude he could choose any other moment he wished to make his presence known. In fact, he must be tracking me a good part of the time. Otherwise, how would he know I was in Oxnard? I supposed it was possible that he, like Jelicka, regularly went to Shooter's Paradise and just so happened to choose that particular Saturday to go for target practice. But this would have been a coincidence in a sea of other coincidences, which meant he had been following me. This sent me into a tizzy reconstructing the time line and realizing that Lauren told me about my new private investigator *before* I went on that disastrous date with John, and that meant Frank was already on my case that night. It also meant he might have been watching. *OMG, could this get more embarrassing?*

Notwithstanding my mortification at that thought, knowing that at any moment Frank might be nearby gave me the idea that if I simply paid better attention when I went somewhere, I would see him, and thus be able to confront him. So, in the quest for more information, I called Lauren as soon as I returned from Kiki's the previous evening. I didn't want to bother her, but I was hoping she could get a message to Frank somehow that I needed to talk to him as soon as possible. Otherwise, his paranoia—my word, not his—about not creating a digital connection between us meant I had to wait until he physically appeared. Fortunately, she said she would.

Work on that Monday started off slowly, but one of my pet projects—negotiating a four-million-dollar deal for a legend in the music business, Wylie "Big Mouth" Cotton, now broke, to become spokesman for a growing fast food empire—had been given the green light. This was a deal I was proud of; not only because it had been my idea to track the old bluesman down, but because Big Mouth really needed the money and, if I was to believe him, booking that gig meant he could save his family.

Steven sent a cryptic, innocuous text: "Call me"—the kind I used to respond to right away but which I'd been ignoring for over a week. And at another point that morning, Sameer appeared at the edge of my cubiffice, head wagging, to tell me about the latest sexting scandal plaguing Bronco's tight end and client, Tyroil Wallace-Ibrahim, who'd just been busted, threatening his lucrative Gatorade contract. Sameer was also curious about how my online dating was progressing and whether I had dated a farmer yet. Not wanting to land another blow, I said, "On one level, we are all farmers, don't you think, Sameer?" He seemed to like this answer and walked away smiling.

Jamie summoned me into her office at noon to discuss several ongoing deals and to check my progress on Picturegate. From all outward appearances, she and Titania were still getting on famously. It was looking highly unlikely that the two of them would break up in time for Jamie to be open to the idea that the woman on the picture button might be her lithe and lovely love bunny—or that Titania masterminded my takedown to advance her career.

No, if I showed Jamie the button of Titania and the guy kissing *now*, while she and Jamie were still an item, I still believed one of two things would occur: (A) Jamie would say it wasn't Titania on the button and think me a desperate woman with absolutely no evidence to exonerate myself; and (B) She'd think me a malicious, spiteful bitch trying to destroy the happy couple. There would be no winning with that button; not if it's all I have.

No matter how bad things looked, I still had approximately forty-eight hours to come up with convincing evidence, not that I had any idea where I was going to get it—*thanks a lot, Frank Sexton*—which would prove that my impending social network sabotage was no longer a threat to the solid industry reputation of Talent Partners. But I suppose the truth was, even if I produced that sort of proof, it would be impossible to absolve myself of *all* wrongdoing—at least in Jamie's eyes—because, after all, it *was* me in the pictures and she had seen them. She would always know. That's the thing about the Internet, too. It's a wonderful tool until somebody wants to use it to take someone else down, which they can easily do with doctored photos, mug shots taken when they were teenagers, or with words on Facebook. It's left for the person wronged to clean it up, and that costs money. Once a rumor is out there online, it never completely goes away.

"Well?" Jamie interrupted my thoughts. "Is there anything you can say or show me in your own defense?"

"I'll have something for you by Wednesday," I said with conviction.

"Have you found out who sent the pictures?"

"A couple of strong leads, but I don't think I should say anything until I know for sure."

I sounded confident, but I feared the worst. What I wanted to tell her was that she shouldn't fire me over the stupid photographs when they could have been sent by anyone who was pissed off at me. There had to be someone—though I hadn't been able to think who—who was angry enough or malicious enough to try to sabotage me. I knew I should broaden my pool of candidates, but Titania was still the most likely person.

There seemed no sense in saying anything more. Besides, at the end of the day, pinpointing who didn't like me wouldn't have made any real difference. Jamie's only concern was sparing the agency embarrassment. It didn't matter who was making the threat or why—it just needed to be stopped.

I knew that I needed to be more pro-active. I'd been too complacent, relying on Frank Sexton who, so far, had been a disappointment, and hoping something that could help me would just appear. *Enough.* As uncomfortable as it made me, I *would* defend myself because I wasn't ready to give up my career. *I was going to confront Titania.*

CHAPTER 19

WHEN I left work that evening and stepped onto the second floor of the parking structure the agency shared with a department store and blue chip law firm, I spotted Frank Sexton leaning on my car. My first inclination was to smack him one, as soon as I got close enough, for taking so long to resurface. But seeing as that would be unproductive, I smiled and continued walking toward him and my trusty nine-year-old Rav4, which I'd been advised by Jamie, on more than one occasion, to trade in for something more "appropriate." There had been more than a few memos sent in which Talent Partners suggested its agents drive a Lexus, Audi or BMW. Now I was very glad I hadn't obliged because I *owned* my Rav4 outright. Buying or leasing a new, Talent Partners-approved vehicle would have meant a car payment at a time when my future livelihood looked uncertain.

It was actually good to see Frank. He wore khakis and had on a white oxford cloth shirt, just like the previous two times I'd seen him but, contrary to my first reaction upon seeing this outfit, I found it comforting, rather than that he suffered from a lack of imagination. The only thing new was the pair of mirrored aviator-frame sunglasses he had on, making him look as though he came out of a 1980s cop drama.

"Hello, Frank," I said, as I rummaged around my purse for the car key. That was one thing about the car I'd change if I could. It pre-dated keyless entry, so I was always looking for my keys.

"Get in quickly," he directed, doing a scan of the area.

"Hello to you, too," I said, once inside, watching him slip in beside me. "Why haven't you contacted me? I've been dying to know if you found anything. It was all I could do not to follow you out of Shooter's Paradise."

He smelled clean, and my nose picked up the scent of expensive cologne, which I did not remember from our earlier meetings.

"You handled that very well, by the way." He pulled the door closed.

"It wasn't easy, trust me. Where have you been? It's been over a week!" My voice sounded whiney and thin; I'd better pull myself together.

"I told you I'd be in touch when I had some information to impart."

I let out my breath. "Well, given my situation, one might have thought you'd have 'gotten in touch' before now if, for no other reason, than to tell me you didn't have anything."

"What would be the point of that?"

"Because I've been freaking out, that's why." *Dial it back, Quinn.*

"That's why I'm here now," he said, calmly.

Was he deliberately being obtuse? Why did this guy continue to grow on me?

"There have been some recent developments I came to inform you of."

"Could you be more specific?"

"I will get to that."

What was he waiting for? I stared at him for a beat or two. His face was directed forward, out the windshield—no expression, save for a barely perceptible twitch of his jaw muscle.

"Drive," he said.

"Drive?"

"Yes, drive," he repeated, all Schwarzenegger in *The Terminator*—the first Terminator, when he was all hunky and sexy. There was more than a passing resemblance.

I peered out the opening of the parking structure to the rear-facing windows of Talent Partners' offices a floor above. The sun, long past mid-point, glinted off the tempered glass guaranteeing that if someone was watching, we wouldn't have known.

"Where am I driving?"

"Anywhere you like."

"A tour of stars' homes?"

"If you wish."

"That was supposed to be funny," I said, but judging from his reaction, he clearly hadn't found it so.

I pointed the car toward the down ramp and onto the exit, over the "don't-back-up" spikes and out through the access alley. I had vague plans to go pole dancing later in the evening but, at that moment, one direction was no better than another. I turned east, toward my apartment.

"The man you call *Yankees* is a private investigator," he said, once we'd hit Wilshire Boulevard.

"Another private investigator is following me?"

"He's not following you any longer."

I flashed Frank what must have seemed a panicked expression. "You didn't do anything to him, did you?"

"He's in good health."

"Good, because I don't need any more trouble by adding a dead body," I said, relieved.

"Several days into my surveillance, I saw a man matching the description you provided sitting in a car outside your apartment. I followed him, observed him from a distance, and subsequently approached."

"Are you allowed to do that? I would think there would be some sort of secret private investigator code of conduct?"

"He would not tell me who hired him. That's standard. But I determined it was this man who took the photos of you at Narita."

I swerved to the curb and put the Rav4 in park. "But that was several days ago, and you're just telling me?"

He turned his body to face me. "Please, Ms. Cunningham, try not to get upset. It has been necessary for me to keep my distance. There was always the possibility that some other plot was afoot. It was also necessary to wait so as to better ascertain who it was who hired this man."

"Was this before or after I saw you in Oxnard?"

"I believe it was after."

Way to keep it vague, Mr. Sexton.

"How'd you do, by the way?" he asked, surprising me.

The question, being so off topic, threw me.

"Your target practice."

"Fine, not as well as last time, but…" I stopped, finding myself getting angry. "What—? Are we making nice conversation now? By the way, how did you know I was there?"

"I was there before you. It was simply a matter of tapping into your phone and determining your destination prior to your arrival."

"Oh, really? Simply a matter of tapping my phone?" I knew spying had gotten easier, but was he serious? Something told me no. "That's not true," I said.

"Correct. It's not true. I put a GPS locator on your friend's car."

I flashed on Udi and his supposed embedded chip—the reason given by his friend Nissim and Nissim's oversized associates for knowing he'd died and showing up at Maddie's to collect his body. But I wasn't sure I should believe that, either, though I'd seen it in enough movies.

"You didn't put a GPS locator on my friend's car."

"Correct again. But I could have."

Now he was playing with me—something I would not have thought he would know how to do, given his by-the-book demeanor. Did this mean there was a sense of humor in there somewhere?

"So you did follow us," I said in a softer tone.

"I was in danger of losing you briefly. Your friend, Angelica, drives very fast."

"It's Jelicka—and yes, that's her speed."

He said nothing but sat back against the car door, assessing me. There were opinions and thoughts going on behind those polarized lenses—positive ones, I hoped—but he was none too generous about sharing them.

"So you've been following me this whole time?" I already knew the answer.

"In between pursuing other leads, yes. I've kept my eye on you," he said quietly. "Just as I said I would." It almost sounded like a pass, and I felt a flip-flop in my chest.

"So how come the only time I've seen you was at the shooting range?"

I couldn't see his eyes, but I'm pretty sure he rolled them.

"If you're doing your job, I'm not supposed to see you, right? Okay, that was a dumb question. You wanted me to see you."

"I have also been watching your boss, Ms. Harris, and have followed Ms. Cibulkova as well."

"And?"

"The two of them have met eleven times that I am aware of, outside of the office where intimacies were likely exchanged."

"Hmmm...that's an interesting way to put it. Covers a lot of things, don't you think?" A teasing quality had trickled into my voice. I felt the desire to tease him further but kept it in check.

"It could, yes. Ms. Harris attends many screenings and also spends a good bit of time on the treadmill at her gym."

"The treadmill, huh. I would have thought she was more of an elliptical type. What about Titania's workout routine?" I joked. *Miss Moldovan Molotov had quite the hot bod.*

"She does an assortment of exercises, including extensive Pilates poses," he said, missing my tone. He paused. "You were right about her, Ms. Cunningham."

"What?" What did he mean? "What was I right about?"

"She is bisexual and has a boyfriend by the name of… " He pulled out his little pocket pad and flipped a couple of pages.

"Yes!" Partial vindication anyway.

"…Boris Sizmansky. I obtained some photographs." He put his pad away and produced his phone with a few racy pictures on it.

"Wow, you sure did." I scanned the grainy shots of Titania and Boris in degrees of nubile nakedness assuming a variety of provocative poses.

I couldn't tell what Frank actually thought about the duplicitous bi-babe, but chances were, if he was like other guys, he enjoyed visualizing two women together—even if one was decidedly hotter than the other. However, the idea of inserting a guy other than himself into that lesbian lusciousness put an immediate kibosh on the first visual.

The shots were incontrovertibly Titania—unlike the female image on the picture button I'd found. And the guy was definitely the same. Same chin, same pecs, same beautiful washboard stomach. Jamie would for sure have a reaction to *these* pictures.

"These are really good; really good resolution, too. Were you outside her apartment with a telephoto lens? Or did you somehow install a remote camera?"

Glancing at Frank's tight lips, it was clear he had no plans to supply the details of how he'd obtained the pictures, and maybe I didn't want to know. Those lips were tight, but they looked soft.

He closed the phone and started to put it away.

"I hope you'll email me a few of those; they might come in handy."

Pulling the phone out once more, he opened it, making a display of doing as I asked. "I am sending an encrypted email to the company. They'll make sure you get them. These are for your private use only, for purposes of keeping your job," he warned.

"Of course," I said, and meant it. Boris was cute and everything, but the only use I had for the pictures was to prove to Titania that I could hurt her if she didn't come clean.

He turned his face to glance at the passenger rearview mirror. "It's better we keep moving," he said, disturbing my daydream in which Jamie tossed Titania out on her ass.

"I was headed home." I put the car back in drive and pulled out into the steady stream of cars on Robertson Avenue. "And after that, to dance class."

"As you wish," he said, after which the conversation summarily died. After going several long city blocks without a peep, I decided to continue on by myself.

"How is that going, the pole dancing?" I asked myself. "It's going very well, thanks for asking," I responded. "How long have you been dancing, Ms. Cunningham?" "Oh, about two years, and please, call me Quinn." "What is it you like best about pole dancing, Quinn?" "Well, let's see...I really like the platform shoes, plus it's great exercise—not to mention a terrific stress reducer while also being a very expressive form of dance." "Wow, that's amazing. You must be..."

"Okay, that's enough," said Frank. "I'm not much of a conversationalist."

"Do ya think?" I said, teasing.

"When I'm on the job, I'm thinking about a lot of other stuff, not small talk."

This comment begged two questions: What was the other stuff? And how would he be at conversing off the job? I found myself interested in both.

We continued along in silence for another couple of blocks. "Think you'll ever do anything with it—the pole dancing, I mean?"

So he *could* make conversation! "Like what?" I asked, encouraging him.

"What do other women do with it?"

"Some dance for their boyfriends or husbands. Others work at strip clubs. Too bad I'm over thirty. It might have been something to explore if I get fired."

He cleared his throat. "That won't happen."

Did I detect in his voice more concern about my future than he perhaps intended? Or was I just wishing I had. I glanced over at him. He was facing forward, lips—nice lips—tight. If only I'd been able to see what his eyes were doing behind those lenses, it would make it a whole lot easier to know how to behave.

"I hope you're right. I'd sure miss the employee insurance plan," I said, as we passed by the trendy shops north of West Third. "Do you want me to drive you back? We're going to be so far from your car. How will you...?"

"I'll get myself back."

He was so damned *capable*, which reminded me of Vicki's comment about finding a guy to get her through an apocalypse. Frank seemed like a great candidate for the job. But he was so stingy with words, it would be awfully quiet before the apocalypse arrived. Maybe if I kissed him, his lips would loosen up and stimulate another form of lip loosening.

Turning onto Melrose, I realized I was now driving

aimlessly and would have to turn around to get to my apartment. I wasn't sure why he thought it was better to keep moving. Besides, he'd already moved me a little just sitting in a parked car, and he hadn't even touched me. Certainly, my little problem at work did not rise to the level where someone would hire another someone to tail me. So why were we driving around? I had an *ah-ha* moment—someone might not be tailing *me* but might be tailing my private investigator.

"Frank?"

"Yes?"

"What's the real reason you have me driving us around? What aren't you telling me?"

As it was rush hour and the car was moving, I couldn't turn to look at him, but I felt his body flinch.

"Is the reason you just show up all the time and you won't let me call you because you're involved in something other than my little problem?" If Frank was a full-time employee of a corporate espionage company, which he was, there probably *was* something else afoot.

"No," said Frank, offering nothing more.

"Is it a girlfriend?" I asked, getting an idea. "I know! In an ironic twist, you have a girlfriend who's having *you* tailed, in which case, what must she think!"

"No, Ms. Cunningham. There's no girlfriend."

There was another pause, again with no additional information. I was concentrating so hard on a way to get a rise out of him—to find out what else might be going on—that I ran a red light.

"Please concentrate on the road, Ms. Cunningham. In fact," he was once more checking the rearview, "pull over when you can."

"My *name* is Quinn!" I said, angry that I couldn't seem to penetrate his tough exterior.

I saw an empty spot and swerved into it without slowing, which made him reach for the handle above the door to steady himself. He had the good sense not to complain about my driving, as he faced me and removed his sunglasses.

"I have told you what I intended to. However, before I get out of the car, I want you to tell me all about your boyfriend, Steven."

CHAPTER 20

*T*HOUGH I immediately felt the absence of Frank's solid and comforting presence once he got out of the car, I also felt lighter than I had in awhile, knowing I could now prove what I had suspected about the self-serving, two-timing Titania. And notwithstanding Frank's request that I dredge up my relationship with Steven—the details of which I would have preferred to keep buried—part of me hoped it was Frank's romantic speculation about me that made him ask. That said, he refused to tell me his reasons unless and until he discovered something legitimate that related to my case.

I was also sad to see him walk away because, in my mind, he'd solved the case and now he might not have reason to make an appearance ever again. I realized I would be very happy to have him around, even if his part in the proceedings was over. Unlike on TV, I come to find out, a private detective doesn't bust down doors and make arrests unless he or she is pushing the limits of his or her authority. A P.I. finds out things his or her client wants to know and turns that information over to the client to do with as he or she sees fit.

Frank had found out that Titania was a switch hitter. Now it was up to me to go to Titania and, depending on how that went, to Jamie. The piece of the puzzle I did not yet have, which Frank said he'd continue to work on, was connecting Titania to the pictures that were sent to Jamie. So far he hadn't been able to gain access to the database that would tell him. So there was still hope I might see him again.

After an invigorating dance class, I stopped at Whole Paycheck to spend a good portion of it picking up nuts, gluten-free bread, yoghurt, and local organic produce and had the thought that, considering all the money I spent in the place on a weekly basis, maybe I shouldn't have been so quick to dismiss *Dateafarmer. com*. A non-stop supply of organic produce, though boring as an all-day-slash-everyday solution to hunger, would still be great if I lost my job. And it was superior to becoming a bag lady, that's for sure.

I returned home and poured a glass of Pinot Noir made from grapes grown in the Santa Rita foothills. That might sound hoity-toity, but it's actually the only bit of impressive wine trivia I know. Someone told me once that any Pinot Noir from the Santa Rita foothills region of Santa Barbara County was a sure thing and, so far, that piece of advice has held true.

After a few savoring sips, I set about preparing a beet salad with walnuts and goat cheese, which I ate while catching up on unanswered emails and planning my strategy for exoneration the following day.

My personal email box was stuffed with missives of all kinds. Frank's pictures were there, along with Muffia emails and action requests sent by every environmental, animal, and political group I'd ever heard of. There were also at least forty emails sent by *NowLove* alerting me to prospective matches: "*ClassyChassis* sent you a wink," and "*Pantheon* wants to meet you," they beckoned cheerily. The handles of these heartthrobs ranged from *Quasi-CoachPotato* and *JohnGaltWasHere* to *Bioforce*—all of which I deleted for sounding either too lazy or too egotistical. There were also a few emails from a guy named Gary, aka *ManforYou,* whom I'd been corresponding with before my date with John.

Curious, I clicked on the most recent.

> To: Miss_Quinn@thecloud.com
> From: GBLevchenko@yahoo.com
> Subject: Us
> Where'd you go? I thought we were having a good time.

If tossing sexy *bon mots* back and forth constituted a good time, we'd been having a ball, but did I want to get back into that game? I found myself thinking about Frank as I took another sip of wine. Frank didn't seem interested so, *why not?*

> To: GBLevchenko@yahoo.com
> From: Miss_Quinn@thecloud.com
> Subject: Us
> I li Gary, how goes the dating?

I hit *send* and clicked over to my main email account to read one of numerous emails from members of The Muffia—this one the first in a thread started by Jelicka.

> To: TheMuffia
> From: MissJelickaG@aol.com
> Subject: Shut 'em down
> Thanks, Kiki, for a scrumptious lunch on Saturday. For those who couldn't make it (missed you), K laid out a spread and served up some tasty Sangria (recipe pls), while showing us what she's dealing with at the house next door. Oy, she wasn't kidding about the cement animals. We noshed on garlic shrimp while listening to the owner planning his porn shoot—which M says is illegal without a permit (not to mention tacky in a residential neighborhood), so we're going to shut 'em down, ladies. Who's in?

Before I could continue reading the multiple responses in the thread, *Ding*—another email from Gary hit my "dating" box. He must be up late trolling, too.

> To: Miss_Quinn@thecloud.com
>
> From: GBLevchenko@yahoo.com
>
> Subject: Us
>
> I was hoping to meet you then you disappeared. What are you doing now? Wanna Skype?

I'd already taken off the make-up, and my hair was in a knot on top of my head, so there'd be no Skyping for me tonight. We didn't know each other well enough for him to see me like that anyway. Hell, I'm not sure I want someone to ever see me like that.

> To: GBLevchenko@yahoo.com
>
> From: Miss_Quinn@thecloud.com
>
> Subject: Us
>
> No can do, but I'm ready to talk on the phone, tomorrow maybe?

Hitting *send*, I clicked on a response from Maddie to Jelicka's email:

> To: TheMuffia
>
> From: MSC@MSCMediate.com
>
> Subject: re: Shut 'em down
>
> Pending no school functions, I'm there. BTW, K, I found a slew of businesses linked to that address, including a sports drink, a DVD workout program, a Twitter follower generator, and yes, porn. There were also job postings on Craigslist linking to that

address. Anyway, you look at it; they shouldn't be doing what
they're doing, so we WILL shut 'em down!

Pretty much everyone said they wanted to be there, which
meant that when the time came for the bust, half of us would
actually show. A couple of Muffs commented on liking *When
Will There Be Good News?*, which was gratifying, and three or
four mentioned their dresses for the upcoming benefit. All of
them had something to say about my online dating pursuits when
Ding—another email from Gary popped into my box.

> To: Miss_Quinn@thecloud.com
> From: GBLevchenko@yahoo.com
> Subject: Skype
> Come on, just for a little bit? I'd like to see you. It'll be fun.

Fun? I didn't think so. The answer was still no, but apparently he wasn't getting it.

> To: GBLevchenko@yahoo.com
> From: Miss_Quinn@thecloud.com
> Subject: Skype
> Some other time, Gary. I'm not much of a Skyper.

I hit *send*, clicked back into the Muff thread, when *Ding*—
Gary sent another email.

> To: Miss_Quinn@thecloud.com
> From: GBLevchenko@yahoo.com
> Subject: Skype
> Come on. We can watch each other.

If I hadn't known it before, I now had a firm grasp of what

he meant by fun. Well, it was time to put an end to the euphemism.

> To: GBLevchenko@yahoo.com
> From: Miss_Quinn@thecloud.com
> Subject: Skype
> I'm not getting naked on camera, Gary.

Ding—

> To: Miss_Quinn@thecloud.com
> From: GBLevchenko@yahoo.com
> Subject: Skype
> You might really like it.

Ding—

> To: GBLevchenko@yahoo.com
> From: Miss_Quinn@thecloud.com
> Subject: Us
> I might. But I'm not doing it.

Ding—

> To: Miss_Quinn@thecloud.com
> From: GBLevchenko@yahoo.com
> Subject: Skype
> Money back guarantee.

Sheesh, he was persistent. Before I had a chance to think about how to respond, *Ding*—he emails me again.

I *knew* I shouldn't have answered that email. There'd been a reason why I'd gone on a date with John over Gary—though at present I couldn't remember the reason—when the reality was neither of them was a good fit. In fact, they were both the lowest of the low hanging fruit—so low as to be already on the ground. And it was my own fault. All my life it seems, most of the guys who come on to me are the ones I don't want. I was kidding myself if I thought it would be any different now that the meat market has moved online. The nice guys—the handsome, smart, quiet guys who had it all going on—didn't need to expend energy getting a date. Women found them. So if I wanted one for myself, I would need to expend more energy than I was currently exerting to get one. For now, though, I just needed to shut Gary down and explain why.

I left out that I knew a porn purveyor who could help with distribution. Let him figure out how to do that on his own.

Hostile? Perhaps. But was it "nice" of him to jump to masturbation? I think not. Gary was not a gentleman, nor was anyone else I'd met on the website. Frank was a gentleman, but he wasn't interested. But could I have him wrong? Maybe he was one of those nice, handsome guys who had it going on but was used to women making passes at him. That's it; I just hadn't expended enough energy. *Well, if I ever get another chance...*

In that spirit, I deleted all the *NowLove* emails having to do with winks and nudges, and so-and-so-wants-to meet-yous in my inbox. And I got back to what mattered—my Muffs.

From: kookykiki@hotmail.com
To: TheMuffia
Subject: re: Shut 'em down
Dear Muffs, Thanks for all your support. As soon as I know for sure that they're inside shooting, I'll put out the APB on the 911 and come over asap! xxK

Closing the laptop, I sat back. *Men.* The whole subject was tough—organic chemistry when you're an art major kind of tough. So tough that busting a porn ring seemed safer and easier by comparison.

CHAPTER 21

"HI, TITANIA," I said, catching up to her as she stepped off the elevator into the lobby of the Talent Partners Building at about noon the following day. She was dressed provocatively, per usual—pretty pumps, bare legs, slim leather skirt, and a crisp, white blouse unbuttoned to reveal just a hint of cleavage into which a tiny gold pendant dangled. She was a hot little number, no matter which sex she favored, and the male security guard registering the building's daily visitors gave her a flattering stare.

"Hi, Quinn," she said, haltingly—as if she suspected I was about to give her bad news. The girl was no ninny.

It was lunchtime and we weren't alone in the lobby.

"I wanted to talk to you about something," I said, drawing her toward me.

Her overly-mascaraed eyelashes fluttered open and closed—a few times in succession—like a baby bird testing its wings before it actually knows they work.

"Um...okay," she said, inching toward the building's front entrance. I began inching along next to her.

Glancing over my shoulder, I fortunately didn't notice any Talent Partners clients or employees—only those I presumed were affiliated with the building's other occupants. I leaned in, not like Sheryl Sandberg recommends, but just so as not to have my voice bounce around the marble-enclosed foyer. "Are you trying to get me fired?"

She stopped, not looking at me, and opened her handbag as if searching for something. "Whaaa...t?"

Oh, come on, you heard me. We were standing just inside the building now, in front of the doors—not a great place to pause.

"Let's keep moving, shall we?" I pushed on the revolving door, each of us in our separate glass compartment as the door spun around its center before spilling us onto Wilshire Boulevard.

"So *are* you?" I asked again.

"I don't know what you're talking about." She started walking, long strides now, her heels clicking on the cement sidewalk.

"Don't let me keep you from doing whatever you were going to do. I'll just walk alongside."

She gave me a sideways glance. "I was going to Chipotle."

"Me, too!" I said with glee. "Don't you love the bowls? I prefer barbacoa myself, so was quite disappointed when the whole thing happened with the pig farmers." I could see in her face that she thought I was nuts. It was fun.

"Ahh, I usually get the salad."

"The salads are good, too, but I find they're really just like the bowls except with more lettuce." *Enough with the mundanities.* "How did you get the pictures?"

Again she gave me the vacant, *"Whaaa...t?"*

"You know 'what.' The pictures," I said again. "And just in case you send pictures to a lot of people, I'm talking about the ones you sent to Jamie."

She stopped for a second, me a beat later, and said, "I don't know what you're talking about." Then she started off again.

Of course she's going to say that. I knew she was going to say that but stupidly held out a misplaced hope she'd own up to sending them.

"Are you denying you sent Jamie pictures?"

"Ahhh…"

"So you *admit* it?"

"What pictures are we talking about?"

"The pictures of me."

That seemed to get her. "Where would I have gotten these pictures of you that you think I sent to Jamie?" Now she was defiant.

You're not handling this right, Quinn. She should be cowering by now. Let me just say, I don't like conflict. For all my snarking, I generally avoid ever having to directly confront the source of my snarkiness. But this was my career on the line, and I really didn't want to be— nor was I qualified to do—anything other than a talent agent. If I was to hold on to my job, that meant conflict. Muff Maddie the Mediator told me just to keep my voice steady and take long, slow breaths, just as I do when I say my aphorisms. *Yes, yes, yes…*

"That's part of what I wanted to talk to you about," I said calmly.

"I did not send any pictures of you because I did not have any pictures of you to send," she said in a clipped voice.

"But you're saying you *did* send pictures to Jamie."

"Yes, but…"

"Ah-ha!" I said victoriously, remembering too late that was precisely how Maddie told me *not* to behave.

"The pictures I sent to Jamie were not of *you!*"

"So you had someone else send those pictures," I said. *Very clever.*

"What pictures?" She appeared now to think I was certifiably insane.

"Of course you can't admit it; I get it."

A cute guy with a nice build entered my field of vision. "Hi,

Titania," he said, pulling his Don Draper shades low onto his nose and smiling appraisingly. Though I was not on a first name basis with him, I recognized him as one of ours; I'd seen him at the last company barbecue. But to him, I wasn't even there. Such are the young and beautiful.

"Oh, hello, Sam!" said Titania, sounding very girly and sexy all of a sudden, in contrast to how she was talking to me. I could tell just how much of Titania was put on and artificial; it seemed like a rather large percentage.

"Are you really gay?" I asked her once Sam was out of earshot.

She swung around to face me and I recognized an expression of—horror, maybe?

"I mean, it's just that you don't really seem gay to me," I continued, "what with all the men and everything."

"Sam and I are just friends." She resumed her march to Chipotle.

"That's good, because otherwise, the guy you perform regular body locks with might get upset."

"I don't know what you're talking about." This time she said these words with more vocal power than I'd heard up to this point.

"You seem more 'bi' to me," I said. "No judgment, of course; just sayin'… "

She stopped again and turned on me. "Who told you this?"

"An itty bitty birdie. I don't know what kind."

"You're making up lies because Jamie is going to fire you."

Oops. I do not believe she meant to say that.

So...Jamie had let it slip; a faux pas, to be sure, but it probably wasn't actionable. Meanwhile, I could see a noticeable frisson developing in her girlfriend's demeanor—tiny glimmers of fear were detectable in Titania's eyes and voice, but she hadn't yet cracked.

She looked away from me. Then, as if suddenly realizing where she was, she led us into the closest open building, through a glass door. Once again, I found myself in the make-up department at Barney's. *Excellent.* I needed lip liner and had more than enough room on credit after returning the Natacha Marros.

"You have no proof," she whispered, as we approached the currently unattended Jo Malone display.

How presumptuous to think I'd make any accusation without the ability to back it up.

She stared at me in horror as I picked up a bottle of Mimosa & Cardamom and sprayed some on my neck. "Actually, that's inaccurate," I said, sotto voce, continuing to spray the cologne the length of my forearm. "*We* do have proof. *Mmmm,* that smells good. Doesn't that smell good?" I said, offering my wrist.

"We?" Her face went blank—an expression I hadn't seen in all the sucking up she did around the office. She appeared to be suffering from incomprehension disorder, and the puzzling thing was, it seemed real. Did she really not know what I was talking about?

"It doesn't matter who *we* are," I said. "We just want to know what it is you want."

The thing about being around actors as long as I have is you learn to spot the real from the fake pretty quickly. In the business of show business, the real and the fake are on display, side by side, all the time. So if Titania was acting, it was an Oscar-worthy performance.

"Please don't tell Jamie," she implored. "I *need* this job."

"Funny you say that, Titania, because I need my job, too, and I'm not going to let you take it from me." Maddie probably would not have recommended that I said that, either. *Too sarcastic; too argumentative.* I put the cologne down.

"You're not going to tell Jamie, are you? Please don't, please—" She was really scared now.

"I don't have to tell her if *you* tell her that sending those pictures was just a joke."

"But I didn't send her any pictures!" she protested. "Can I ask what they were of? I mean, what you were doing in them?"

"It's not important," I said. "Let's do this—I won't say anything to Jamie about your boyfriend and you somehow get her to believe those pictures will never hit the Internet."

"But I don't know… " She took a big gulp of air—a sort of pre-sob. Now she was in Jennifer Lawrence territory with the acting chops. Tears were forming at the corners of her perfectly made up eyes. Hopefully that mascara was waterproof. "I'll do anything; I'll do whatever you say," she begged.

I don't think anyone has ever begged me for anything— maybe an actor begged me to get him an audition for a Christopher Nolan movie once, but nothing like this. I tried to figure out what to do next, scrutinizing Titania until a Barney's fragrance specialist appeared, bearing down on us in pursuit of a sale.

"We're sampling," I said as we moved away from the counter, heading in the general direction of handbags.

Was it possible Titania had *not* been the one who sent the pictures of me purportedly threatening the *Hello Kitty* conventioneers? Leaving aside the question of who, if not Titania, *had* sent them, this smoldering Moldovan with the big dreams whimpering in front of me clearly felt threatened by what I knew about her and sexy Mr. No Clothes. It sounded like she was willing to do anything I asked to prevent my intel from getting leaked to the wrong people—namely Jamie Harris, our mutual boss. Maybe we could make a deal.

I found myself in a situation that was new to me—*I was a blackmailer.* I might get in trouble for this, I thought suddenly. But was it really blackmail? Even if all I was doing was scaring

Titania into thinking I *might* reveal what I knew to Jamie? Even if what I'd be sharing was simply that Titania was not, in fact, gay but had a boyfriend? That's not blackmail—*I don't think.* In any event, I'd made no direct threat.

Instead—*oh my God*—instead, maybe I should be worried that Titania would try to hurt *me!* Really hurt me, I mean, as in physical pain. My brain started racing.

Titania might be part of some Moldovan Mafia, able to put out a hit for less of a reason than the one she had for getting rid of me, which was no less than her livelihood and the MM's access into the Hollywood machine.

But that would be dumb, wouldn't it? Of course it would. After all, I had said *we* had proof of her non-gayness. That meant not just me. So if she had *me* snuffed out, the proof would still exist, along with the threat. Even with me gone, Frank and The Muffia—just as powerful a force as the Moldovan Mafia, for sure—would come down hard on her and her associates. I decided I was safe and turned back.

"We're cool for now," I said. "I'm not going to say anything to Jamie. But I'll remember what you said—about how you'll do whatever I ask. So just remember you said it."

She nodded, regaining some of her characteristically cool demeanor. I smiled and made a beeline for the Armani counter. Lunch hour was fast disappearing, and there was still lip liner to buy and a steak bowl to eat. But as we parted company, a chill ran over me—like I'd stepped from a warm taxi onto a New York City street in January. If Titania was telling the truth about the pictures, then someone else sent them, and I was back to wondering who.

There had to be someone who, up to that point, had remained silent—someone I might not have even met but who would like nothing better than to see me fall.

CHAPTER 22

LATER THAT day, Frank Sexton was sitting on an orange and pink cushion in the reception area at S-Factor waiting for me. I walked out of Studio One after a mind-blowing hour of pole jockeying during which I helicoptered to the sounds of Nicki Minaj's "Out of my Mind" and the classic, "Love is a Battlefield" by Pat Benatar, and there he was, looking so out of place I did a double-take. Twice in one week he'd sought me out—and I was very happy to see him.

It wasn't that his being there was unexpected because his sudden appearance into my life was always unexpected. No, the reason it was odd was that men rarely come into S-Factor, no matter how much they might want to—whether their interest is borne of curiosity or prurience. It's as if they believe that inside the place, women are concocting a witchy brew that is equal parts magical, enticing, and terrifying. They desperately want to partake of what's getting cooked up but they fear it could well be their undoing. Even if a man isn't afraid of a spell overtaking him, he might stay away just because he doesn't want to know how the tricks and treats a woman bestows on a man get to his table. He wants the mystery.

Knowing what little I did of him, Frank probably couldn't care from witches' brews anyway and, glancing out the window, I could see it had been raining, which went a long way toward explaining why he had chosen to wait inside.

K-Love, coming out of the studio behind me, saw Frank and quickly stepped between us. Clearly, she'd recognized him from our encounter a week or so earlier and smelled trouble.

"Can I help you?" she said as he stood. "You don't look like the type who's here for dance class."

"You never know," said Frank, with a smile. "But I'm here to see Ms. Cunningham." *This guy was really growing on me.*

"It's okay," I said, though K-Love looked none too sure.

She raised an eyebrow, curious about what was happening between Frank and me. Then she flipped her hair, like I'd seen her demonstrate countless times in class when she's stickin' it to the pole, and moved back to rejoin my classmates still coming out of the studio.

I turned to Frank and found him looking down at my shoes. Still sporting my pink bling Bordello platforms, I had a couple inches on him, and I don't think he liked it.

"Are those comfortable?" He glanced up and met my gaze.

"Depends on what you do in them, I guess." Sheesh—I hadn't meant to sound so provocative.

In my defense, an empowering ninety minutes on the pole has been known to make a lioness of even the most timid pussy-cat. The whole idea is for a woman to learn how to unleash the creature within when she's in a safe space so that she can do it any time she wants. I was still a work in progress.

Watching his reaction, I realized Frank might actually be a little afraid of me, which took me aback. *That couldn't be why he kept his distance, could it?* I realized it could.

He cleared his throat. "I need to speak to you about a new development in the case." That sounded ominous.

"Can you give me a minute?"

He nodded and turned to the door. "I'll be outside."

"Frank?" I called after him, remembering I hadn't told him

about my conversation with Titania. "I have something to tell you, too."

He nodded and I watched him step outside, where it appeared to have stopped raining.

I took off the Bordellos and put each into its own pink satin bag. I said my goodbyes, assuring K-Love that I could handle the man who'd again shown up unannounced and left.

"How do you dance in those shoes?" Frank asked when I came through the door. A few drops of rain dripped onto my face from the wisteria wound around the archway over our heads.

"Waltzing or tango shoes, they are not. But they're built pretty well for pole dancing shoes. They wouldn't have fallen apart running for a plane, I'll say that much for them." I wiped away the drops, his eyes not leaving my face.

"Is that something you do?"

"The airport?" I remind him. "The pictures? The reason I know you?"

He studied me as though this was not at all relevant then did one of his scans of the area, presumably checking for danger signs.

"See anything?" I asked as we started for the parking lot.

On second thought, he wasn't afraid of me. Instead, I got the feeling he thought I was silly.

"The rain has stopped," he said, announcing the obvious.

"I meant something more significant. This new development, for example." I stopped as my cellphone vibrated. I pulled out the device and looked at the screen. Steven. How long was he going to keep calling me before he got the clue? I dropped the phone back in my purse.

"Can I ask you a question, Frank?"

"You can ask another question, yes."

It took me a second to catch up with his humor. "You can

be a real jokester, can't you?"

He had stopped a few steps beyond me and now came back. "Is that your question? If so, the answer is 'not particularly.' "

Why was it so hard to read him? Never mind, I already knew why, but I still wondered if I could get him to let his guard down. I bet Lauren, Jelicka, or even Sarah could have figured out how to crack his shell. At forty-two, I had the dating experience of your average twenty-year-old.

"How do you always seem to know where I am?" I asked.

"It's my job."

"And that's it?"

"Yes."

Clearly I would not be satisfied. "Okay, so what's the new development? Sorry, that's four questions."

"That's five questions. Do you have any more? I'll answer them."

"Why don't you have a girlfriend?"

This question, though on my mind, just slipped onto my tongue and now it hung out there. But his expression remained unchanged.

"Because I don't."

It made me happy he didn't have a girlfriend, but *sheesh*, I might as well be asking if he had a piece of gum for all the emotion he put into it. He stopped and pulled a pack of Trident from his pocket and offered me a piece.

"No, thanks. Are we going to do this all evening? Oops— another question. How many is that?"

"Seven." He popped a piece of gum into his mouth.

"By the way, I was good at math."

"I know."

"You *know*—?"

He pulled his Don Johnson sunglasses from a pocket and slipped them on. *Cute.*

"I looked it up," he said. "This kind of thing isn't hard to find these days. Pretty much public knowledge."

Taking a deep breath, I willed myself to hold on to the vestiges of what had been a fantastic class. There was no end to the things he might know about me, which hardly seemed fair. If I could look him up, maybe the crush I had on him could be quashed. I took another deep breath and let it out. "You must have found something else, right? Otherwise, why are you here?"

We were standing at the edge of the parking lot where anyone coming or going from the little shopping-cum-office complex where S-Factor and Katsu-ya are located could see us. Frank started across the lot and gestured for me to follow.

"Steven Zucker has been sitting in his vehicle at your apartment building."

It sounded insane. Why would Steven be at my building? "When?" I managed to ask, trying to remain unperturbed by this information.

I was aware of the pulsing male energy pouring out of him—thick and decisive—and I loved it.

"Have you had any contact with him since you and I first met?" he asked.

"No!" I said, denying vehemently the mere idea of such a thing. "I mean, he's left a few messages, and I've tried calling him back a couple of times. But I haven't actually *talked* to him since—well, not since I got back from Japan when we… " *Don't be so explicit, Quinn!* "I haven't seen him since the day after I got back from Japan."

A piece of me wondered if Frank's curiosity was strictly about the case, or if it was something more. Did I dare hope part of his concern might be personal?

"You communicate through texting, leaving messages…that kind of thing?" he asked.

"No!" I said again. "I never really even called him, unless I knew he'd pick up, because he told me not to; same with texts. He said his wife sometimes got hold of his phone and if she saw the texts or calls coming in from blocked numbers, she'd suspect something. So no, I don't—I mean, I *didn't* text or leave messages, though I confess to a few slip-ups."

Frank's body language said he didn't believe me.

"Really," I said, staring into those mirrored lenses. "The only time I ever phoned him was when he gave me a specific time to call. For the most part, it was a one-way street. And lately, we haven't had *any* contact. There's been no need for it because, well, it's over. And I told him that; I told *you* that."

We'd arrived at my car and he faced me over the hood. "Regardless of what you told each other, I saw Steven Zucker parked in front of your building in what appeared to be an agitated state earlier today."

I knew that state. "But why would he be at my building? Why not just call me?"

Frank said nothing.

"Nix that," I said. "He *has* called me, and I haven't picked up."

"Why not?"

"Because… " I let it trail off, hoping he wouldn't push the issue, but that was a stupid idea—like hoping the on ramps to the 405 Freeway would be open.

"Because?" he prompted, doing another scan of the area.

Not wanting to say something stupid and make him think less of me, I opened the door of the Rav4 and got in, Frank taking the passenger seat, just as he had the last time. I didn't want to give him the *because*, which was I didn't completely trust my resolve where Steven was concerned. Admitting that, however, only made me look weak and I wanted to give Frank the best impression. He and I might someday…

Might someday what, Quinn? Did I really think Frank and I were going to ride off into the sunset together? *Come on, you're just attracted to him because you're desperate and hate Internet dating.* He's not your type, remember? And you're probably not his!

In fact, he probably considered me damaged goods, without any sort of moral compass, given that I conducted a two-year relationship with a married man.

I looked through the windshield out toward the western sky, which had turned to blue with refracted hues of orange, yellow, and pink in the gloaming. Glancing over at Frank, I saw his faced tipped to the sky as well, in an expression of wonder. "We live in a beautiful part of the world."

"We do," I agreed, still watching him. I thought maybe I found myself interested in him precisely because he was not my usual type; that type being pretty, slick, and unavailable. Frank was neither pretty nor slick, and that last item—availability— well, I only knew what he told me, but I'd been around him enough to get a sense that he was telling the truth. After a few minutes' hesitation, I figured it was only right I tell him the truth, too.

"The reason I didn't pick up his calls," I began, "is because I didn't want him to charm me back. He's always had this power over me. He no longer does, but I guess that's why. I knew how unhealthy the relationship was, and I couldn't do it any more, his being married and everything. This time I've been completely committed to staying away and I think I can resist anything he tries, but still—I'm a little afraid he won't take no for an answer."

I rolled down the window of the Rav4 to let in some air.

"But this time, you're serious," he said. "That's the difference. This time, you're a woman who knows her mind. And from what I've seen, you seem more than capable of keeping him at a safe distance."

"Thanks for the vote of support." *Maybe he doesn't think I'm just a silly, pole-dancing, glorified babysitter.*

"Besides, I'm here now." He smiled, one side of his mouth tilting up a little higher than the other.

"Frank's here so nothing can happen?" *He was so hard to read.*

Was he saying he was my very own knight in shiny sunglasses?

"Which means, you don't need to worry about him hurting you," said Frank. "He won't get the chance."

I gazed out through the windshield again feeling vulnerable and safe at the same time. Frank wasn't saying Steven didn't want me, nor that he wouldn't try to get me back; he had faith I'd be able to resist him if that happened. He had faith in me. And that meant he cared more for me than he let on—certainly more than he was required to. His job description was only to find out who was sabotaging me, not protect me from horny, insistent ex-lovers.

"That's good to know," I said, playing it cool; I tried to be hopeful but unassuming.

Frank made another survey of the parking lot. It must be habit because seriously, who was he worried might show up?

I suddenly remembered the Moldovan Mob and realized I hadn't told him about my tête à tête with Titania.

"I almost forgot," I said. "I talked to Titania about the pictures."

"Hold that thought."

"Hold that thought?"

"You'll see why in a second."

I didn't argue.

He faced me in the seat. "I want you to arrange a meeting between you and Steven."

This was a bad idea. "I don't know—if he's sitting in a car

outside my building, he might be cracking up or something. You said he seemed agitated."

"I'll follow you home tonight," he said reassuringly, "just in case he's still there. It will be perfectly safe."

I felt the last of dance class slipping away and the tension returning to my neck and jaw. How does one get oneself into these situations? Yes, to live fully requires a certain degree of risk-taking, but I think that the people who say that mean we should all 'go sky diving' or 'try eating frog's legs,' not 'have an adulterous relationship with a guy who's going insane.' "

"I don't see the point," I protested.

"After completing the investigation into Ms. Cibulkova, I have determined that though she is lying about her sexuality, there appears to be no connection between her and the pictures sent to Ms. Harris. My suspicion is that your situation at work involves Steven in some way."

"Steven sent those pictures?" *That seemed ridiculous.* On the other hand, it was true that Titania had seemed honestly stunned by my accusation that it was she who sent them, claiming not to know anything about it.

"You were going to say something about Ms. Cibulkova?" he asked.

"Yes, I was going to but—" This new suspicion of Frank's had me reeling. "Okay, let's say you're right and Titania wasn't the one who sent the pictures. That doesn't mean Steven would feel so jilted, he'd send them hoping I'd get fired. Besides, the pictures were sent before our last... " *Ugh—had to be honest.* "Before we got together for the last time."

Reaching for my bag, I pulled out my phone, which must have vibrated four times since I'd last checked it because there were four texts from Steven—all various permutations of: "I need to talk to you as soon as possible." The texts filled the screen.

"Well, something's up." I showed Frank the screen. "Think I should I call him back?"

Frank nodded. "Yes."

"What am I going to say?"

He checked the mirrors and scanned again. He must be on some sort of internal timer. I was beginning to find it very comforting.

"Tell him you got his messages, and ask him what he wants to talk about. If he says he needs to meet, tell him you're on your way home."

Preparing to make the call, I first scrolled down through Steven's texts to those below his. *Sheesh,* you look away for a few minutes, and suddenly there are more texts and emails than you can deal with. I inhaled sharply. There was a one from Kiki:

> Calling all Muffs! The neighbors are shooting! Get here asap.

"I'll call Steven, but we or I have to stop somewhere first."

"Not advisable," Frank said.

"I have to. I promised. But it won't take long."

Frank shook his head. "Tomorrow *is* the day you have to explain the photographs to your boss, isn't it? That doesn't leave much time."

He was right, but Muffs didn't let Muffs down, and I thought there was a way to do both.

"I told a friend I'd help her with something, and we didn't know when it was going to happen. Turns out it's now. She needs me—us if you care to come along." I pivoted the face of the phone toward him so he could read Kiki's text. "You'd probably enjoy it." I smiled.

"Is this one of the women from the shooting range?"

"No, but they'll be there, too."

"Then they can take care of it."

"It's not going to be a shoot out!"

He sighed. "I only meant your friends seem quite competent."

That they were. And Kiki would understand if I didn't show, but I'd given my word. "Look, it's on the way. Really—half an hour." I held up my phone. "I'll call Steven and arrange for a meeting after."

"Okay, let's go," he said, opening the door to the Rav4.

"Having you there will give us legitimacy," I said, connecting my headset. "We're going to bust an illegal porn ring shooting a movie."

His eyebrows shot up. Apparently 'porn' and 'ring' were the magic words. "Well, then…I'll follow you."

My index finger was poised to call Steven as I watched Frank get into his nondescript dark blue sedan. I didn't want a confrontation with Steven, and I might have avoided what was now going down had I just listened to Maddie. She'd suggested Steven might be involved that day at Babalu—an idea I'd obviously dismissed. I just couldn't get past the idea that Steven would go to all that trouble to get me fired. Well, we were going to find out. Putting my car in gear, the phone was ringing as I drove out of the lot with Frank on my tail.

CHAPTER 23

THOUGH KIKI had prayed and asked the Lord to shut down the unholy house next door, the prayers hadn't worked. But she was not the type to wait for divine intervention. Determining the Lord helped those who helped themselves, she decided to take matters into her own hands.

For three days, she watched as the neighbors loaded in equipment and put up light poles in the backyard in preparation for filming. She'd also seen several large-breasted women going in and out of the house. For three nights in a row, she had the Muffs on standby—ready to go over there and do whatever we could in the way of moral support, physical presence, and evidence gathering. Now, according to Kiki, the shoot was about to begin, and tonight we were going to shut them down.

When I pulled up with Frank right behind me, it was clear that things were already happening. There was no place to park, for one thing, and if you didn't look closely, you might just think someone was having a party. But the windows on the first floor were blacked out, and the second floor was lit up throughout. We got out of our cars and headed toward Kiki's. As we walked to the door, I filled Frank in on as much as I knew.

Kiki had been expecting *me*, not me and some guy she didn't know. But at this point, she'd take all the help she could get, and Frank certainly looked official, which I knew would be a plus.

We knocked on the front door and were let in by Rachel, who was drinking a Pellegrino and dressed like Jenna Jamison.

"Whoa, Rachel," I said. "Talk about a career opportunity. You are sizzling."

"Just playin' my part, babe," she said. "You know me—it's all in the packaging."

I introduced Frank, who was nonplussed by the hot babe, and the three of us made our way to where Vicki was busy getting her video gear ready. Kiki emerged from within, also dressed provocatively in a low-cut black bodysuit, wearing too much make up, and a "big hair" wig on her head. Saul appeared with a cheese and veggie platter and said he'd dropped Troy off at a friend's house for the duration. There were more introductions. Maddie arrived, followed by Jelicka—both of them dressed for the occasion in matching animal print outfits designed to show off their shapes.

Each of the Muffs gave Frank an appraising stare. I knew they were trying to reconcile what he looked like with the fact that he wasn't my type. I was able to pull Maddie aside and explain that he was the private investigator I'd told them about and *that's all.* I worried that one of the Muffs might recognize him from Shooter's Paradise—particularly Maddie, since I'd pointed out his disappearing form as he walked out of the shooting range. But no one said anything, so consumed were all of us with the mission at hand: *Shut down the porn palace.*

Frank leaned in and said to me, sotto voce, "We can't spend a lot of time here if we're going to take care of the Steven problem."

"He said he'd be at my place in an hour. That should be plenty of time to do what we need to do here," I told him.

From Kiki's yard, we could see a number of light stands with 10K's mounted and shining into what must have been a second floor bedroom. In the eerie spill of illumination, the cement giraffe looked like a long-necked peeping Tom.

"So catch me up, here," said Frank, addressing Kiki. "You're doing this because the city hasn't been responsive?"

"I've called the city fifty times…"

"Useless," Jelicka interjected.

"They finally came out but said they found no proof of a business," Saul said with disgust.

"It was like, *come on*," said Kiki. "There are 45 cars parked up and down the street every day belonging to the employees, and the lame-o supervisor tells us 'the owner was having some friends over.' "

"Waste of space," said Jelicka.

"Exactly. Our tax dollars hard at work," Kiki agreed.

"But now that they're actually shooting over there without a permit and us getting proof, we should be able to nail 'em," said Maddie.

"What do we do if they're just kinky perverts shooting themselves?" Rachel bit down hard on a carrot.

"The worst that could happen is it'll be embarrassing for everyone," said Saul. "But I think we can all see they're not just living in that house. They're doing something they shouldn't be."

"It's the zoning," clarified Maddie unnecessarily.

"They could even be involved in sex trafficking," Rachel said, riled up. "I can't wait to get the Scumbags—"

"The key is catching them in the act—cameras out and naked bodies with the cameras rolling. We get that kind of proof, we're good. And us saying on camera the location and all that."

"Camera's ready," said Vicki. "All the footage will be time stamped, and there's even a GPS feature to stamp the longitude and latitude where the footage was shot."

"The plan," said Kiki, "is for Rachel to get inside first. Whoever's on the door is probably not a key player on their team.

He'll think she's part of the shoot and let her in."

"Do you have a 'B' Plan?" Frank asked.

"Don't worry, I'll get in," said Rachel with enough confidence he didn't ask anything more. "I'll open that door—there—along the side of the house." She pointed to a spot on the other side of the eight-foot cement wall, "and let you all in."

"Vicki's the main shooter, but if you get to the room first, everybody start shooting using your phones or whatever," instructed Kiki.

"We ready?" I said, trying to move it along.

Jelicka and Maddie both gave the thumbs up sign.

"All in," said Rachel defiantly. "Smash the subjugators."

Saul looked at his watch. "Police response times in this neighborhood are on average eight minutes." He pulled out his phone and dialed.

Kiki said, "Let's go," and we were off.

Frank threw me a look and addressed everyone. "Are you concerned that these people might be armed?"

The Muffs stopped, quickly assessing this possibility, but determined we would appear to be "non-threatening" females worthy of being in a porn film and thus dismissed the idea as so much unnecessary worry.

"On the other hand, *he* could throw things off." Jelicka gestured toward Frank. "No offense. But this was supposed to be the bumbling bimbo posse, not the kind of thing that makes a man draw a weapon. But if he's with us that could cause problems."

"I'll stay out of sight. Consider me back up."

"Me too," said Saul, seemingly on hold with 9-1-1.

If what I'd previously observed about Frank was any indication, and had this been his case, he would have shut them down already. So I gave him a lot of credit for letting us do our thing. Saul, on the other hand, was a mild-mannered tax attorney, hardly the take-no-prisoners type. He seemed quite content and proud to let Kiki take charge as he began explaining to the 9-1-1 operator what was happening.

"Can I talk to you?—later of course," Jelicka said to Frank as the group headed toward Kiki's front door. "I'm curious what it's like being a P.I. Quinn was supposed to ask you, so I hope this isn't coming out of nowhere."

"Be happy to," said Frank. "Maybe next week."

Rachel hesitated before opening the door to put on enough lip gloss that we could see ourselves reflected in her lips. Suitably reflective, she left the house with a purse over her shoulder. Saul followed close behind, still on the phone, with the family Labrador retriever, Otis, on a leash. He would be within sight of the neighbors' front door when Rachel rang the bell. The rest of us waited, counting off the time.

Two minutes later, Saul's text hit Kiki's phone and she read it out: "She's in. Police on the way."

Maddie, Jelicka, Kiki, and I went to the side door of the neighbors' house, while Frank positioned himself near the back door. As soon as the neighbors realized what was happening, they'd try to flee, and Frank would be there to hold them until the cops came. Meanwhile, Saul, with dog and camera, staked out the front and would direct the police as soon as they arrived.

Minutes ticked by. Suddenly, the side door opened and Rachel was there, whispering to us and pointing in the direction she wanted us to go. Vicki was already shooting as Kiki ran ahead. This was not part of the plan. Outside, a dog started barking. Was it Otis? Just then I heard Kiki yelling at somebody and screaming up ahead of us, inside the house. *What was she doing?!*

"Why did she run ahead?" said Maddie. "Hurry up, Vicki, or they'll have their clothes back on by the time we find them."

Vicki momentarily turned off her camera so she could move faster. Hopefully, Kiki had the presence of mind to shoot what was happening. *Unlikely, or she wouldn't have abandoned the plan and run ahead.*

My phone buzzed. It was a text from Frank:

The police are here. Time to leave.

That was fast. "The police have arrived," I reported to the others in a loud whisper.

We headed toward the foyer and the stairs, each of us with our phones out, hoping to capture some incriminating footage. The group of us was on the first landing when the front door opened, and male voices could be heard in the foyer. As we reached the top of the stairs, we inched our way down the hall toward the voices. Kiki sounded out of control. Rachel and I looked at each other. *What was Kiki thinking?*

Not more than a few feet from the door behind which people were yelling, the door burst open. A man and woman, robes hastily wrapped around their obvious nakedness, bolted out and collided with Maddie, while I got the whole thing on my phone. These two were followed by one of Kiki's neighbors, a short swarthy man we'd seen in the backyard—the "director," most likely. Then we saw Kiki emerge from the room.

"I got it all on digital recorder. You are bad, bad people, and I can prove it!" she yelled after their disappearing bodies.

She got it!

"Why'd you run ahead?" said Rachel. "You might have wrecked everything."

"Sorry, I got excited."

"Where are they going?" said Jelicka, concerned, as we watched the three porn makers hastily run in a direction away from the stairs.

"There's another stairwell," said Kiki. "But Frank's outside, right?" She called to the cops who were coming up the front staircase. "They're fleeing out the back. Quick!"

Two of the cops reversed course, while the third, the most senior among the uniformed officers with short-cropped gray hair, escorted us down the front stairs.

"You ladies mind telling me what's happening here?"

"Don't jump to conclusions, Officer," said Kiki. "And FYI, we have a lawyer here."

Maddie turned to me again and mouthed a silent, "Whaaaaat?"

Moments later, Frank and the two other officers came into the living room, where we'd gathered, surrounded by unused pieces of film equipment. Saul came in through the front door with Otis.

"If anyone else is up there, I suggest you come down now," Senior Cop called out. Almost instantly, a door opened, and two more presumed crewmembers came walking down the stairs with their hands up.

"All right, who's going to tell me what all this is about?" said Senior, looking from Frank to Saul, completely leaving out the Muffs.

"They broke into my house," said the swarthy man.

"Oh, come on, your people let us in," said Kiki.

"Hold on a second," said Senior whose badge said Holt.

"My wife can tell you." Saul gestured to Kiki.

"I don't think she wants to."

"Look," said Kiki. "We have been trying to get the attention of the city for months about the illegal businesses being operated out of this house, and the city has done nothing, so we decided to prove it ourselves."

Kiki continued to explain as Frank sidled up to me. "Our work is done. We need to slip out and leave your friends to answer questions."

"Won't the cops notice?"

"I identified myself outside. They'll be in touch if they need us."

Nice to be part of the brethren, I thought. But then, the Muffs have a pretty tight bond, too. I caught Maddie's eye and she nodded she understood.

"Let's go."

CHAPTER 24

"IT'S GOOD to see you," said Steven, his lips quivering, his eyes searching. "How I've missed you, Quinn."

It was nice seeing him, too, but there was not going to be any romance novel-type make-up sex, and I knew better than to encourage him in any way, shape, or form.

"Why did you need to see me so badly?" I said, cool as the overcranked AC at the Peninsula Hotel.

"I had to talk to you, babe. You weren't returning my calls." He was really edgy, like he was on something maybe. His clothes— usually so carefully chosen and well kept—appeared slept in, and his hair was a disaster, far beyond its usual deliberate level of dishevelment.

"You told me never to call you," I said, avoiding his eyes. "Besides, I didn't think there was anything more to say."

He picked up *When Will There Be Good News?* from the table next to the front door. "Book club?"

I nodded.

"When *will* there be good news?" he said. "I'd like to know the answer to that question myself." He licked his lips.

"Steven—sorry, but can you get on with it?"

He put the book down. "There's something I've just found out and it involves you." He walked to the window and peered between the slats of the shutters.

"Why are you acting like you were followed?" I asked.

"Claudia," he said. Claudia was his wife.

"Claudia? You think Claudia followed you?"

"I'm looking around because she might have *had* me followed."

"Either way, it strikes me that if you are being followed, one of the last places you should be is at my apartment."

Oh, yeah, I forgot to say—we were in my apartment. But this time, I knew my resolve would remain strong because Frank Sexton was also inside, hidden, listening to everything that was being said. Watching Steven in his "agitated" state—as Frank put it—and learning about Claudia, I now knew why he'd been sitting in his car in front of my apartment; she had kicked him out.

"I had to risk it. I needed to see you, even if it meant coming here." His eyes softened, his voice cooed. It had always worked before, so he must have thought *why mess with success?* But studying him now, I found, to my great relief, that I was no longer attracted to this man who'd been my illicit lover for far too long.

"Steven, don't flirt with me. We're done."

"I know; I know we are but… "

He looked ready to cry, and I wondered what Frank was thinking listening to us.

"You said you had something to tell me, and we shouldn't be in a public place."

"Quinn, please—"

"So were you thinking you'd get me up here and we'd have sex and be back to how it was at the beginning? The only beginning you can go back to is the first page of a book."

I sounded quite convincing, I thought.

He made a step toward me, and I could tell he wanted to sweep me up and make promises. I recognized that particular grand gesture.

"Something's changed. It could mean a whole new beginning for us." His tone was obsequious—no other way to describe it.

The thing I wanted, above all else, when we were "together" was for us to be a legitimate couple. And the only way that could happen would be if something else occurred first. A divorce from Claudia was what he had promised me early on in our relationship. He said it was inevitable—that he and Claudia were incompatible; that there was no love between them anymore and that they never had sex; that she was smothering the kids, and that he felt his sole purpose as a husband was to supply the funds to continue the family's upward progression on the socio-economic ladder. In short, his reasons for wanting a divorce could be described as the stereotypical litany of complaints that drive a married man to cheat. But when he and I were new, those reasons hadn't sounded so stereotypical; I'd wanted to rescue him. *Silly me.*

For two years I'd been hoping he would tell me they had filed the paperwork, the custody of the children amicably decided, and the divorce imminent. For *two years* I had asked him, no pleaded with him, to tell me when, and he had promised me, "soon." But there had, of course, always been some reason that "now was not the right time."

It was, therefore, a relief to *not* feel the quickening of my heart; nor the hope that he would tell me the divorce was official. In fact, at that moment, I found myself hoping that the change he was referring to was *not* an impending divorce.

"You're splitting up?" My voice sounded as hollow as I felt.

"It's inevitable, I think. Claudia's gone off the deep end. Probably delayed post-traumatic stress after Kyle was born."

"Kyle… your son?" *He had to be kidding.* "That was five years ago!"

He glanced down. He must think I'm even stupider than I thought he thought I was.

"Well, we don't really know why," he said. "But she's been acting erratically, and that's why, well one reason I'm here. God, it's good to see you, Quinn."

"Will you please get to the point?"

Frank would probably prefer that Steven get to the point as well. He was probably crouching in the kitchen or the closet—uncomfortable, waiting, and listening in case his services were needed. I wasn't sure where he was hiding because I'd given him my key to go in first. I let myself in with the spare.

"It was Claudia who sent those photographs to your boss," said Steven.

"Wait. Claudia?! That doesn't make sense."

"Not everything makes sense, Quinn."

"And you let it happen?" My mind tried to twist into a scenario where this was any kind of reasonable.

"I just found out," he protested.

"That can't be true."

"She's been having you and me followed…for months."

"Months?"

"Yes, preparing her case."

"A case for what?" The only thing I could think of was that Claudia was after sole custody of the kids. He didn't answer me but instead moved closer.

"You just came from pole dancing, didn't you? I can tell by the way your face is flushed."

"Wait, you can't just drop the subject. What case is Claudia supposedly preparing?"

"Will you put on those pink shoes I like and dance for me?" The distance between us had narrowed considerably. "You know, you've never danced for me, Quinn."

"Steven, we are done."

His voice dropped another five notes. "I've heard that before." It was so low and resonant it was like his voice box had moved to his groin.

I backed up, which was as close to a dance move as he was going to get. "Stay there."

"You look so lovely, Quinn." Suddenly, his hands were on me, my arms captured between them.

"You need to go, Steven. Steven—!"

And in a flash, Frank was on him, leaping from behind the couch and pulling Steven off, tossing him on the floor. So skilled a tosser-offer was Frank that not a single piece of furniture was touched on Steven's fall.

"Was that necessary?" Steven asked, rubbing his temple as he sat up. "You might have told me you had someone here."

"Shut up," said Frank. "The lady said she was done with you and you weren't listening. You deserve more than you got."

"Is this your new boyfriend?" Steven asked, dismissively. "Kind of rough around the edges."

Steven was the one being coarse.

OK, so…I liked Frank stepping in to defend my honor. Nothing like that had ever happened to me; it was the stuff of the movies I had a peripheral hand in making but was never in. But I wanted Frank to know that as much as I appreciated his putting Steven down, I was the one with a greater reason to do so.

I slapped Steven's face as hard as I could.

"Owww! Why'd you do that?"

"Because," I said, feeling empowered, "he's right. You weren't listening to me, Steven. That's for all the women out there who don't get listened to."

Steven's hand shifted from his head to his cheek, and I was tempted to slap him on the other cheek but restrained myself.

"Sit down, *Steve*," Frank demanded, indicating the chair he'd fetched from the dining area. "Tell us about your wife having you and Ms. Cunningham followed."

Steven babbled on and on, but the upshot was Claudia had known Steven was, if not unhappy, certainly discontented. When he stopped soliciting sex, she'd suspected there was another woman and finally hired an investigator to follow him to me; and from there, follow me wherever I went. The P.I. was also tasked with getting pictures of Steven and me *in flagrante*, as well as any she might use to humiliate Steven or me separately. For example—she was hoping to hurt Steven by proving I was a poly-amorous slut, but that hadn't happened (not that I hadn't tried for something with Viggo). All the investigator was able to get was a picture of a crazed-looking me with the *Hello Kitty* conventioneers at the Narita Airport. Apparently, Claudia had been charging the P.I.'s services using her Visa card, and one day Steven, going over the bills, spotted several unexplained charges. When confronted, she at first denied everything. She finally came clean, but not before sending the pictures to Jamie Harris at Talent Partners, whose email address is public knowledge.

Claudia had all the evidence she needed to establish the affair that her husband and I were having, but that wasn't enough. She wanted to take me down and thought if my character were ma-ligned and I got fired, Steven would find me uninteresting and ultimately dump me. If he was as shallow as he now appeared, she was probably right. My fall from grace might also serve as a warning to any other would-be mistresses that her husband might take up with.

And the P.I. she'd hired to tail me? It was *Yankees*, of course; aka Freckles, the man at the Narita airport who helped me after I fell and to whom I, regretfully, spoke so harshly to. No wonder he had it in for me, too.

All this meant that Titania was telling the truth when she said she hadn't sent Jamie any pictures of me, though she still could have been lying about not having seen them. I was pretty sure that as Jamie's lover and assistant, she'd seen them in the process of screening Jamie's emails. In any event, Titania really didn't matter now. At this point, I should be able to assuage Jamie's concerns that I was not going to embarrass the agency. We just had to make sure that Steven would now do the right thing by Claudia and me.

"So that's what you're going to do, Steve," said Frank, deliberately leaving off the "n."

"You're not a judge," said Steven, acting like a brat. "You're not even a cop."

"Yeah, but he was with the Navy Seals that took down Bin Laden," I said.

Steven shot a look to Frank, a fearful respect there all of a sudden. I had no idea if Frank had been in Seal Team Six. But it seemed like he could have been, and saying it had the desired effect.

"I'll take care of it," Steven said, defeated.

"Go back to Claudia," I said. "She obviously loves you enough to fight for you."

Steven looked none too sure about that.

I felt bad even though there was no reason to anymore. I'd made a mistake and was now trying to fix it. It's not like I was the first woman to have made this particular error. And falling in love with a married man wouldn't get me pounded with rocks unless I was a Muslim woman living in rural Turkey.

Steven rose to leave, and it was all feeling sort of final.

"She has your word you'll make sure there's no trace of the photographs?" Frank asked.

"Yes." Steven looked at me. "I'll make sure. What would be the point now?"

As he walked out the door, I felt a twinge of sadness, but that's all it was. No breakup is ever "all good," and saying it belittles what was there.

"It wasn't Team Six," Frank said after Steven had gone. "It was Team Twelve. We were nowhere near Bin Laden's compound. What gave it away?"

"From the first day I met you, you struck me as one of those really capable, no-bullshit types. But it was just a guess."

"Don't tell me," he said. "You recognized the character from the movies." There was an almost imperceptible smile on his face, but I couldn't tell if he was teasing me.

"You know," I said, smiling, "movie characters are often based on *real* people. They're just 'embellished,' with timelines speeded up for full effect. But I'm sure if someone were to put Frank Sexton in a screenplay, no embellishment would be needed."

Except, of course, if a screenwriter were writing the script for Frank and me, he'd need to add the scene that hadn't happened—the one where the handsome private detective and the woman he's protecting make crazy, undeniable love in the midst of playing a dangerous cat and mouse game involving international forces of evil wielding the technology sector's most advanced weaponry. *The guy's right, Quinn; your life is not a Tom Cruise/Matt Damon/Dwayne Johnson/Jason Stratham movie. But oh, how I wanted it to be.*

What I really wanted was for Frank to take me in his arms and hold me; the holding would hopefully develop into more active movements. He liked me, I could tell for sure now, but that didn't mean he felt romantic toward me. Slugging Steven had been within the purview of any decent man seeing another guy abuse a woman, let alone Frank Sexton, P.I., who was supposed to be watching out for me. Any man worth anything would have done the same thing in his situation, so I shouldn't interpret his chivalry as any sort of testament to how he felt.

On the other hand, I didn't feel him pushing me away. And I wasn't making it up when I'd caught him watching me a few times when he thought I wasn't looking—like at Kiki's house.

Maybe there was some rule or protocol in his company against having sex with your clients. But hell, that rule gets broken all the time, doesn't it? What about *Klute?* Or *Someone To Watch Over Me?* There I go with the movies again, but it can't be said enough: *Movies are sometimes based on real life!* Clearly, life and art had merged dangerously in my head.

"My life wouldn't make much of a movie," he said, his hand reaching into his pants pocket and coming out with his phone, which he flipped open.

Was he just being modest? Or did he really think himself uninteresting? Either way, his humility seemed refreshing after all the male bravado I'd been exposed to in my own line of work.

He snapped his phone closed. "I'll check with the office to-morrow, but I expect your case will be closed—unless there's something else that needs to be done."

There *was* something that needed to be done, starting with him planting a kiss on my lips. I hadn't even thought about the case being over. *Oh no*—if there was nothing else for him to investigate, that meant I might never see him again, and I didn't want that. I don't *think* it was just that he made me feel safe— even though he was paid to do so. I don't *think* it was because I didn't know anyone else like him who does what he does and did what he did. I think it was all that and more. Even his clean-cut appearance had grown on me—his traditional off-the-rack Brooks Brothers clothes and the throwback sunglasses he wore. I liked his quirky sense of humor and his way of catching me off guard.

If anything was going to happen between Frank and me, it

was clear I would have to make the first move. Just as I'd realized when I was deleting winkers and other bottom feeders sent by *NowLove*: The good guys take more work. As much as I wanted him to pursue me, Frank was the kind of guy who needed a signal.

"If they close the case, does that mean we won't see each other again?" *If he doesn't get that this is something I didn't want to have happen, I'll need to get a hammer.*

"I don't think there'd be a reason to, unless you intend to file a complaint about me." He smiled so enigmatically I couldn't read a deeper meaning.

"No complaints here," I said, while sending major vibes for him to jump my bones. *Sheesh, how blatant did the move need to be?*

"Not even when you were losing your mind because it took me so long to get back to you?" He was smirking. *What did that mean?*

"Oh, that, well… " I drifted off, frustrated that he was either not picking up on or ignoring my subtext. *How quickly new concerns obliterate the previous ones.*

I had to think of another reason for us to see each other. I considered asking if he wanted to have lunch sometime—maybe meet me at Katsu-ya for old time's sake. I could simply tell him I wanted to see him again, but that seemed too direct. How far was I supposed to go with this signaling business? I felt as though I'd already told him I liked him in several different ways, and he'd chosen to ignore me. How much more could I lay myself out there before I appeared desperate? *Screw it,* I'll just be obvious.

"So what will you do now, Frank? Get assigned to another damsel in distress?"

"This was kind of a unique situation." He shook his head. "It'll probably be another corporate espionage case—theft of trade secrets, that kind of thing. I don't generally do damsels."

"Too bad for the damsels." *Could I get any clearer?* "This one liked having you around."

He knew what I meant now and held my gaze. I could see his brain working as he figured out what to say next. *Please, please don't make it be about the weather.* I stood close to him in my stocking feet, he in his basic brown loafers. And he was just a teensy bit taller than me—*perfect.*

His mouth opened and closed just as quickly. It felt like he was going to move in to kiss me. I know I didn't make that up. But he didn't, and that enigmatic expression of his returned. He glanced at the table where my book lay. Safer territory.

"When Will There Be Good News? Is it good?"

"Excellent."

Picking up the book, he opened it, perusing the dust jacket. "I read a lot—pretty much anything."

"If you like police procedurals, you'd like it—even though it's written by a woman, if that matters to you."

"It doesn't. I'll put in an order." *Right answer.* He put it down. "Well, good night, Quinn."

A slight wave of embarrassment washed over me even though I felt like he'd been tempted; I could even see it. But he hadn't accepted my invitation. A guy like Frank wasn't about to get involved with somebody like me—a shallow, Hollywood type with a history of adultery. No, he was too high-minded, I concluded. He just nodded, opened the front door, and was gone.

I stood with my back against the door for several long seconds, playing the events of the last couple of weeks over in my head, and wondering if there might have been anything else I could have said or done. But short of throwing myself at him physically, I decided there hadn't been.

Flipping off the light in the entry, I headed for the bedroom ready to call it a night. I took a sharp inhale realizing when he'd said good night, he'd called me Quinn.

CHAPTER 25

WITH THE mystery of who sent the photographs solved, I knocked on Jamie's open door the next day to tell her.

"Come in."

She barely looked up from what appeared to be frenzied note taking. It was immediately clear that something was off. She was not her typically put-together self—her hair not so coiffed, her outfit not so pressed. At 10 a.m., with very little of the day gone, it was unusual for her to have a hair out of place.

"What is it?" She was also in a snitty mood.

"I'll be brief." I stepped closer to her desk so as to avoid being overheard. "I came to tell you that the pictures were sent by the wife of an ex-lover of mine—that's another story and this isn't the time. But essentially, she had both her husband and me followed by a private investigator with instructions to take any pictures she could use as evidence or to shame us. They have money, so following me to Japan was apparently not a problem. Anyway, when I fell running for the plane, the guy tailing me saw an opportunity to get some of those embarrassing pictures and when the wife saw them, she decided to send them to you to make my life hell."

"I see." Jamie continued making random marks on her note pad. *Was she doodling? It didn't look like work.* "I hope the investigator hit her with a big bill for sushi expense."

"Excuse me?"

"It was a joke, Quinn. I don't condone adultery, but there are limits to what is acceptable behavior on the part of the wronged spouse. Sounds like she crossed it."

Maybe I'm off the hook. "Thank you," I said, suddenly remembering there was more I needed to fix. "The pictures have been deleted from the wife's phone and computer, and the private investigator is no longer in the employ of the wife. So other than the investigator who was told to destroy them, you are the only person with those pictures."

Jamie nodded her head, appearing to ponder the possibilities. "What about the marriage?"

"No idea," I said flatly. "It could go either way, but I want you to know I don't feel good about the affair and if I could go back, I would never have started it."

Jamie was definitely doodling. I could see a little face on the pad—was it frowning? She was giving me nothing, and I realized I'd better point out what was, to me, obvious, just to make sure she fully understood.

"If you're wondering whether those pictures might still make an appearance on the Internet, the answer is 'no'—that is, unless *you* decide to put them there."

She glanced up.

"Not that you'd do that," I said quickly. "Only that I don't believe there's anyone else who has access to them, so Talent Partners will be spared any backlash." I finished with a flourish, hoping to hear something from Jamie about how the matter was now well behind us, and we can forge ahead into many new celebrity commercial ventures—maybe even *Hello Kitty*!

She pursed her lips and made an effort to smooth her hair. "Could you please close the door, Quinn?"

Suddenly, it seemed she had nothing but time for me, but

something was lurking behind her eyes. If I didn't know better, I'd say it was pain.

"Sure." I quietly pressed the door shut, hearing the latch catch.

"How did you find out about all this?" she asked.

I considered the downside of telling her. Could I have figured everything out on my own? Sure, eventually. Would I be satisfied the pictures were destroyed just because Steven said they were? No. Having Frank had made all the difference. *Frank.*

"I had someone helping me."

"Another investigator?"

"Yes, a friend's husband's company let me borrow him." I figured that much couldn't hurt.

"I see," she said, deep in thought.

I waited for more, but she just kept doodling.

"Can I ask 'why' you asked if someone helped me?"

She looked up. "I was just wondering what else your private investigator might have found out."

"What do you mean?" I knew what she meant, but I sure as hell wasn't going to volunteer anything.

"It's no secret that you and… " She hesitated. "You and Titania don't like each other."

"I don't mind her, really. She's just so… " I was trying to form the word *perfect*, because that's what Jamie had called her, but my lips wouldn't obey.

"Not really," Jamie snapped, reading my mind. "What I'm asking is, in the course of the investigation, did your private investigator follow Titania at any point? Did he try to find out if she might have been the one who was behind the pictures? And don't deny you suspected her. I ask because that would have been—if I were you, that is—*she* would have been my first choice for who would have sent those pictures."

As demonstrated by her halting language, Jamie was

uncomfortable discussing any of this—at least with me.

"Oh, well, sure," I said. "I mean—yeah, I did. That is—I did think she might, you know, have thought—or wanted to get me fired. But there seemed so many other people... "

I wasn't doing much better.

"And? Did he follow her?"

Clearly, all was no longer blissful with the happy couple. Jamie was desperate for information. *I* knew that Titania wasn't gay, of course, but it was now clear that Jamie had also begun to think something was amiss with her perfect princess. But did she suspect another woman of stealing her beloved's affections, or did she know Titania liked cock?

"He *did* follow her, didn't he?" Jamie shot back before I could respond to the first question. "What did he find out?"

"He knew pretty early on that she didn't send the pictures." Hopefully, that would be enough to satisfy her curiosity.

"You're not telling me something, I can see it. What else?"

Ugh. Is it right to tell your boss what she doesn't really want to know, even though she's begging for it? *It's a no win; lose big or go home.*

"Titania has a boyfriend," I said.

She stared at me.

"You wanted to know what he found out, and that's what he found out. Titania has a boyfriend."

She continued to stare.

"Frank—the investigator—got the guy's name but... "

"This is *such* a violation... "

This was the Jamie I knew, her rage boiling up.

"I know; not ethical at all," I said. "Pretending to be lesbian."

"The audacity."

"Incredible."

"The nerve."

"A...*dick*? It's disgusting."

I didn't know what to say.

"Get out!" Enraged, her face the shade of Chanel's Pink Posey, she began moving toward me. *Shit.*

"I'm sorry you found out, Jamie," I said, backing away. "You wanted to know and you're my boss. What was I supposed to…?"

"Get out now!"

Was I fired? I ventured a tentative, "Permanently?"

She stopped, processing what I just asked.

"What? No, just get out of my office. And don't say anything about this to anybody." Her hand reached for the doorknob and stopped, adjusting her manner. "Thank you, Quinn." Then she flung the door open, and I scooted through the opening, mumbling lame apologies for upsetting her. There was a small gust of wind behind me as the force of the closing door was accompanied by a *thwunk* that probably was heard in Chinatown.

There, staring at me, were the faces of my concerned colleagues, all of whom also answered to the temporarily (we hoped) unhinged Jamie Harris—to wit, Carolyn, Rafe, soon-to-be exassistant Titania, and Sameer, who remained seated, gazing at me with worried eyes, head waggling.

"She just needs a minute," I said. "A deal went bad, and she needs to figure out how she's going to handle it."

As I said this, I made the effort not to look directly at Titania while, at the same time, trying not to completely avoid her. Instead, I allowed my eyes to meet each of those listening—*yes, acknowledge them and move on*—exactly like I'd learned at Toastmasters during college.

"Shit, not the Beyonce PSA against body mutilation," said Carolyn with concern.

"No, I think that's still a 'Go.'"

"Not the Alex Rodriguez/Brian Williams 'Tell the Truth' project," said Sameer.

"No."

"Then what is it?" asked Titania.

Now I *had* to look at her. *Did she know?* Maybe she could see it in my face. Warning her was an option—one I considered for about two seconds. It was two seconds too long.

The door to Jamie's office opened and there she stood, restored to full power with a smile on her face. Her skin was no longer that deep shade of emotional-looking pink, but was back to its usual Bobbi Brown Perfect Neutral and her hair had been brushed into place. Clearly, she was making an effort to seem her normal self.

Back when Jamie had first confronted me with the pictures, I was so angry with Titania, I'd imagined something like this happening. Dreams of schadenfreude had me hoping Jamie's takedown of the Moldovan would go according to this script but, now that it was happening, it didn't feel sweet at all. I just felt bad for the girl. I was also a little thrown because I thought Jamie at least possessed the wherewithal to keep it together until the end of the day, at which point she could ream the little Twitiot in private.

"Hello, everyone," she said, surveying the floor. "You're all hard at work, I see."

It was obvious none of us was working—let alone with any diligence. But each of us got the message and turned our faces to what was on our desks. Our mental focus, however, was still fixed on what we suspected was about to become a raging storm.

"Good." There was a long pause while she surveyed us all. "Titania, could you come in here, please?"

I felt Titania's stare, daggers for eyes, as she crossed to Jamie's office. I did feel guilty, but Jamie would have found out about her eventually, I reasoned. In fact, if Jamie's demeanor was any indication, she'd already known something was amiss when I arrived that morning, possibly even suspected that Titania had a boyfriend.

Had I promised Titania I wouldn't tell? No. Did I owe her some allegiance? Not really. If I owed anybody, it was Jamie, whom I had known far longer. And she was my boss. It was a pretty clear-cut situation, far easier than trying to decide whether you should tell your best friend that her husband is screwing around. But did I feel good about getting Titania fired? Not a bit.

As Titania went into Jamie's office and closed the door behind her, I caught Sameer's eye and shrugged, hoping to convey that I had no idea what was about to happen in there. Besides, no one else at the company needed to know.

Life is tough then you die, whether you're born dirt poor in Islamabad or you're a member of the Hilton family. If you can put yourself in another person's situation in a real, empathic way, you'll see there's always some headache for him or her, just like there is for you. Even the rich celebrities I work with go through tough times. They're first-world problems, but that's only because the first world is the world celebrities find themselves in. Let's say they're no longer hot, they're broke, and they get asked to do a Danny Bonaduce movie for $200,000. They never imagined when they co-starred with Brad Pitt or Sandra Bullock and commanded a million dollars a movie that they'd ever be groveling for a "C" horror picture to be shot in Kabukistan. But they have to take it to pay the bills. Don't you think Don Rickles would rather be asked to do a TV show than to have to make the rounds of the low rent comedy circuit at age 87? On second thought, maybe he's just happy he's not in a retirement home.

The point is, I don't know why Titania should have it any

easier than anyone else. I didn't know much about her past, but I'm sure there were struggles back in Moldova and probably a lot more struggles since coming to the U.S. It's all relative; no matter what condition we're born into, the human condition of wanting more than what we have is hard wired. For me, life is a struggle punctuated by occasional bursts of joy—everything, good and bad, shared with the women of The Muffia. I hoped, for her sake, that Titania also had some good friends who could help her through.

CHAPTER 26

THE ALZHEIMER'S benefit was a week away, and by this point, Lauren had enlisted all of the Muffs to help her. She'd put Maddie on the board, not only for her ability to keep the meetings moving, but so as to expand fundraising efforts into the legal community; Vicki was in charge of lining up the video crew to shoot the event, along with doing some tasteful social networking; Jelicka was the perfect pick to acquire items for the gift bags that would be handed out to guests; I was supposed to be lining up celebrities as both guests and auction items; Kiki was the logical choice to set up a first aid plan and to book the emergency personnel; Sarah, the ex-possibly-soon-to-be-rehired Williams-Sonoma employee, and arguably the Muffia's most accomplished chef, had been working with participating restaurants to develop the ideal menu; Paige was making calls, and Rachel was in charge of the art. All in all, the Muffia might as well have been credited first on the Volunteer Committee.

Since the mystery of who'd sent the pictures had been solved and the threatened Internet exposure quashed, I'd been able to keep my job, which had made it far easier to contact all those celebrities. Titania's ouster had so far not provoked the feared backlash from the Moldovan expat community and, though I remained vigilant when out late at night, I was pretty sure the threat was gone for good as well.

Kiki's porn-producing neighbors had been shut down, the Muffs were enjoying my book club choice, and all seemed right with the world, even if there was still no man in my life. I was *so* okay with it, I even cancelled my membership on *NowLove*, determining that life is too short to go on bad dates, and I really wasn't the gambling type. At least if you meet a guy in the course of living your life and decide to go out with him, you have some information ahead of time—what he looks like, how he talks, and how he presents himself. You can read his body language, too, so the whole enterprise isn't as big a risk.

I also decided I loved volunteering. I loved fundraising. The feeling of being able to contribute to something important was stupendous, and it was amazing how different and energized I felt worrying about something other than what I was going to wear—not that I'd given that up entirely. I really got it this time, on a visceral level: it can't be all about you. Yeah, we hear it every day, but there's a reason *why* we hear it—we need to be reminded. At least I do, or did. As I said, this time I got it.

Frank had vanished for good, it seemed, which made me sad because I felt like there had been something kindled between us at the end. I considered asking Lauren to find out if there was, in fact, a work protocol that might keep him from contacting me, but she had enough to worry about with the benefit.

Though it hardly compares, I now empathized even more with Maddie's feelings about Udi. To wit; it was easier for a woman to put a man (or try to put a man) out of her mind than to imagine him not having her in his. So, apropos Frank, I tried not to think about him, but he still popped into my head. I'd gaze out a window—between attempts to lock-in a contract renewal for Naomi Watts' Clairol campaign or a booking for Will Ferrell to hawk Windex in Malaysia—and visualize Frank turning to face me as he pulled off his mirrored shades and say, "Ms. Cunningham, would you come this way…?"

It was okay, though. The mind wanders, and K-Love says to let it. Though the mind may wander, thankfully, it does return.

CHAPTER 27

FLOWERS SPILLED out of Grecian urns, tiny lights criss-crossed the patio and doves cooed in several large, white, antique birdcages strategically placed around the opulently accented home. Elegant women served imaginative-looking hors d'oeuvres, while spring-themed cocktails, along with any other alcoholic beverage one desired, were available from well-tended bars positioned around the palatial site of the benefit.

Lauren had outdone herself. It wasn't all Lauren, of course. She had lots of help from the Muffia—all of whom she'd comped—and her sister, Kristin, had flown in from Chicago a week earlier to help with the final arrangements. Kristin was a publicist and known to the Muffs only by reputation. Among other coups, she had been the party planner for Chelsea Handler's vodka launch—an event each Muff remembered for all the free bottles of vodka we got post launch. The two sisters had overseen the transformation of the swanky home of the head of E! Entertainment (and Kristin's new squeeze) into a *luxe* fantasy location, and from all outward appearances, it was going to be a party no one would want to miss.

Kristin met E!'s CEO, Keith, at the vodka launch, and the two had hit it off immediately—funnily enough over Alzheimer's disease. Turns out Keith's father also had the "Big A" before he passed. Anyone who's witnessed the ravages of Alzheimer's disease first hand has a dreaded fear of getting it himself. So the fact that they'd both experienced this devastation created an immediate bond between them

Like Vicki says, " 'In the end, it's either the big "C" Cancer, "A" Alzheimer's, "S" Stroke, or "H" Heart Disease that'll get you. And that's exactly what it's going to cost to keep you going—CASH.' "

"Rachel, you look so nice, but what's with the red cloth bracelet?" Sarah said, joining Rachel and me standing in line for one of those themed drinks. "It doesn't go with your outfit."

"I'm trying a new outlook," said Rachel. "It's from Ruth."

"Ruth who?"

"Bible Ruth," I said, speaking figuratively. "It's a new religion she's trying."

Sarah looked puzzled.

"It's not new," Rachel said.

"New to you," I said. "Sorry, I should have been more precise."

"How did *you* get it?" Sarah asked.

Rachel smiled. "It's not actually the one she wore."

"Duh," said Sarah, realizing. "I'm so gullible. I didn't even know you were religious."

"I'm more spiritual," Rachel said. "A searcher."

"Does that explain why you became a lesbian or why the guys you date end up in paintings with their faces removed?"

Thankfully, Lauren appeared. She walked up and threw her arms around me. "Quinn, thank you. What a gorgeous dress!"

"It's a Cate Blanchett cast-off from the Golden Globes." One of the amazing perks of my job is having access to the designers who want stars to wear their gowns. This particular dress was a couple of years old but had never been worn by Ms. Moore. It was a shimmery, navy blue taffeta, strapless and fitted through the bodice to a skirt that went out from the waist; very simple, but so elegant and chic.

"Everyone just *loves* Viggo," Lauren was saying. "I completely understand why you have a crush on him. And not only did he agree to be auctioned off for the cause, but he donated one of his paintings! I had no idea he was so talented. When I talked to you that day and you said he'd probably prefer to paint a kitchen, I wasn't expecting oil on canvas."

"Oh, he's really good," said Jelicka, joining the group, a cocktail with some sort of plumage firmly in her grip.

"I think he's a tad overrated." Rachel wasn't as enthused.

"It turns out Viggo's grandmother had dementia, so he really wanted to be involved," I explained. "He's even interested in being on the board for the next one."

"What do you mean, 'auctioned off'?" said Sarah.

"Sold to the highest bidder," Lauren replied.

"To do what exactly?" Sarah frowned.

"Well, to go..." Lauren started.

"It's one way to get a date," interjected Jelicka with a snort. "Unfortunately, I have to watch my pennies until my crooked career path straightens out."

"When Viggo came on board, he pulled in a lot of his cute celebrity friends, too," I said.

"Really, who?" said Jelicka as Madelyn approached the group of us, her date in tow and not wearing a kilt. *Was this the Scot or a last minute replacement?*

"And if it weren't for Quinn, we wouldn't have gotten any of them," Lauren said.

"Come on," I protested. "That's not true. You would have gotten them without me." It wasn't false modesty talking, either. The cause spoke for itself.

"Possibly," said Lauren, "but you were the one who got everything going."

The Muffs are generally great about giving credit where

it's due, and it's always nice to be acknowledged. But on this one? I just made a few phone calls.

I glanced over at Maddie's boyfriend, whom I still assumed was Rory, standing patiently by her side. She hadn't told us he was so handsome; or maybe I'd forgotten. This man with her tonight was extremely good looking—good looking enough to be auctioned off for charity with the celebrities—but was he, in fact, the Scot?

The mystery was solved when she introduced him as Cullen. Cullen I'd heard *all* about; Cullen I remembered. And if I'd gone to Babeland that day when Maddie went vibrator shopping, I would have met Cullen. I couldn't remember what she said about why it hadn't worked out with him, but maybe now they were giving it another try.

"We're not sleeping together," she said, sotto voce, when Cullen went for drinks. "Just so you know. He's only my date. It's probably no surprise, but I couldn't take it anymore with the jolly Scot—too much effort trying to be his bonnie lass."

"Well, Cullen's pretty hot," I said.

"Not when you've seen him with his mother. It's actually a huge turn off."

"She won't be around forever," I pointed out. "Besides, isn't it nice he cares about his mother?"

"Yes, but you need to experience the two of them together to fully understand just how odd their specific mother-son relationship is."

I supposed I would, though it was probably a question of degree; many mother-son relationships being fraught.

"The trouble is I think Udi's spoiled me forever," she said. "I've tried to date, but I still think about him. Then *you* call me to say you saw him… " She gazed around the room, clearly trying to get her emotions in check.

I reached out to touch her arm. "I said I was sorry."

"I know," she said, softening. "I like your dress."

"I like yours." She had on a simple black chiffon sheath at cocktail length, but her calves were the real draw.

"Anyway, Cullen is very sweet and available—if you're interested."

Part of me *was* interested. But I still had my own obsession. I hadn't told the Muffs about my crush on Frank Sexton yet but I planned to come clean at the next book club. I guess I'd held off telling them because I worried my feelings for Frank weren't real. I supposed a shrink would say they came from a mistaken belief that he'd saved my life. The thing was, he *did* save my life. Anyway, I wasn't interested in handsome Cullen.

Kiki, dressed in a long, pale yellow gown that showed off her well-toned body, appeared with Saul just as Lauren's sister, Kristin, entered our little circle, holding the arm of an older woman—seventy, perhaps—wearing a peach-colored St. John knitted suit. Lauren greeted the woman with a kiss, and it was instantly obvious that this elegant woman was their mother.

"Hello, dear. What a nice party."

"It is, isn't it?" Lauren said. "I hope you're having a good time."

"Yes, dear. But where is the birthday cake?" Mom's eyes widened, a look of mild panic appearing. "Where is the cake?"

"The cake will be here," said Lauren, doing her best to reassure the older woman.

Mom pulled her arm away from Kristin's and did an emotional one-eighty, snarling, "I *told* your father you didn't like carrot cake, but he doesn't listen."

A few of us glanced at each other, instantly on alert that "Mom" was not at the same event we were. A couple of awkward seconds went by, then Lauren smiled and whispered conspiratorially to Mom: "We'll just dump that cake on his head."

Another couple of awkward seconds passed, and Mom burst

into giggles.

"We'll smoosh it all over him," Kristin agreed. Mom giggled some more. It was the giggle of a schoolgirl. Clearly, both daughters had learned how to steer their mother into safer territory.

"I think she needs another Derazapan," Kristin whispered. "I'll get it."

"What are you talking about behind my back?" Mom snapped. "I'm not in crazy town, you know."

Kristin once again dodged. "Mom, these are some of Lauren's friends in L.A., and they've come to celebrate with you. Ladies, this is our mom, Joy." Joy beamed at us.

So far, Joy was aptly named fifty percent of the time. We all chimed in with our hellos.

"You're all so *pretty*," Joy said, giving us her appraisal. She spotted Jelicka's shoes. "Those are hooker shoes."

Jelicka held up her glass. "You're right."

Joy's brow suddenly furrowed, and she extended her hand out toward me. It looked so frail it might break, her skin so thin you could see her skeleton. The several rings she wore no longer fit, and the weight of the gemstones threatened to drag them off her fingers. "Who are you people?" she asked, as if Kristin hadn't introduced us.

"They're all Lauren's friends, Mom," Kristin repeated.

Joy knew there was some formality that was supposed to take place, but the details were no longer clear. Her hand sort of hovered for a second or two—elbow bent, rings slipping—as I raised my hand to meet hers. Then, she suddenly pulled hers back as if burned, her left hand coming up to grab the right one.

"You stupid, stupid boy. Get back in there. Don't do that!" said Joy, slapping her right hand repeatedly with the left, as Kristin tried to calm her.

"Mom—your hand is sorry."

"Bad boy; bad, bad. Get—"

"Her caregiver went to the restroom," said Lauren quietly, by way of explanation. "It seems to have set her off."

Kristin wasn't having much success in calming their mother down. Joy was now trying to lift her dress up so she could look underneath. "Something is getting into my panties," I heard her say.

Kristin and Lauren exchanged a look, and Kristin began leading Joy away. "Mom, guess what!" said Kristin, full of excitement. "They have fresh lobster tail over there."

Joy suddenly stopped. "Goody-goody. Can we watch them crawl on the floor?"

"Of course we can!"

As Kristin led Joy away, across the floor to the buffet tables, Lauren said, "I hope by the time they get over there, Kristin can take her mind off the lobsters because the ones they're serving will never crawl again."

"It's got to be so difficult," said Sarah, with great empathy. "I had no idea."

"Brutal," I agreed.

"Not to mention just plain sad," Rachel said.

"My parents aren't there yet, but it's coming," said Sarah.

Lauren sighed, a look of resignation on her face. "But what do you do, you know? She told us never to let her get like this, but now it's too late."

Not much you can do. Personally, I'd rather die, but it was obvious to any half-wit that when you actually get as old as Joy, you don't feel that way anymore—or else you don't know how you feel.

"So now you know what it's been like," said Lauren. "Generally, she's funny and easy to deal with, but if she starts taking her clothes off, we're going to have to take her home."

"Oh, God, my dad has started taking his clothes off in public, too," said Sarah. "Maybe it's already started."

Over Lauren's shoulder, I saw Viggo approach the

microphone. He looked dashing in a tuxedo with his hair a little wild. Glancing around, I saw most of the women lower their cocktails and give him their undivided attention.

"While you're enjoying your drinks," he began, "I'd like to get you all thinking about one part of the evening that will be coming up later. It's the live auction when you'll be able to bid on any one of us you see standing here."

Eight gorgeous men, including Viggo, stood for our pre-bidding pleasure. Not all were Hollywood actors. A couple of them were stars behind the scenes, and one had to be the finest-looking neurosurgeon ever. Viggo also directed the attendees' attention to the silent auction items and encouraged everyone to bid. What an asset he turned out to be. *Sigh.*

As we all sat down to dinner, Paige arrived with Richard, her on again/off again/live-in/kicked-out significant other. She looked fabulous in a red and black dress with marcasite jewelry. There was no sign of the supposed shiner of a few weeks before, but something was different—it was subtle, but it was there. She looked rested and then some.

I glanced at Lauren and Sarah, both of whom had seen Paige soon after the alleged tennis ball incident and denied she had any plastic surgery. Neither of them gave anything away now, either. Though we generally don't keep secrets in The Muffia, a person's privacy is still something each of us has a right to. Oh, what did it matter? Paige looked great, seemed to feel great, and plastic surgery isn't something one should be concerned about at an Alzheimer's benefit.

Richard had a few more gray hairs since the last time I'd seen him, but he was a distinguished-looking man. Paige was wearing her engagement ring, so I guessed all that must be back on, too. For a couple of years, Paige and Richard had been attempting to blend their families. But like the proverbial oil and vinegar, they just kept separating. Now maybe the mix was right.

I took Paige's hand and examined the ring.

"For sure this time," she said. "In two months—a very small affair at his family's place in North Carolina. You're all welcome to come, but we know how far away it is."

"How to make a girl feel welcome," I said.

"Seriously, it's going to be very low key. It may end up just being us at the courthouse with a party after."

A few courses of inspired food landed at our places delivered by attractive volunteer servers, all of them standing up for the cause. And before we knew it, it was auction time.

The auctioneer was a SmartCar-shaped man hailing from Witchita named Walker Talbot. He wore a tight-fitting suit made of shiny gray sharkskin, and he looked completely out of place among the chic, overwhelmingly dressed-in-black crowd. George was the one responsible for Mr. Talbot's presence at the benefit, and I knew Lauren was concerned about people judging him by his size. But it wasn't long before the man's larger-than-life smile and attitude won everyone over. He started the auction off with a trip to Paris that Maddie bid on first, knowing full well that she'd be outbid soon thereafter. The price became too high for any of us almost immediately.

There were four pieces of donated art to auction off, including a painting of Rachel's that she must have done before the "Nude Men Without Faces" series. It fetched a thousand dollars. The next piece was a drawing—a lesser Chagall, according to the art appraisers—that had come from Lauren's father-in-law's collection and had been in his closet for twenty years, such was the family's art collection that they could leave a Chagall in the closet. Walker, the auctioneer, whipped the bidders into such frenzy, recounting Chagall stories that he pulled out of who knows where? And by the time bidding ended, he'd gotten the price up to $300,000. It was a huge amount of money for Lauren's organization, the still too-long-named *Alzheimer's*

Search for the Cure at the Sweet-Busch Center for Neurological Research, or in its acronym form: the ASC-SBCNR. I'd decided Sweet-Busch really was the most uplifting way to spin the name, but there was no ideal way to say it.

Walker kept his lively patter going in between auction items, tossing in the occasional celebrity joke. But during the bidding, he was at his best, getting the most out of his audience for each of the items. As coffee was served, it was time for the guys to be auctioned off.

The prospective bidders—women mostly, though there were a few men—drew closer to the stage with their bidding paddles held tight. Maybe they were there for the illusory promise of love, or perhaps they had endorsements or business deals they wanted to propose. I noticed Jelicka in the group and wondered what was on her mind. She hadn't *seemed* drunk, and she'd claimed not to have the money to bid. Maybe she just wanted to get a closer look at Matthew McConaughey.

I stayed seated, taking small forkfuls of dulce de lece cheesecake. Neither my heart nor my bank account could handle the pressure of bidding. It would have to be enough just to enjoy the handsome hunks from afar.

"None of these gents look substantial enough to me, Ladies," Walker began. "Now, I *might* be willing to offer myself on the auction block, if that would solve the problem..."

There was laughter and a couple of hoots. "Do it," someone yelled.

"The damnable truth is, I don't have a clue about how to auction off all these skinny boys. Sure, they're movie stars, but not one of 'em's got enough body fat to keep a woman warm at night."

"Hey, we know where you live, Man," called out the handsome doctor, to a chuckle from the crowd.

"Now, I don't want my bias keepin' me from doin' a good

job here; I just need a little help. So I'm bringin' up to the stage a lovely lady so she can point out the fine attributes of these gentlemen from the female perspective. Please welcome to the stage, the *gore-gee-us* and talented—ladies and gentlemen, you know her from *Desperate Housewives* and as Ann Ewing on the new *Dallas* —Ms. Brenda Strong!"

Brenda, who was an old friend of Madelyn's and happy to donate her time—another one whose life had been hit by Alzheimer's—made her way to a second microphone, because it was clear that Walker wasn't about to give his up. The two of them quickly established a comfortable, folksy rapport as they discussed the qualities of each of the men to be auctioned off.

Walker would say so-and-so's too skinny and not much for a woman to love on, or he'd roast him for some other reason. Then Brenda would take over and tell the crowd how handsome, smart, and fun so-and-so was and how a woman will have a blast going on a date with him. Walker would counter, "All right, fine, but can he ride a hog?" And so it would go.

When it was Adrian Brody's turn to be auctioned, he came to the microphone and said, "I just want to be on record here. I can ride a bull, and I can probably ride a hog." He looked over the crowd with some trepidation. "But I thought we were just going for lunch."

Brenda and Walker, who were acting like a couple on the new *Dallas*, continued to spar as they encouraged people to bid higher and higher for each of the men. Some of my tablemates had wandered off, leaving only a few of us there to enjoy the show.

Viggo was the last to be auctioned, and bidding was instantly lively. Like the others, Brenda started it off at two hundred bucks. It went immediately to three hundred, followed by a jump to five hundred, then a thousand, and up it went. Viggo looked a little uncomfortable—actually, they all had looked uncomfortable—but

I'd been watching Viggo's face for longer than the others, so I thought he was easier to read. Every time the bid increased, he'd give a little smile and wave at the person who raised her paddle. And as I watched the bidding climb higher and higher, I again started to think about Frank. Actually, it was less like thinking and more like pining. I was still hoping, Frank being such a practical person and all, that he would have seen through all the Hollywood crap to the real me—the girl from Fresno with the mother who covered her furniture in plastic and a dad who restored old generators in his spare time.

Finally, Brenda said, "Sold to the woman in the gold suit," ending the bidding. I'd met the woman who won earlier in the evening. She was about seventy years old and an avid collector of contemporary art. *Maybe she'd also buy some of Viggo's paintings.*

Walker came front and center, "Ladies, as you can see, I'm a large man who hails from the southwest, enjoys a good steak, and a drive in the country in a big car with quality air conditioning. I like to talk—but I'm told I'm a good listener—and I will make you feel like the center of the Universe. So what am I bid? Let's start it off at two hundred…can I get two-hundred bucks?"

There were several women who stuck their paddles in the air. Perhaps they liked steak and big cars, too, or wanted to be the center of Walker's Universe. Brenda took over the bidding with a joke about people tooting their own horns, but Walker said he was just as happy to have her toot it as long as she kept saying nice things about him. The bidding was up to five hundred by that point, with Walker wanting to show off a tattoo as inducement for women to bid higher.

I sensed a presence next to me and turned, expecting to find one of the Muffs returned from the ladies room. But it was Frank Sexton sitting down next to me. My jaw dropped open.

"Aren't you going to bid on Walker?" he asked. "I know you had a thing for Viggo Mortensen, so I waited until bidding was over on him to come talk to you."

His sunglasses were off and his eyes mischievous. It was so good to see him. "How'd you get in here?"

He gestured over his shoulder. "I flashed my military I.D."

"That must come in handy."

"Oh, yeah. Instead of thanking me for my service, they just waved me in." He paused. "How come you didn't bid on Viggo?"

"A little steep for me. And he's a client, so it's not like I can't hang out with him."

He nodded, glancing around the room, scanning like I'd seen him do many times.

"George and I spoke earlier today about another matter," he ducked his head, "and he told me about his wife's benefit tonight and that you'd be here."

Could it be he had come to see me? I didn't want to flatter myself, but it sure sounded that way. And he was doing it his usual way—showing up unexpectedly. Suddenly, I wondered if he had something to tell me.

"Has there been a new development?" I asked.

"Actually, there has."

So that's why he's here. A wave of disappointment washed over me. "Oh."

Behind me I heard Walker say, "Come on, Brenda, you can get more than $600 for this fine, masculine specimen."

Brenda gave him a gentle punch in the arm. "I'm running this show, Mister."

"I'm just sayin' that's a steal for one entire long afternoon of good times with yours truly. Tell you what, we'll finish up with a fine steak dinner at Boa. I'll spend more than $600 takin' care of whoever wins."

I immediately felt a wave of nausea, thinking about my horrible date with John.

"Something I said?" Frank asked.

"Just got a taste of some bad meat. Sorry."

He smiled. "I know what you mean."

"You know about my bad date at Boa?"

He hesitated. "I do."

I felt my cheeks warming, which meant they were turning red—so much so they were probably the color of my dress.

"So embarrassing."

"Forget about it. The guy was a jerk."

"I'll say." I looked off, wondering when he was going to give me an update on my case, because he'd made it clear he hadn't come to ask me out.

"Since it's been about three weeks, I thought enough time had passed…"

I turned to face him, ready to hear what he had to say.

"…that I might ask you out."

I didn't think I'd heard him correctly. "Wait…What?" *He said he'd come to give me an update, hadn't he?*

"I'm sorry if I startled you."

"I'm not startled, really." I was *very* startled. "I guess I should sort of be used to you doing unexpected things."

"You look very pretty tonight, Quinn."

I had a vague awareness of the bidding coming to an end for the date with Walker and his mock surprise about not fetching a higher sum. It was like the dome on that TV show had plopped down over Frank and me, only Frank wasn't behaving like Frank—telling me I looked nice and using my first name. I mean, it was great, but he wasn't the Frank I knew. "Would you like to get a drink?" he asked, offering me his arm. *Who offers their arm these days?*

I put my arm through his, and we began walking past a cage

of doves cooing, toward a bar tucked back in one corner of the mansion. Through the fog, I heard Walker announce the final item of the evening: an all-expense paid 8-Day trip via Netjets to a private island in the Maldives—complete with a gourmet chef, unlimited massages, private yoga instructor, access to a small yacht, various other seafaring equipment, as well as a constantly-replenishing, fully- stocked mini-bar.

Somewhere down the list of this fabulously unbelievable and unaffordable trip that I could only hope to go on one day, I tuned out—overcome with imagining myself there, opening the mini-bar, pulling out a bottle of Evian, and heading down for a couples massage with Frank on the beach.

It was like he read my mind. "Sounds pretty great."

"So great I can almost feel it," I agreed, as the frenetic bidding started behind us.

"What will it be?" Frank asked me, stepping up to the bar.

"White wine, please." The bartender heard me and poured a glass of Sauvignon Blanc. I was still dreaming of the beach until Frank gently withdrew his arm to give the guy a tip. *Who knew he could be so gentle?*

"Do you go to a lot of these things?" Frank said, putting the wine glass in my hand.

"Not as often as you'd think with my job, but when you only book commercials, you don't get to walk the red carpet. And big charity galas like this are pricey."

"Tell me about it," he said with a wry smile.

"Did you...?

"Forget it; I wanted to support the effort." He said it so matter-of-fact; no hint he was seeking a compliment. "I also bid on a silent auction item."

"What did you bid on?"

"A pair of vintage sunglasses worn by Don Johnson on *Miami Vice.*"

I studied him. "Don't you already have a pair of those?"

"Mine are fakes and if I win that pair, I probably won't wear them. It's just the idea of owning a little piece of history."

"Hopefully, they'll come with a Don Johnson seal of authenticity."

"I can take care of that," Frank said, grinning. "I saw Don Johnson walking around here somewhere."

Really? I glanced around but didn't see a dark blond wearing a white suit with a pale blue shirt under it. "You must have really liked that show."

"It was formative," he said, cracking a smile.

The bartender handed Frank a drink, and we moved away from the bar.

"Actually, I preferred *Hill Street Blues* and *Seinfeld*," Frank said, "but there wasn't anything from those shows to bid on."

"The auction committee was remiss. I'll make sure next year we get some representative memorabilia."

"I'll be there." He pulled out a couple of chairs at one of the tables along the wall that appeared to be abandoned.

I'd lost track of the auction. Presumably, somebody had won the fabulous trip. The DJ had begun and people were dancing. I think I saw Maddie and Cullen out there. Meanwhile, I was still trying to deal with Frank's metamorphosis from the uptight, on-a-mission type, to a conversant and attentive "date"—because that's what it felt like; he was acting like my date. I'd fantasized about him looking at me the way he was now doing, but since I'd given up on it ever happening, I wasn't prepared. And I was a little scared, too.

"I see you've kept your shoe selection a little more sedate this evening."

I looked down at my sexy, strappy, black three-inch heels and smiled. They weren't what I'd call sedate, but compared to the pink bling platforms, they were loafers.

"Well, you know, I try to keep the pole dancing to myself. Just remember, if I hadn't been wearing pole dancing shoes at Narita Airport, I never would have met you."

"Then I'm glad you wore them."

"Me too."

He lifted the glass of wine from my hand and put it on the table alongside his own drink, and took my hand in his.

"They tell us to wait six months to a year after the conclusion of a case before approaching a client—not that I've ever approached one before. I'm sorry if you thought I wasn't interested."

"Oh, that's okay," I said, my heart beating harder. "You know, you had to… "

"The thing is, if I waited much longer, somebody might snatch you up."

He said all this with no guile, and I felt his sincerity. Under all that gruffness was a very kind man.

"You're a pretty good actor," I said. "I never would have guessed that you…actually, I was hoping there was a reason you weren't…you know."

He looked at our joined hands and squeezed. My gaze followed his and I squeezed back, just as he lifted my fingers to his lips and kissed.

A throat cleared nearby. It wasn't Frank's, and I knew it wasn't mine. "Excuse me, um, Quinn?"

I looked up, disappointed to be shaken from the moment.

Sarah was standing a few feet away. If it had been any other Muff, she probably would have found another way to get my attention at such a sensitive moment, but there were sometimes judgment issues with Sarah. And where was Nate? I hadn't seen her husband all evening.

She looked at Frank, then to me. "Um, sorry for..." she said awkwardly, extending her hand. "Hi, I'm Sarah." That's right, she hadn't been at Kiki's the night we busted her pornographic neighbors. "Sorry, Quinn, but you just disappeared! Lauren's been trying to round everyone up so she can bring the Muffs to the stage and thank us."

"Okay, well," I said, glancing at Frank.

"Of course you need to be there," Frank said, standing. "You need to be acknowledged with your friends. You've all done a terrific job." He leaned in and whispered in my ear, "To be continued."

"Hope so."

"I guarantee it. I'll be here when you get back."

My feet were rooted to where I stood, and Sarah started pulling on me. "Sorry, but we gotta go. I'll bring her back."

"All right already," I said, aware of a warm and welcome wooziness—like after a great massage. "What's a few more seconds going to matter?" I looked back at Frank, who was smiling at me with his crooked smile as Sarah charted a path to the stage, never letting go of me.

"There isn't time to dawdle. Lauren wants to make a speech right now. Who is that guy anyway?"

"That guy… is my new boyfriend."

Sarah was moving so fast, we almost knocked down a tiny old man whom I think was a famous director from the 70s.

"Sorry," I said. "You know, we don't have to go this fast; it's not like this is *The Amazing Race.*"

"Since when do you have a boyfriend?" she said. "I knew about the married guy but...wait; that's not married guy, is it?"

"Doesn't even have a girlfriend, unless it's me." I grinned and kept moving.

"Wow, it must feel good not to be an adulteress anymore."

"Hey!" I yelled, as we barely averted another collision. "Watch where you're leading us."

Frank could have been lying when he told me there was no

girlfriend; like Steven, at the beginning, told me there was no wife; like Titania had lied to Jamie. But I was choosing to believe him. Where would choosing the opposite get me, anyway? Exactly nowhere.

Lauren was effusive in her remarks, lavishing each of us Muffs with thanks for our specific contributions to the event's success. She was gracious and funny, with an anecdote about each of us. From the stage, I looked out and spotted Frank standing off to one side watching and listening. I just knew he was one of the good ones, and I wasn't going to blow it.

When Lauren had concluded and thanked everyone, George stepped in to give her a hug. He was so proud of her, as were we. Who cared if she hadn't cracked the book I picked for book club next week. I glanced at the faces of the other Muffs, and in each one I saw love and admiration.

I whispered to Maddie that Frank had shown up and that I'd probably be slipping out momentarily. Sarah might say something about the guy she saw kissing my hand, but Maddie knew the whole story after that night at Kiki's and would keep things in perspective.

"Why not slip out now?" she asked, with a glint in her eye.

"You're bad," I said. "It's not like that. If anything, I'm feeling very prudish with him."

"That's a good sign," she said. "Good luck."

I saw my opportunity to rejoin Frank and quickly headed down the stairs at the back of the stage only to bump into Viggo at the bottom of the steps.

"Hi, Quinn." He gave me his full-wattage smile. "What a great event. Really well done."

"Lauren did a great job," I said, as I began to angle past him. "And thanks again for participating. It wouldn't have been nearly as successful without you and the other guys."

"My pleasure. Hey, I was wondering if you might like to have a drink with me sometime—like after this winds down maybe."

I stared at him, flabbergasted. He had been the object of my fantasies for months, and it was hilarious that now he was in my way instead of being my destination.

"Thank you, that is so nice… "

"But no, right?" He smiled again. He was heartbreakingly handsome. But now that's all it was.

"Thank you, though. I'm very flattered."

I turned from Viggo without a trace of regret. And there was Frank, who'd been listening to the entire exchange. Frank nodded to Viggo, who seemed surprised at my choice and again offered me his arm. "Ready?"

A girl could get used to this…

CHAPTER 28

" '*I* HAVE NO idea how to love another human being, unless it's by tearing them to pieces and eating them.' " Rachel was reading from *When Will There Be Good News?* while the rest of us were chowing down on bangers and beer, in keeping with the book's Scottish setting. "I mean, isn't that just exquisite?"

"Don't you think it's a little gruesome?" Lauren said. "Doesn't sound like love to me."

"Not to mention depressing," added Jelicka.

I sighed. "It's not literal."

"Is that what the serial killer says?" Clearly, Sarah hadn't read the book...again.

"The police officer," said Kiki. "Louise."

"Seriously?" Sarah was disgusted.

"She's so in love, it hurts," Paige clarified. "Louise Monroe is a great character, don't you think? Tough, but with a conscience. A real girl's girl."

"Absolutely," Maddie said. "She felt real to me. She was successful, but also conflicted, and the author shows the reader that living in the gray area is possible—something I work on every day."

"I know *that*," Sarah said, adding a dollop of mustard to her banger. "My life is all about the gray area. But I'll wait on that 'til the roundy."

We all empathized with Sarah's husband and house problems and were ready to listen whenever she wanted to bring them up.

"It was still an interesting pick for book club," said Lauren.

"One of the reasons I love our book club," I said, "is because we get introduced to books we never would have read otherwise. I really liked this one, so I wanted to share it. And you all have turned me on to books I wouldn't have read, either. Like that book "Snow." I would never have read a book about girls killing themselves in Eastern Turkey if it wasn't for...whose pick was that?"

There was some grumbling. It hadn't been a popular pick.

"Mine," said Rachel. "Not everyone agreed with you, Quinn."

"Well, I thought it was worth reading," I said, with Madelyn in agreement.

Vicki stood to reload her camera, which was focused on the table in a wide shot. "I read crime novels all the time, but I didn't know this author, so thank you, Quinn. Now I'm going to read all her other books."

"Okay, I know I didn't read it," said Jelicka. "But why is it called *When Will There be Good News?* The title is terrible and gives the impression there's no good news in the whole damn thing. Who'd want to read that?"

"Atkinson likes odd titles, but you remember them because they're odd," I said.

Jelicka had grabbed a copy of the book and opened it. "No kidding. What's *Started Early, Took My Dog* about? Hope there's a dog in it."

"Here's another beautiful passage," Rachel said. " 'Love wasn't sweet and light, it was visceral and overpowering. Love wasn't patient, love wasn't kind. Love was ferocious, love knew how to play dirty.' "

"You keep selecting the same quotes," said Paige. "What's *that* about?"

"She's right, though. Love *does* play dirty," I agreed. "Or it *can*, anyway."

"Rachel, what's the matter?" said Kiki in a quiet, calming voice. "Why are you so hostile?"

"I'm not hostile."

"You are. I don't think I'm the only one who's noticed." Kiki looked at me, then Maddie. A few of us nodded our heads.

I whispered so only Rachel could hear, "I didn't say anything."

"She's sad, I think," said Sarah. "Just plain sad."

Rachel sat back with a sigh.

Sarah cut through the crap to speak the truth.

"I *am* sad," Rachel said. "I'm actually more disappointed by all the assholes I've chosen to spend time with. Disappointed in myself is more like it." A tear was forming in the corner of her eye. "I don't know where I'd be without you guys."

"Maybe even sadder?" Jelicka said, which drew a scant smile.

"I really wish sometimes that I could have been happy in a same sex relationship but goddamnit, I love men's bodies too much."

"I understand that," said Jelicka. I threw her a look. "I'm not kidding. If I didn't like sex with men, what would I need one for?"

Lauren snorted. "How about conversation, friendship, strength, love, joy, a travel companion, security…" She was rattling off a list and, thanks to Frank, I had a sense of what she was talking about.

"Spoken like a truly happy woman," Maddie said. "Let's be honest, here. None of us would mind having a significant other who was 'all that,' but we've gotten to the point in life when we realize that settling is not an option."

"Right," said Rachel. "And I have to learn to pick a different type—kind of hard when your picker is broken. I need to work on getting my picker fixed."

"Here's a passage I marked," I said, opening my copy of the book. " 'There had been another man once. The kind of man she could have imagined standing shoulder to shoulder with, a comrade-in-arms, but they had been as chaste as the protagonists in an Austen novel. All sense and no sensibility, no persuasion at all.' "

"Now *that* I like," Lauren said, spooning more fried kale onto her plate, without regard to that diet she was always on. "I mean it's sad, but it's not so violent."

"I underlined that one, too," Maddie said. "That's what Louise is thinking about what's-his-name, the guy she let get away—"

"Brodie," said Rachel.

"Right, Brodie—before they meet again after all that time." Maddie's hand went to her heart and she sighed. I felt bad for her, knowing she was still missing Udi.

"I'm sorry you guys. I have to get going," said Kiki, as we wrapped up the roundy-round. "Big day tomorrow."

"Who's next, Paige?" asked Maddie.

"Why do you all always ask *me* who's next? You were able to figure it out by yourselves at Rachel's."

"But we *like* it when you do it," Lauren said. "We missed you last time."

Paige smiled, a smile that still looked a little tight, post-plastic surgery. She shook her head. She could protest all she wanted, but she liked her role as head Miss Bossypants. "Well, I happened to check before I came tonight and it's Kiki."

"Perfect," said Jelicka. "My side of town."

"The side of town you used to complain about driving to," Lauren pointed out with a grin.

"Well, I'd never lived in the valley before. It's actually pretty nice!"

Kiki and Maddie, the long-standing Valley-ites, looked at each other and laughed.

CHAPTER 29

*I*T'S EXCITING and amazing and, I now realize, very rare to be crazy for somebody who's also crazy for you. When you're young, you can lie on your bed for hours staring at the ceiling and pining for someone in an all-consuming, obsessive torrent. But as you get older, you don't have the time or the luxury for that sort of dedicated, self-absorbed longing. When you get older, you have to work, and work becomes the balm that eases all the unrequited pining. So in those scant moments of idleness, when you find yourself pining for the same person who's pining for you, it feels all the more gratifying.

Nothing happened between Frank and me the night of the benefit or, for that matter, the night after. But *nothing* isn't exactly right. We talked and cuddled until we fell asleep in each other's arms. It was perfect. I don't want to jinx us by saying too much while things are so new, but I have a really good feeling about him. He's still not really my type—but my type, like Rachel's type, has only led to disappointment. So many of Frank's positive qualities have overcome what I previously thought of as deficiencies. We're going slow, so there isn't much to report on the sex front; but if his kiss is any indication, I think it's going to be great when it happens.

The biggest hurdle in life for me has been choosing what to believe in. They say we can trick our minds into believing many things. If we physically smile, we'll start to feel happy. If we tell ourselves over and over that something good is going to happen, oftentimes it does. In sports, and in the pursuit of many other endeavors, those who coach those in pursuit say we should act "as if." Act "as if" we are already a great tennis player. Walk across the stage "as if" you are the character you are playing; go into that business meeting "as if" you deserve to be there and can make the deal. I hope I am still destined for great things, but I think it's more important to believe that anything is possible, even "happily ever after," so I am going to act "as if" I'm already on my way.

Things don't need to be all tied up in a bow. And who wants them to be when there's still so much life to live—because even the tightest bow can loosen, and life is long. *Yes, yes, yes; thank you, thank you, thank you.*

EPILOGUE

A MONTH AFTER the benefit, one Sunday morning when Frank and I were drinking coffee, reading the newspaper, and starting to feel very comfortable with each other, Lauren called to say she and George were headed to Japan on Tuesday for an International Beer symposium at the Kirin headquarters in Tokyo.

"Can you recommend any good restaurants?" she asked. "Or any other can't miss sights?" She had the idea that since I'd been over there with a major celebrity, I would know all the trendiest places. It wasn't true, but I did nothing to disavow her of the assumption.

I had, in fact, saved a few of the nicer menus and some other mementos from the trip. *But where were they?* It had been a couple of months since I'd come home, and I couldn't remember where I put it all.

"Hold on," I said. I gave Frank a kiss on the cheek and went looking for my Tumi bag. That stack of stuff must still be in the rolling bag that I took over there.

"Should I call back?" Lauren asked.

"Nope, got it all here," I said, opening an outer zipped compartment and pulling out the collection of pamphlets, menus, and other miscellaneous pieces of paper. "Just have to find the menus."

I brought the stack back to the couch where Frank was sitting, a football game on the T.V. with the volume down low—what a guy— and began looking through it.

"Everything has an English subtitle, so it should be easy to write the names down," I said.

"That's good, because the only Japanese word I know is 'sushi.'"

I started giving her some names as I continued through the stack, while Frank periodically turned his face to me, his eyebrows raised.

"Sound Lady; write that one down," I said. "It's a pedicure place. Really good, but I have no idea why it's called that. Probably got lost in translation."

Frank raised his eyebrows again, and I threw a pillow at him.

I turned the pamphlet for Sound Lady over, and there was a piece of paper on top of the stack beneath it. It was handwritten and in a foreign language, but it wasn't Japanese. I lifted it off the stack and turned it over.

"Huh," I said, causing Frank to glance up.

"What?" said Lauren. "Sound Lady offers more than just pedicures?"

"I'm not sure. This piece of paper—I don't know how it got into my stack of brochures and stuff. Looks like Hebrew."

Frank moved closer, examining the paper. "It's Hebrew," he mouthed silently.

"Is it important?" Lauren asked. "Just go to the next one."

"It *could* be important," I said. "If I could just..." I closed my eyes for a few seconds, mentally retracing my steps as I tried to figure out how it might have ended up in my bag.

Could Udi have put it there? I didn't see any other explanation.

Holy Muffia, here we go again...

THE END

Praise for Ann Royal Nicholas'
THE MUFFIA Series

"Who can resist a book about a book club where the members refer to themselves as "Muffs"? Meet Madeleine Scott-Crane, a savvy 42-year old single mom and mediator as she and her six friends take their monthly meetings to an unconventional—and often shocking level. Nicholas's romp through suburban Los Angeles is sexy, edgy and laugh-out loud funny. With a few of life's lessons thrown in along the way, *The Muffia* is smart, sassy and simply irresistible—just like her heroine. A must-read.
—Hannah Dennison of The Honeychurch Hall Mysteries & The Vicky Hill Mysteries

"I just loved this book. Such a great read. It really speaks to women of all ages but especially those in their 30's and beyond. What a great surprise from a new author!"
—Ely Pouget, actor & producer. CSI, The Mentalist, The 3Tails Movie: A Mermaid Adventure

"5 Stars. Nicholas deftly walks the tightrope of the sexual landscape unfolding around her—of the young, the older and the in between."
—David Glynn – Artist

"LOVED this book. It's good, not so clean, fun. And 50 Shades of Great Writing. An empowered woman who knows not only what she wants, but who she wants, and how many times a day... I recommend it highly."
—Becca Petersen, Amazon Verified Purchaser

"A great read, couldn't put it down. *The Muffia* should be required reading for every book club in America. It's fun, sexy and smart. Hope this is the beginning of a series. Loved it."
—Susan Hito Shapiro, artist, filmmaker and attorney

"I didn't know what to expect when I bought my wife this book on the basis of the *Godfather* style font on the cover. The blurb on the back sounded sort of fun—a story about a bunch of wacky women in a book club (my wife's in a book club). I started reading it on my flight home and I have to say it held my attention (I'm usually reading Malcolm Gladwell or the Wall Street Journal). *The Muffia* is well written and that vibrator shopping chapter cracked me up. Now I'm wondering what else my wife's book club gets up to beyond reading books."
—Jeffrey Malibu, An Amazon Verified Purchaser

"The Muffia Book Club babes may talk like sailors when they meet, but they are sensible, condom-packing ladies. Soon enough, you're reading about vibrators and female sex aids, as discussed by a group of "cliterati" (the author's term, not the reviewer's), as if it were a gardening club comparing the virtues of daisies and sunflowers. The literary proposal is that of a "whodunit?" and both in flavor and presentation, *The Muffia* is urbane, erudite, and ironic."
—Stephen Siciliano of Sidewalk Smokers Club, Highway Scribery, Vine Voice

"Best serious love/thriller/comfort read ever! Wish I could go back in time and be those women! Their lives are serious and dark and fun!"
—Linda Mohan, Amazon Verified Purchaser

"I live in LA, where *The Muffia* takes place, and these women are spot on. They're so realistically drawn, that I could swear I even know a few of them personally! Very enjoyable."
—Amazon Kindle Verified Purchaser

"Ann Royal Nicholas writes in a breezy style making this the perfect beach or airplane read when you don't want anything too demanding or heavy. *The Muffia* is the first in a series and I can't wait to read what the smart and wacky Muff women will get up to next. I also really liked that the author and her book club are giving 10% of sales to women's causes. That's cool!"
—Amazon Kindle Verified Purchaser

ABOUT THE AUTHOR

Ann Royal Nicholas is an author (*The Muffia* and *Homegrown: The Terror Within*, published under the pseudonym Cialan Haasnic), a journalist (LA Times, Vine Times Magazine), an essayist ("Of Wine and Men," printed in Penguin's *In My Mother's Kitchen*, an award-winning filmmaker (*Univers'l*), screenwriter (*Big Bang Theory*), playwright (*Villa Thrilla, Petting Zoo Story*) and actor. She's a graduate of the UCLA Writers Program, former Managing Director of the Ojai Playwrights Conference, a mediator and single mom.

Find out more at annroyalnicholas.com and annanicholas.com

www.ingramcontent.com/pod-product-compliance
Lightning Source LLC
Chambersburg PA
CBHW032052050726
47590CB00001B/234